BY JOHN FEINSTEIN

The Sports Beat Series
Last Shot: Mystery at the Final Four
Vanishing Act: Mystery at the U.S. Open
Cover-Up: Mystery at the Super Bowl
Change-Up: Mystery at the World Series
The Rivalry: Mystery at the Army-Navy Game
Rush for the Gold: Mystery at the Olympics

The Triple Threat Series
The Walk On
The Sixth Man
The DH

Foul Trouble
Backfield Boys

BACKFIELD BOYS

BACKFIELD
BOYS

JOHN FEINSTEIN

FARRAR STRAUS GIROUX
NEW YORK

Farrar Straus Giroux Books for Young Readers
An imprint of Macmillan Publishing Group, LLC
175 Fifth Avenue, New York, NY 10010

Copyright © 2017 by John Feinstein
All rights reserved
Printed in the United States of America
Designed by Elizabeth H. Clark
First edition, 2017

1   3   5   7   9   10   8   6   4   2

fiercereads.com

Cataloging-in-Publication Data is on file at the Library of Congress

ISBN: 978-0-374-30592-5

Our books may be purchased in bulk for promotional, educational, or business use. Please
contact your local bookseller or Macmillan Corporate and Premium Sales Department at
(800) 221-7945, ext. 5442, or by e-mail at MacmillanSpecialMarkets@macmillan.com.

*This is for Andrew Thompson (USNA '96) and
Jim Cantelupe (USMA '96), who taught me a lot about
football but more about loyalty and friendship*

PROLOGUE

TOM JEFFERSON WAS STARING INTO THE RAPIDLY SETTING SUN, HANDS on hips, wondering what to do next. It was just a game of touch football on a November afternoon, but he didn't want to lose to the private school kids.

Every Friday, eight boys met in Riverside Park for public school versus private school bragging rights. Tom and his best friend, Jason Roddin, along with Mike Roth and Marc Posnock, were the public school team—all seventh graders at Junior High School 44, which was four blocks east of the park.

The private school guys, all kids they had grown up with on the West Side of Manhattan, went to McBurney, an all-boys school about a mile away, off Central Park West.

The publics had the two best players: Tom and Jason. But they also had the two worst: Mike and Marc. The privates had figured out if they double-teamed Jason and forced Tom to throw the ball to Mike or Marc, they could slow Jason down—no easy task since Jason was stunningly fast. His nickname was "White Lightning"—with good reason. Like Jason, Tom had earned a nickname, too: "Bull's-Eye," because he never seemed to miss a target.

Now it was getting close to five o'clock and the sun would soon be down. There were no lights in the small park, and everyone had agreed a few minutes earlier to two more possessions. The privates had scored to make it 6–6. Since there were no field goals or extra points, the boys simply counted each touchdown as one point.

So it was now up to the publics. If they didn't score, the game would be a tie and they would have to buy the ice creams at Carvel since the privates had won the week before. In other words, a tie was a loss.

It was third down. Needless to say, the privates had been playing deep to keep Jason from getting behind them. They'd gladly give up an open pass in front of them to either Mike or Marc. Tom had to figure out a way to get the ball to Jason.

"What do you think?" he asked, as the four of them stood in a small circle a couple of yards behind where the ball sat on the ground.

The privates were standing back from the ball, hands on hips, taking deep breaths. Everyone was tired.

"We got two options," Jason said, because the question was clearly directed at him. "We can throw it underneath and then try to score on fourth down, or go for all of it now."

"No way they're going to let you get behind them," Tom said.

Jason grinned. "Don't look up, but you know the trash can down by the trees?"

"Sure," Tom said. The landmark was far down the right side of the field.

"Fake like you're going to throw it to me underneath, and then just throw it right at that can."

Tom understood. Marc and Mike both nodded. Their job was to spread out as far as they could to keep the defense at least a little bit honest.

Steve Holder, the slowest player on the privates, picked up the ball and flipped it to Jason—the touch-football version of a snap. Steve would slowly count to five and then rush Tom, forcing him to throw the ball whether or not someone was open. Tom could pull the ball down and run, but he wouldn't get very far. Speed was not his forte.

Tom took the snap and instinctively spun the ball so his fingers were across the laces. He had done it so many times in his life that it required no thought. He dropped back a step, just to clear a little space between himself and Steve as he heard him counting.

"One-one-thousand, two-one-thousand . . ."

Jason had started from the right, running about ten yards up the field—which ran roughly fifty yards between the oak trees at either end that represented the end zones—and began to cut toward the middle. Kenny Medley went with him, Johnny Strachan lying back as a deep safety.

Just as he heard Steve say "Four-one-thousand," Tom faked, beginning his throwing motion, then stopping. Jason, who had paused for a split second as if expecting the ball, suddenly pivoted right and was past Kenny in the blink of an eye.

As he sprinted in the direction of the goal line, Johnny, who had hesitated for an instant after Tom's fake, scrambled to get back. It was too late. Jason was a blur. Tom came up on his toes and let go of the ball, feeling absolutely no strain on his arm or shoulder, wanting it to drop into Jason's arms just as he went past the trash can.

The ball arced through the darkening sky, and Tom could see Jason running under it with Johnny helplessly trailing him. Jason made the catch in full stride, raced past the tree, and held the ball up triumphantly.

Tom threw his arms in the air, doing his best Tom Brady/Peyton Manning imitation as he raced across the grass and dirt to congratulate his receiver. All four of the publics gathered to high-five one another. The privates stood and watched, then joined the circle to exchange handshakes and fist bumps.

Johnny bent over, hands on his knees, still trying to get his breath back.

"You know something," he said between gasps. "You two should play real football someday. You're pretty good together."

"Yeah," Kenny said. "Bull's-Eye to White Lightning. You guys could make history."

"History?" Jason said.

"How many great quarterback-receiver combinations had the black guy throwing to the white guy?"

Tom and Jason looked at each other.

"Should we make history?" Tom said.

"Yeah, we should," Jason said. "Let's talk our mothers into letting us play real football when we get to high school."

Tom laughed. "You're right," he said. "That *would* be making history."

Sweating and laughing, they all grabbed their jackets and backpacks and crossed Riverside Drive, heading in the direction of the Carvel two blocks away on Broadway.

PART 1

1

THE FIELDS JUST KEPT ROLLING PAST THE CAR, MILE AFTER MILE.

"Did it take this long the last time we came down here?" Jason asked.

He was sitting in the back of the Jeffersons' silver Honda Accord. Mr. Jefferson was behind the wheel, a smile on his face even though they were more than five hours into the six-hour drive.

Riding shotgun, Tom laughed at his best friend's latest complaint. "Last time, we flew to Washington, remember?" he said. "We rented a car in D.C., so the drive was two hours, not six. But I promise you we drove past every one of these fields."

"All these cows, too?" Jason asked.

"Yup. And the sheep and chicken farms."

Jason laughed. There was no way he would be in this car right now if not for Tom, who had convinced him that going to a jock boarding school in Middle-of-Nowhere, Virginia, was a good idea.

Jason and Tom had grown up five floors apart in an apartment building on West End Avenue near Seventy-Seventh Street. They had met in the first grade at PS 87 after Tom's father, Alan Jefferson, a salesman for an athletic gear company, had been transferred from Chicago to New York. Tom's mother, Elaine, an elementary school teacher, had found work as a substitute teacher at PS 87, just over a two-block walk from the apartment building.

Jason's family had lived in their apartment since before he was born. His dad, Robbie, was a New York City police detective. His mom, Julie, was also a teacher, working at a nearby private preschool.

The parents became friends through their sons. Almost from the beginning, Jason and Tom were the best athletes in the PS 87 schoolyard. They started out playing punchball—smacking an orange rubber ball with their fists, rather than a bat, but otherwise following the rules of baseball—and soon graduated to stickball, basketball, and touch football.

It wasn't until they crossed Seventy-Seventh Street as sixth graders to go to junior high school that the two boys were part of any organized teams. There was no football team at their school, but they were starters right away on both the basketball and softball teams. Both badly wanted to play football. Their mothers weren't in love with the idea, but their fathers were.

One night, when the two boys were in seventh grade, the Jeffersons rode the elevator from the eleventh to the sixth floor for what the parents called "cocktails," although the mothers drank wine, the fathers drank beer, and the boys drank soda. They all sat around the Roddins' living room and talked about a football summer camp that Mr. Jefferson had heard about from some of his coworkers.

"They're called seven-on-seven camps, because it's not real football but skills football," he explained. "You don't have linemen, except for a center to snap the ball. Everyone else is either a receiver or in the backfield at quarterback or running back. There's no real tackling either."

"How is it football if there's no tackling?" Mr. Roddin asked.

"First question I asked, Robbie," Mr. Jefferson said, smiling. "The camp is about helping kids develop their skills— running, throwing, catching, running pass patterns, defending pass patterns, reading offenses and defenses, things like that. There's almost no hitting at all."

Jason and Tom both loved the idea. They were determined to play for a real team when they got to high school, and this was a chance to enhance their skills.

The mothers weren't quite as enthusiastic.

"Okay, there's no tackling at this camp," Mrs. Roddin said. "But why aren't we sending them to a basketball camp somewhere, or a baseball camp? Aren't those the two sports we want them to focus on?"

"Maybe," Mr. Roddin said. "But I think that's ultimately up to the boys, isn't it?"

"Since when?" his wife said almost instantly.

Jason still winced at the memory of how sharp his mother's tone had been.

"Well, if Jason wants to play football or *doesn't* want to play football, I think that's up to him, Julie," Mr. Roddin said. "I think Alan feels the same way. I don't think we'd ever push either one of them to play football—or any other sport—but I don't think we should tell them they *can't* play a sport."

Mrs. Jefferson had said very little up until that moment. Now she jumped into the fray. "You don't think we could say no?" she said. She looked at Mrs. Roddin. "Julie, have you and Robbie ever had that conversation about football? Alan and I haven't." She then turned and looked directly at Mr. Roddin. "How can you possibly act as if playing football is the same as basketball or baseball or any other sport? Have you been living in a cave the last few years? Aren't you aware of how dangerous the sport is?"

"As a matter of fact, I've studied the stats pretty carefully," Mr. Roddin said. "And for all the panic going on, the fact remains that the odds one of the boys will get a concussion or suffer a severe head injury are pretty low. Even with all the new technology that makes it easier to identify a concussion, the rate for high school football players is, according to most studies, only about twenty percent."

"Twenty percent!" Mrs. Jefferson practically jumped out of her chair. "Robbie, I want you to think about this for a minute: If the boys were about to get on an airplane and the pilot told you there was a twenty percent chance it would crash, would you let them get on it?"

There was a long pause. For a moment Jason thought that question would end the debate.

It was Mr. Jefferson who finally responded. "If that flight was the only way they could get where they wanted to go, yes, I would."

"Well, then you need to have *your* head examined," his wife answered.

. . . . .

And yet, here they were, on a Sunday evening eighteen months later, on their way to Thomas Gatch Prep School in central Virginia, just outside the tiny town of Scottsville and not far from the campus of the University of Virginia in Charlottesville.

TGP had been started by a sports agent named Thomas Alan Gatch and several partners in 1999—in fact, a twentieth-anniversary celebration for the school was already being planned for 2019. Mr. Gatch also now served as head-of-school, the equivalent of a public high school's principal.

The way Mr. Gatch had explained it to the boys and their fathers when they first arrived on campus for the seven-on-seven camp in the summer prior to their becoming eighth-graders, he'd gotten the idea to start TGP from his former employers at IMG, the giant sports-management agency that represented hundreds of athletes, ran professional sports events, and in the 1980s had purchased a tennis academy in Florida with the intention of turning it into a full-fledged high school—one where every student was an aspiring college athlete. The IMG Academy had been hugely successful, and Mr. Gatch believed he could not only copy it but better it.

"The difference between us and IMG is that we really *do* stress academics as much as sports," he had told the boys and their fathers on the day they arrived. "My background is in education. I was a history teacher once and then a high school principal. That's why we're smaller by design, so we have a better teacher-student ratio. We pay our teachers as well as we pay most of our coaches, so we get better teachers."

Jason had googled IMG Academy and was stunned to find that more than twelve thousand athletes passed through it every year—though only half of them attended full-time and lived on campus. The tuition was more than $70,000 per year—plus living expenses.

Gatch was considerably smaller—about fifteen hundred full-time students—and had only recently added golf and tennis to its curriculum. The focus was on team sports: football; boys' and girls' basketball, soccer, lacrosse, and swimming; plus baseball for boys and softball for girls, since softball was a scholarship sport for girls in college. The school website boasted that TGP fostered traditional values in its "student-athletes," on and off the playing field.

It wasn't quite as expensive—tuition was $55,000 plus expenses. But, like IMG Academy, it offered scholarships for especially gifted athletes whose families didn't have that kind of money. Jason could still remember the two fathers' eyebrows going up the first time Mr. Gatch mentioned that. He knew there was no way either his dad or Tom's could afford to spend that much money a year to send their sons to high school.

The deal the fathers and sons had made with the mothers was

simple: the boys would be allowed to attend the summer seven-on-seven camp, and once it was over they would all reconvene. The brochure for the camp explained that doctors and trainers were present on-field for every practice or game. If a boy had suffered any sort of prior injury, he needed a doctor's letter clearing him to play. That soothed the mothers—somewhat. Jason was pretty convinced they were hoping that one of two things would happen: their boys wouldn't like the camp or they wouldn't do well enough there to consider going on to play high school football.

But Tom and Jason had both loved the camp. Jason enjoyed playing wide receiver and especially enjoyed catching passes from Tom. Through their Friday touch football games in the park, and later in the JHS 44 schoolyard, they had figured out that Tom had the stronger arm—though Jason's wasn't bad either—and that Jason was considerably faster and was a little better at catching the ball.

During the camp, every kid played every position at some point. The goal was to learn the skills needed to play anywhere on the field and then figure out later exactly where you would end up playing.

"The more versatile you are, the better your chances are of playing on Sundays," the head coach, James "Bobo" Johnson, told the campers, using coach-speak for playing in the NFL. "And when you start playing real football, being able to play on special teams will also help you greatly as you go up the ladder."

There was no special-teams play—kickoffs, punts, field goals—at the camp. There were, Jason learned, camps that specialized in kicking. What's more, special-teams play was considered so dangerous that there had been talk in the NFL about abolishing kickoffs because so many injuries happened when twenty-two players ran full speed right at one another.

There was nothing Jason enjoyed more about the camp than the speed drills—or time trials. He won the time trials in the 100-yard dash, the 40-yard dash, and the 10-yard dash, beating everyone among the 150 campers on every timed occasion. His 4.58 forty drew oohs and aahs from the coaches and the other campers, and he enjoyed busting the stereotype that white boys couldn't run fast.

"Wait till they find out you're Jewish," Tom joked. "They'll want to drug-test you."

Tom's forty time was 4.77, which put him midpack among the other campers. But he had the most accurate arm in the camp—maybe not the strongest, though it was strong enough—but without doubt the most accurate.

By the end of the camp, they'd both made their mark and Coach Johnson had told them he'd be in touch with their parents.

"You boys belong here," he'd said to them. "You could be a great team, and you could help make *us* a great team."

He then made it clear to both boys that he wouldn't let money stand in the way of their enrolling at TGP for the ninth grade. A subsequent scholarship offer for each boy changed everything.

. . . . .

Of course it hadn't been that simple. Neither Elaine Jefferson nor Julie Roddin was at all happy with the idea of her son going to a jock school 350 miles from the West Side of Manhattan to be—worst of all—a football player.

But when Mr. Gatch personally offered full rides to both boys, and when the fathers supplied the mothers with a list of where the 350 graduates from TGP's class of 2017 were going to college, they gave in—grudgingly.

"It won't do Tom any good to go to an Ivy League school if he can't remember his name when he's forty," Mrs. Jefferson said when her husband pointed out that six of the thirty-four football-playing seniors were going to the Ivies.

That had set off another round of the fathers pointing out the percentages and the mothers saying that *any* risk was too much risk. For their part, the boys had pleaded and a compromise had been reached: Tom and Jason would be one-and-dones: not one *year*—as with college basketball players, who played for a year before leaving for the NBA—but one *concussion* and done.

"First time it happens, Jason," Mrs. Roddin said, "that's it. Football's done."

Only with that understanding did the mothers finally sign off on accepting the scholarships.

· · · · ·

And so, as more and more cornfields and cow pastures raced past the window, Jason leaned back, closed his eyes, and imagined himself running under passes perfectly thrown to him by Tom.

He could see the headlines in the newspapers around the state of Virginia now—not to mention on ESPN's weekly high school highlight show: BULL'S-EYE TARGETS WHITE LIGHTNING IN TGP VICTORY.

This was going to be fun, he thought.

If they ever got there.

2

THEY STOPPED FOR DINNER IN CHARLOTTESVILLE. A FRIEND OF MR.
Jefferson's had recommended a steak place just off Route 29
called the Aberdeen Barn, down the road from the campus of
the University of Virginia.

"So here I am, a couple miles from the school founded by
old Mr. Jefferson, having dinner with *two* Mr. Jeffersons," Jason
said, grinning, as they walked inside.

They were walking in the direction of the hostess's stand,
where two young women were smiling at them.

"Do me a favor and shut up," Tom said.

"Reservation for Jefferson," his dad said to the two young
women.

If the name carried any special meaning around here, the
hostesses didn't show it.

"Yes, sir," the taller one said. "Table for three, right?"

As Mr. Jefferson was nodding, Jason said, "You realize, don't you, that you're about to seat Thomas Jefferson?" He pointed at Tom.

The shorter of the two, a pretty brunette, didn't miss a beat. "Thomas Jefferson, it's a pleasure," she said. "I'm Martha Washington."

That was funny.

"Let me guess," Mr. Jefferson said as they walked to their table. "We're not the first people to come in here with the last name Jefferson."

"Or the first name Tom or Thomas," Martha answered, handing them menus as they sat down.

"But do you get Sally Hemings in here a lot?" Jason said, trying to keep the banter going.

Martha smiled. "Absolutely. But she has to come in the back door," she said as she walked away.

"Girl's funny," Mr. Jefferson said.

Jason knew about Sally Hemings from the early American history section of his social studies class. She was the slave who became President Jefferson's mistress after his wife died; the two had had several children together.

"She's got guts saying that to a couple of black guys," Tom said.

"I think she figured we could handle it," Jason said.

"What do you mean *we*?" Tom said. "Did I miss the part where you became black?"

"You always say I run like I'm black," Jason answered.

"I'm sure she was aware of that," Mr. Jefferson said, just as a waitress arrived at the table to take drink orders.

"First round of drinks is on the house, gentlemen," she said. "Courtesy of Martha Washington. My name is Sally, and I'll be your server tonight."

Jason stared at her name tag. It actually said SALLY. *Amazing,* he thought. *Just amazing.*

．．．．．

They all ordered Cokes. The boys were a long way from being old enough to drink, and even though they were now only a short drive from the school, Mr. Jefferson wasn't taking any chances.

"Remember, after I drop you off, I'm coming back to Charlottesville to spend the night," he said.

"It's great of you to do this, Dad," Tom said.

"Well, there was no way that Robbie could change his schedule," Mr. Jefferson said. "And neither one of your mothers wanted to do the tearful-farewell thing down here after six hours in the car. So that left me."

"Somehow I don't think you'll be tearful," Tom said.

Mr. Jefferson smiled. "Probably not," he said. "But I will miss you both."

Tom's head had been buried in his menu. Now it snapped up and he looked at his father, clearly surprised.

"For real?" he said.

"Of course," Mr. Jefferson said. "Did you think I *wouldn't* miss you?"

Tom shook his head. "No, I figured you'd miss me—us— but I never thought you'd *say* it."

"Well, consider this a first," Mr. Jefferson said. "But not a last."

"Saying it once puts you in the lead over my dad," Jason said, smiling. "Probably an insurmountable lead at that."

Jason knew his dad loved him, but he was a tough-guy cop, not inclined to show much emotion—anger being the exception.

They all ordered steaks since they'd been told that this was one of the best steak houses in the state. Soon they were buried in sizzling platters of meat and several side dishes apiece.

"Good intel on the steaks, Dad," Tom said as they all emptied their plates.

"Well, my guess is, even at a jock training table, the food you'll get in the school dining hall won't be all that good, so I figured I'd better get you a good meal tonight," Mr. Jefferson said.

To top it off, they all ordered ice cream sundaes. Then they were out the door, headed in the direction of the school by seven o'clock.

The sky was slowly darkening overhead. It would be close to sunset when they got to TGP.

They arrived to find a slew of cars in the parking lot, with others pulled up in front of the dorms to be unloaded. They'd been told to report first to Jackson Hall—where all the school's offices were located—to register. After that, they'd head to their rooms.

Two very pleasant women checked Tom's and Jason's names off a list and handed them dorm room keys. They were in Lee Hall, a six-floor all-male building.

"Mr. Jefferson, you're in room 344," one of the staff members said. "Mr. Roddin, you're in 228."

"Hang on," Tom's dad said just before Jason could open his mouth. "I know that the boys asked to room together."

At seven-on-seven camp the dorms were empty enough that all the campers could have their own room. Jason and Tom had had adjacent rooms and had made it a point on their applications to request rooming together at school.

The woman who had handed them their keys was middle-aged, probably about forty, Jason figured. She had her dark hair pulled up and was wearing a blue blazer with a Thomas Gatch Prep School crest; the name tag on her lapel said MRS. WILLIAMS.

She smiled at them. "Yes, well, we get a lot of requests for room assignments, especially from boys and girls who are from the same hometown," she said. "We think it better to start fresh, make new friends. It isn't as if the boys won't be seeing a lot of each other, is it?"

Jason was fine with the idea of making new friends. He just didn't especially want to share a room with one of them.

"We should have been informed," Mr. Jefferson said. "At least that way the boys wouldn't have been taken by surprise. They've been counting on rooming together."

"Well, next year they can put in a request for that, and maybe it will be granted," Mrs. Williams said.

She looked past Mr. Jefferson to a father, a mother, and their son standing behind them.

"Welcome to TGP," she said to them. "Can you give me your name?"

As politely as possible, she had just said, *I'm done with you—move on.*

Jason and Tom looked at each other, then at Mr. Jefferson.

"Do you want me to take this up the line to someone in authority?" Mr. Jefferson said. "She's just doing her job."

"Couldn't be more officious, I'd say," Tom muttered.

Jason was pretty certain that *officious* wasn't a compliment, but he wasn't sure what it meant.

Tom, who often read his mind, said: "Obnoxious when asserting authority. As in, *I'm in charge, don't question me.*"

That said it all, Jason thought.

Tom turned to his father. "Let's leave it for now," he said. "We don't want to be the only ones complaining on the first day. We'll see how it goes. If we don't like our roommates, we'll try to make a switch."

Jason figured Tom was right.

The three of them walked back to the car and, as instructed, Mr. Jefferson pulled around to the back of Lee Hall. It was not a football dorm per se, but all the school's football players were among those who lived in the building. The basketball players also lived in Lee Hall.

The boys unloaded their things, and Mr. Jefferson stayed with the car while they first carried Tom's stuff to his room. Tom's roommate was sitting on the bed watching TV when they arrived. He jumped to his feet and introduced himself.

"Anthony Ames," he said. "I'm from Marietta, Georgia."

He was a black kid, clearly a lineman: about six foot three and, Jason guessed, at least 240 pounds.

18

Tom introduced himself, shaking hands. "And this is Jason Roddin. We're from New York City."

"The NYC boys. I heard about you." Anthony shook hands with Jason. "You're White Lightning, right?"

"That's me. And this is Bull's-Eye. He's slow as sin, but he has the best arm you'll ever see, no doubt."

"Well, we'll find out, I guess," Anthony said. "Need a hand?"

The two friends thanked him but said they were good. They left to go deal with Jason's things.

"I like him," Jason said.

"In five seconds?" Tom said.

"Yup, I'm a gut-instinct guy. You know that."

They went back to the car and collected Jason's stuff and hauled it up to room 228. It was empty. Apparently his roommate—Jason hadn't bothered to ask his name—hadn't arrived yet.

Jason and Tom walked back to the car to say goodbye to Tom's dad. It was just about dark now, the last bits of dusk fading rapidly. The three of them stood by the car for a second. For some reason, Jason had an almost overwhelming desire to jump back in and leave with Mr. Jefferson. He wondered if Tom was thinking the same thing.

"I better get going," Mr. Jefferson said. "I want to be on the road by six in the morning, and you boys probably have an early wake-up, too."

"Drive carefully, Dad," Tom said, giving his father a hug.

Mr. Jefferson hugged Jason, too, thumping him on the back. "I texted your mothers when we got to the Aberdeen Barn. Do yourselves a favor and give them a call before you go to bed and let them know you're okay."

They nodded, and he slid into the car and was gone. They watched the car turn out of the parking lot, headed back to Route 20 and Charlottesville.

"We okay?" Jason asked Tom as the taillights disappeared.

"We're fine," Tom said.

"Easy for you to say," Jason said. "You've met your roommate and you like him."

"*You* like him," Tom said. "I haven't passed judgment yet."

They turned and slowly walked back into the dorm together.

3

JASON WAS UNPACKING WHEN HE HEARD A LIGHT KNOCK ON THE DOOR.
He opened it and found a tall, gangly kid with a shock of curly
blond hair standing there with several pieces of luggage.

"I'm guessin' you're Jason," the kid said in a very distinct
Southern drawl. "I'm Billy Bob Anderson. Looks like we're gonna
be roommates." He put out a hand.

Jason took the offered hand while restraining a smile. No one,
other than actors, was named Billy Bob in real life.

"Um, sure," Jason said, afraid to actually say *Billy Bob*, because
he was afraid he'd burst out laughing and not be able to stop.
"Let me help with your stuff."

Billy Bob smiled. "Appreciate it," he said. "The coach who
picked me up at the airport just kind of dumped me at the door
after I registered. Figured I'd try to get everything up in one trip.
Wasn't easy."

Jason took a suitcase and a computer bag, while Billy Bob

brought in another suitcase and what looked like a garment bag. Jason had taken the bed nearer the window, so they piled everything next to the other bed.

The two boys sat down on their beds, looking each other over. Billy Bob was around six feet tall, Jason thought, a couple of inches taller than he was. He was pretty certain he was a wide receiver or a defensive back.

"So," Billy Bob said, breaking the silence, "I'm gonna take a guess that this is a first for both of us."

"Being away at boarding school?" Jason asked.

"That too," Billy Bob said. "Gadsden, Alabama, is a long way from here."

"So is New York City," Jason said.

"I reckon," Billy Bob said. "I ain't ever been to New York."

"Well, we're even, then," Jason said, "because I've never been to Gadsden, Alabama."

"And probably never will be," Billy Bob said.

They both laughed.

"That's not what I'm talkin' about, though," the Southerner said. "I was just thinking that I *have* to be the first Billy Bob you've ever met, and I *know* you're the first big-city kid I've ever met. So we're even again."

"Maybe I'm the first Jewish kid you've met, too," Jason said, taking a guess.

"You're Jewish?" Billy Bob asked.

Jason looked at him for a moment, wondering if this was some kind of challenge. But he couldn't see even a hint of malice in the boy's face, just an innocent-looking smile.

"Not a lot of Jews in Gadsden, huh?" he said.

"Probably about as many as there are Billy Bobs in New York City," he said. "Hey, do you really live *in* the city?"

"West Side of Manhattan," Jason said.

"Is it scary?"

"Probably no scarier than it would be to be Jewish in Gadsden."

Billy Bob cracked up again. "Nah, you'd be fine. I'd take care of you."

"And I'd watch your back in the city," Jason said.

"I'll take you up on that someday," Billy Bob said. "For now, I better get unpacked so we can get some sleep. I hear six-thirty comes early around here. And I'm too beat even to scout out where they got all the freshman girls livin'."

· · · · ·

Tired as he was, Jason took a while to fall asleep, wondering what the next morning would bring. After breakfast they were supposed to get registered for their classes and pick up their books. The first football practice was that afternoon. Classes would start on Tuesday.

Tom knocked on the door at 6:20, and Jason introduced him to Billy Bob. If Tom had a first reaction to Billy Bob's name similar to Jason's, he hid it completely.

"Where's Anthony?" Jason asked.

"Out the door ten minutes ago," Tom said. "I think he wanted to be first in line for breakfast. My sense is the boy eats a *lot*."

As they walked to the dining hall, they began filling in the blanks on one another's lives. Jason had been wrong: Billy Bob wasn't a receiver or a DB; he was a quarterback.

"Looks like we'll be competing, I guess," Tom said.

"Guess so," Billy Bob said. "The coach made a big point of telling me that TGP's top two quarterbacks were graduating. Guess I shoulda asked how many guys they were recruitin' at the position."

"My guess is, place like this, they overrecruit," Tom said. "They recruit five guys at a position and let two rise to the top. They figure the others will transfer."

"So you mean there will probably be five or six receivers when I get out there this afternoon?" Jason said.

"More like ten," Billy Bob answered, and they all laughed.

Jason could tell from looking at his best friend that he and Tom were thinking the same thing: this guy could be Tom's competition to be the starter, and he was a good guy. That was less than ideal.

"Well," Jason said, "I guess we'll find out soon enough."

·　·　·　·　·

By the time they made it to the practice field, Jason was too tired to be all that concerned about how many wide receivers TGP had recruited.

The morning was spent shuttling around the campus, which was less familiar than Jason thought it would be—in part because he hadn't gone anywhere near a classroom during the seven-on-seven camp. New students had to pick up their books in each class to give them a dry run on how to find those classrooms the next day.

It was hot, and the late-summer Virginia humidity hung over the campus like a curtain, weighing everyone down, especially as books accumulated in backpacks.

Jason was ready for a nap by the time they got to the cafeteria at lunch, but all the freshmen had to go to a postlunch orientation meeting, during which Mr. Gatch introduced them to every single person working at the school. Or so it seemed.

By the time they were walking down the long, winding hill from the academic and residential halls, it was after two.

"Do you remember the place being this big when we were here last year?" Tom asked Jason.

Jason had been thinking the same thing. The three dormitories—Lee, Jackson, and Monroe—all named for famous Virginians, two of whom had been Confederate generals—were massive.

They had stayed in Jackson the previous summer and, although they had crossed the quad to the dining hall every day, they hadn't really been aware of the four buildings that housed the classrooms. Now they were.

The athletic facilities would have made most colleges proud. The football building had three levels, with locker rooms in the basement, a weight room and administrative offices on the main floor, and coaches' offices and classrooms for team meetings on the second floor.

The two adjacent athletic buildings housed the rest of the boys' teams and all of the girls' teams.

Jason remembered crossing the Columbia University campus with his dad en route to basketball games there. This place was a good deal bigger—and more spread out.

When they arrived at the TGP football building, they had to go through another registration process, checking in at the equipment cage so they could be given all their practice gear and assigned lockers.

When Tom asked if number 10 was available—in honor of Eli Manning—the equipment manager looked at him as if he had asked for the keys to his house.

"We don't even let the seniors pick their numbers," he growled. "Why in the world would we care what number a freshman wants?"

He shoved the gear at him, and Jason noticed the number on the back of the top was 81. Tom was about to point out that 81 wasn't a quarterback's number but stopped when Jason put a hand on his shoulder.

"Later," Jason said softly.

Jason was very pleased with being given number 19. He remembered that Lance Alworth, the San Diego Chargers Hall of Fame wide receiver, had worn 19. He liked that.

"Willis Reed," Tom said, remembering that the great Knicks center had worn 19. "Johnny Unitas, too."

"Lance Alworth," Jason said. "Wide receiver."

"Got it," Tom said.

The freshmen, as expected, were tucked into the back corner of the locker room. That wasn't a problem, though, because the locker room was huge. Jason guessed there were about eighty players getting into their practice outfits—thankfully, they had been told to wear shorts and no pads for the first workout—and the room would easily have space for a hundred players if need be.

Every player's locker had his name on it, lined up alphabetically. Jason found himself between Gerry Richards and Larry Ross. Both were clearly linemen. They all shook hands and said hello and then dressed in near silence. The rest of the locker room was much louder, old acquaintances being renewed. The freshmen eyed one another, sizing everyone up. The older players, who had already proved themselves for at least one year, were a lot looser than the new kids on the block.

Tom and Jason followed the older guys down the hall and onto the practice field. There were actually two practice fields: one had FieldTurf—the currently in-vogue artificial surface—and one real grass. During the camp, they had worked out on the FieldTurf every day, but the coaches had told them the grass field existed because some of TGP's road games were played on real grass and the team would practice on it during those weeks. The stadium, which Jason knew seated about ten thousand fans, was on the other side of the two practice fields and was apparently used a couple of days a week for practice once the season began.

They made their way across the nearest practice field to a small bleacher. Everyone sat down to wait for the coaches. There was clearly a pecking order here, too: the seniors sat in the first two rows, the juniors in the next two, and so on up to the freshmen at the top.

At precisely 3:00, the coaches walked across the practice

field to the bleachers, led by Coach Johnson. Jason had googled him when the possibility of attending the seven-on-seven camp at TGP had first come up. He was fifty-one years old and was what was known as a football lifer. He had gotten the nickname "Bobo" growing up in Macon, Georgia, because when he was born his older sister couldn't say "Bobby," which was what his mother had wanted to call him. He had gone on to "live the dream"—his words in one interview—of playing at the University of Georgia and had been a starting linebacker for three years with a reputation for hitting anything that moved and hitting it hard. He had been honorable mention All-American as a senior and All–Southeastern Conference as a junior and a senior.

But he'd gone undrafted because he wasn't considered big enough at six-two, 220, to play linebacker in the NFL, and he wasn't fast enough to play safety. He had been invited to the Atlanta Falcons camp and been cut, then signed with the New York Giants practice squad—where he lasted, if Jason remembered correctly, for six weeks. Then he'd signed with the Montreal Alouettes of the Canadian Football League, but a torn knee ligament, an ACL, had ended his career.

The next year he'd gone back to Georgia as a graduate assistant. He'd risen through the ranks to become the linebacker coach under Ray Goff. He'd kept his job when Goff was fired and remained there when Jim Donnan and then Mark Richt took over the top coaching spot. But in 2005, Richt had passed him over to bring someone in from the outside as defensive coordinator and Johnson had left to take the job at TGP, assured that

Mr. Gatch wanted to build a football program that competed nationally and had facilities comparable to IMG Academy's.

According to one story Jason had read, it was now considered only a matter of time before Johnson left TGP for either an NFL coordinator job, a college head-coaching job, or a coordinator's position at one of the big-time college programs. In the meantime, though, the Thomas Gatch Prep Patriots had gone 24–2 the last two seasons.

Coach Johnson looked to Jason like he could still play linebacker. There was no sag in his body, no sign of anything resembling a belly. He stood in front of his players ramrod straight, eyes hidden behind mirrored sunglasses, a TGP baseball cap pulled tightly over his head.

"Upperclassmen, welcome home," he said, smiling—an expression that really didn't fit his face. "Freshmen, other newcomers, welcome to your new home."

From there, he introduced the players to the fourteen assistant coaches, some of whom Jason and Tom had worked with at the seven-on-seven camp, and four of whom were new to the staff. Jason knew that Mark Cruikshank, the quarterbacks coach, and Terry Reilly, who coached the wide receivers, were both new. They were young and had been assistant coaches at other high schools in Virginia. He figured a coach who knew none of the players—as opposed to someone who had already worked with some of them—was a good thing for him and for Tom. Everyone would be starting from the same spot in working with his position coach.

"We'll ramp up slowly this first week," Coach Johnson said.

"We want all of you to learn and relearn our offense and our defense. Beginning tomorrow, we'll spend forty-five minutes each afternoon before practice in the classroom so your coaches can teach you the plays and the play calls. By next week, you'll be expected to know them, so be sure you are listening *and* taking notes in your playbooks during those sessions. You'll have academic homework each night, and you'll have football homework, too." He paused as if waiting for questions.

There were none.

He went on. "Today, we just want to go through some basic drills. We'll get you with your position coaches and then work on sprints, agility, ball handling. Linemen, you'll report to the sleds when the skill position guys start on their drills.

"I've introduced the coaches by position, so each of you report to your position coach when we're finished here. If you are in doubt about your position—or you're not sure what your best position will be, check with the appropriate coordinator. Clear?"

There were nods and a lot of "Yes, sirs," particularly from the upperclassmen. Jason felt some adrenaline beginning to surge through him. He couldn't wait to run some sprints and run under some footballs—preferably thrown in his direction by Tom.

As if thinking the same thing, Tom nudged him slightly in the ribs and whispered, "Ready?"

"Born ready, Bull's-Eye," Jason whispered back.

"Okay," Coach Johnson said, raising his voice. "Coaches, spread out! Players report on the whistle!"

He blew his whistle sharply and everyone began scrambling

off the bleachers. Jason kept his eyes on Coach Reilly, who was jogging in the direction of the end zone to the right.

"See you in a few," Tom said, trotting in the direction of Coach Cruikshank, who was headed for the far sideline.

Coach Reilly was holding a clipboard when Jason and the other receivers arrived where he was standing.

"Just to make sure that everyone who is here should be here, answer up when you hear your name," he said.

Jason looked him over. He was young—no more than thirty—and was wearing the same outfit as all the other coaches: blue cap with TGP on it, white shirt emblazoned with GATCH PREP FOOTBALL, blue shorts, and blue-and-white sneakers.

He began ticking off names in alphabetical order. There were, by Jason's count, twelve receivers standing in the circle around the coach. Jason wasn't listening so much as sizing up the competition, trying to figure out whom he was going to be competing against for playing time.

"Jefferson!" Coach Reilly said.

That got Jason's attention. Why was he calling Tom's name? Or was he? It was certainly possible that there was more than one player named Jefferson on the team. But no one responded.

Coach Reilly tried again. "Jefferson!" he said, his voice a bit louder.

Still no answer.

Jason put a hand up. "Excuse me, Coach?" he said in a timid voice.

"You Jefferson?" Coach Reilly said.

"No, sir, but—"

Coach Reilly stopped him. "Let me finish the roll and then tell me why you felt the need to interrupt."

That reply didn't give Jason a warm and fuzzy feeling about his new coach. He waited for Coach Reilly to call his name. He never did. When the coach had finished calling the rest of the names on the list he looked up from the clipboard at Jason. Everyone else was also looking at him.

"And you are?" Coach Reilly's tone was remarkably snide, given that Jason had only said three words.

"I'm Jason Roddin," he answered, feeling his stomach beginning to turn over—although he wasn't exactly sure why.

"Well, Rodding, you aren't on the list of wide receivers," Reilly said. "Could you be in the wrong place?"

Jason ignored the mispronunciation of his name, but he was beginning to think that maybe he *was* in the wrong place. And it had nothing to do with the list he apparently wasn't on.

4

JASON WAS STILL TRYING TO FIGURE OUT HOW TO RESPOND TO COACH
Reilly's question about whether he was in the wrong place when
he noticed Tom and a coach he couldn't identify walking in their
direction.

"Coach Reilly, I think we've got a couple of newcomers who
are a bit confused," the coach said as he and Tom reached the
receiver group.

"Well, Coach Ingelsby, I've got one youngster here who isn't
on the receiver list, so maybe you can clear things up for all of
us," Coach Reilly answered, a snarky smile—at least it looked
snarky to Jason—on his face.

Jason realized then that the other coach was Don Ingelsby,
the offensive coordinator; he'd heard of him but hadn't ever met
him during the seven-on-seven camp.

"This is Thomas Jefferson," Coach Ingelsby said, putting an

arm around Tom. "He thought he was supposed to be with the quarterbacks. I'm betting you have Jason Roddin here with you when he should be with the QBs."

"That explains it," Coach Reilly said.

"Roddin, you need to report to Coach Cruikshank—and you better do it on the double." He smiled the same snarky smile. "Jefferson, better late than never. Welcome."

Jason looked at Tom, who shrugged his shoulders as if to say, *I don't get it either.*

"Coach, excuse me," Jason said, "but there's been a mistake."

"And we've cleared it up," Coach Ingelsby said before Jason could go any further.

Jason shook his head. "No, sir, I don't think so—"

Coach Ingelsby held up a hand to stop him. "Roddin, this is your first day, so I'm going to cut you some slack. But you need to learn that at TGP you don't contradict your coaches—especially on the practice field. When practice is over you can ask your position coach a *question* if you're confused about something. Now I'd suggest you get over to the QB group in a hurry, because you're about five seconds away from a long run and I doubt that's how you want to start your first practice."

Once again, everyone was looking at Jason. Once again, his thought was that the coach had it wrong; Jason *did* want to run—and keep going until he got to I-64 and could hitch back to New York from there.

Instead, without saying another word, he began walking,

then jogging, in the direction of midfield, where the q
backs were gathered.

. . . . .

When he arrived, much to his surprise, Coach Cruikshank didn't give him a hard time.

"Some confusion I take it, Jason?" he said. "We'll straighten it out after practice, okay?"

Jason was surprised by the friendly tone, and by being called by his first name. He just nodded and went to line up for the sprints that were apparently first on the practice agenda.

His adrenaline still up, Jason finished well ahead of the other quarterbacks at all three distances—even the 10-yard sprint, where he finished a full step ahead of Billy Bob, who was second.

"Why are you here?" Billy Bob said quietly as they walked back to the starting line. "I thought Tom was the QB."

"He is," Jason said, but didn't have time to say anything more.

When it came time to throw, Jason didn't do badly, but the star was Billy Bob. The kid could throw the ball over the moon, Jason decided after watching him. He had to admit, the Alabama boy's arm was stronger than Tom's, but he'd still bet on Tom when it came to accuracy. There was one other QB who caught Jason's eye—Jamie Dixon, a rangy kid who looked to be about six foot four and who, he remembered hearing, had been tabbed as the heir apparent to the two quarterbacks who had graduated.

The sun was still blazing hot and the humidity still thick enough to peel when Coach Johnson's whistle brought all the players and position coaches to the midfield area.

"Take a knee," Coach Johnson ordered, and they all did. Tom had veered away from the receivers and was kneeling next to Jason.

"Good first day," Coach Johnson said. He pointed in the direction of the top row of stands, where cameras were set up. "As you know, we tape everything that goes on here. I know it's all digital nowadays, but I'm old-school and I still call it tape. By the time we practice tomorrow, the coaches will have some comments for you based on what they see on the tape tomorrow morning.

"They'll also start scheduling you for individual tape sessions and, once we get all the plays in place this week, we'll spend some time on tape before practices. Tape, gentlemen, is a key to opening the door to football success. Come to those sessions ready to focus and work!"

They were all nodding. Jason felt himself dreading tape sessions already.

"We'll scrimmage on Saturday," Coach Johnson continued, "and that will go a long way toward establishing a depth chart for the opener. We only get two weeks of preseason practice, so come prepared mentally and physically every day." He paused, then finished, "Okay, that's it. Hit the showers."

Everyone stood up, and most of the players began walking slowly in the direction of the locker room. Billy Bob came over to where Tom and Jason were standing.

"So what happened?" he asked, glancing around as if wanting to be sure no one else was listening. "Why'd they switch y'all?"

"No idea," Tom said.

"I think we need to talk to Coach Johnson," Jason said.

"Bad idea," Tom said. "My guess is that this is a place where, if you go over someone's head, it won't be looked on kindly. I think we go to the position coaches."

"Equally bad idea," Jason said. "I was only with Coach Reilly a couple of minutes, but my sense is that he's a serious jerk."

Tom nodded. "Unfortunately, your sense is correct."

"Why don't you compromise?" Billy Bob said. "Go to the offensive coordinator. He'd be the one who had input, if not final say, into position assignments anyway."

"Coach Ingelsby?" Jason said. "He didn't strike me as a charmer either."

"If you're looking for charm, you're in the wrong place," Billy Bob said.

"I've been thinking that most of the afternoon," Tom said.

Jason was about to agree when they looked up and saw Coach Ingelsby walking in their direction.

"Ready or not . . ." Billy Bob muttered, and he turned and headed to the locker room, leaving Jason and Tom to meet their fate, in the form of their coordinator.

· · · · ·

"You guys like standing in the hot sun?" Coach Ingelsby said, taking off his cap to wipe his brow, the hint of a smile curling his lips just a bit. The effect was more frightening than friendly.

"No, sir," Tom said. "But we were hoping to talk to you for a moment."

Coach Ingelsby turned his palms up and spread them. "Talk," he said. "Floor's yours."

Jason and Tom glanced at each other. Tom was a lot better speaking on his feet than Jason, so he took the lead.

"Coach, we think there's been some confusion—"

"About what?" Coach Ingelsby broke in. It was pretty clear that he wasn't feeling terribly patient, despite saying that the boys had the floor.

Tom picked up on the fact that he'd better cut to the chase. "I'm a quarterback," he said. "Jason's a receiver. Somehow I ended up today with the receivers, and Jason ended up with the quarterbacks."

Coach Ingelsby folded his arms. "You boys were both in seven-on-seven camp a year ago, weren't you?"

They both nodded.

"You know we taped everything there, just like we tape practices here, don't you?"

They both knew it because one of the things the camp did was offer to let players buy their tapes to look at and analyze after they went home. They both nodded again.

"So don't you think that the staff looked at your tapes from the camp before we decided where to assign you?"

"Did you look at Jason's sprint times?" Tom asked. "Did you look at how he runs a route and catches anything within his air space?"

"Did you watch Tom throw?" Jason added.

The curled smile disappeared from Coach Ingelsby's face.

"If you two would like to apply for coaching jobs here so you can make decisions on who should play what positions, feel free. If you get hired, I'll be glad to listen to your input on every player we have on the offensive side of the football. Until then, do me and yourselves a favor: keep your opinions to yourselves unless I *ask* for them."

"Do you ever ask players for their opinions?" Tom said.

"No," Coach Ingelsby said. He turned and walked away.

Jason watched Coach Ingelsby stalk across the field toward the locker room without glancing back. "I thought that went well, didn't you?"

Tom didn't answer for a moment, ignoring Jason's joke. He had his arms folded, his helmet dangling from his right hand. Finally, he shook his head.

"Look, these are bad guys," he said. "At least this Ingelsby guy is, and so is Reilly. Haven't seen enough of Coach Johnson yet to know if he's the nice guy we met at seven-on-seven camp or—"

"He's not," Jason said. "Remember, he was recruiting us then—trying to charm us—sell us on this place. He's done selling. We've already bought. My guess is that the real Bobo is as big a jerk as Ingelsby and Reilly, and they're taking their cues from him."

"Probably true," Tom said. "We knew this was a jock factory when we signed up. I think we can live with that, especially going for free. I can deal with being yelled at by coaches, and so can you." He thought for a moment, then added, "But there's something rotten in Denmark."

"Huh?" Jason said.

"Come on, you read *Hamlet* in English last year, didn't you?"

Jason shook his head. "CliffsNotes," he said. "Got a B on the paper. What in the world are you talking about?"

"One of the most famous quotes in literature, 'Something is rotten in the state of Denmark.'"

"Oh yeah," Jason said, still embarrassed but trying to recover. "I remember now. Hamlet says it."

Tom shook his head. "No, Marcellus says it in the first act. But he's saying that something is wrong with the way Denmark is being ruled and—"

"I get it. Something's rotten in the state of Virginia—at TGP."

Tom sighed. "Close enough."

"Well, sweet prince, we better go shower before we get in trouble for being late for dinner."

"*Et tu*, Jason?"

"Whaa?"

"Forget it," Tom said, throwing his arm around his friend. "One Shakespeare play a day is enough. Let's go eat."

. . . . .

They walked over to the dining hall with Billy Bob, who was already out of the shower by the time they got to the locker room but had waited for them.

Even though he'd eaten three meals a day there during the seven-on-seven camp, Jason still found the dining hall—the

Robert G. Durant Dining Hall, apparently named for a donor rather than a general or a former president—overwhelming.

The room was big enough to easily fit every TGP student into it with space to spare. It had seemed relatively empty the previous summer since there were only about four hundred campers—football players, boys' and girls' basketball and soccer players—eating in there every day. The skylights built into the high ceiling seemed to make everything in the room shine.

Now, with the entire student body gathering three times a day for meals, it was quite loud, despite the high ceiling. Even amid the noise, Jason couldn't help but notice that, although no one had been assigned a seat, there seemed to be very few coed tables and that for the most part players from each different team sat with one another.

"So what happened out there with Ingelsby?" Billy Bob asked as they loaded their trays in the cafeteria line. "Y'all in trouble?"

"Not yet," Jason answered.

They filled him in on the conversation.

Billy Bob shook his head. "Makes no sense, really," he said. "They need a quarterback this year, and I *know* good old Coach Johnson doesn't like losin'. In fact, my daddy says there's been talk around the Southeastern Conference that if Brian Daboll gets a job, Coach Johnson might be in line to be the next offensive coordinator at Alabama. *If* we're good this season."

"Why would he leave a job where he has absolute power to be a coordinator and have to work for someone—even if it is Nick Saban?" Tom asked.

"Because the head coach here only gets paid a hundred and fifty grand a year," Billy Bob said. "The coordinators at Alabama make a million-plus."

"Coordinators?" Jason said, stunned.

Billy Bob laughed. "You boys just don't understand the South. *Everyone* in the Southeastern Conference gets paid a lot of money."

They found their table just as the school chaplain was walking to a podium in the front of the room to deliver the premeal blessing. As quietly as they could, they slid into three empty chairs near the back of the room that Tom's roommate, Anthony, had saved for them.

"Welcome home, ladies and gentlemen," the chaplain said before starting his blessing.

"If this is home, how do I run away?" Jason whispered to Tom, causing him to snort with laughter.

"Hey, freshmen, you need to shut up and show some respect during the blessing," some kid hissed at them from across the table.

"Blessing hasn't started yet," Tom hissed back.

The hisser didn't respond because the blessing had gotten under way and he had bowed his head.

"Dear Lord," prayed the chaplain, "we thank thee for our food today. May we be faithful stewards of thy bounty. Grant us the grace to walk where your son Jesus's feet have gone . . ."

Jason wouldn't bow his head for a prayer mentioning Jesus as the son of God (and he thought praying about someone's feet was an odd choice for mealtime). Tom didn't bow his head because he believed that all prayer should be silent and private.

Somehow, the hisser took time out of his own praying to make note that neither of them had bowed his head or murmured an *Amen* when the chaplain finished. "What's the matter, you big-city boys don't believe in God?" he snarled.

Jason started to answer, but Tom put a hand on his arm in an I-got-this gesture.

"How about we all mind our own business?" Tom said.

The hisser glared at Tom but said nothing.

The kid next to him, whom Jason recognized as Ronnie Thompson, one of the other quarterbacks, looked at Tom and said, "Are you Muslim or something? You pray to Allah?"

"I'm not, but if I were, so what?" Tom said. "You pray to whomever you want, and I'll pray to whomever I want, and we'll leave it at that."

"Except you guys don't pray at all, do you?" the hisser said.

Billy Bob jumped in. "Fellas, I'm a good old boy from Gadsden, Alabama, and I go to church every Sunday and pray to the Lord Jesus Christ, just like you do. But at this school we've got folks from all over, and we all"—he glanced at Jason and Tom—"better learn that not everyone's the same as us. Now can we all just eat? I'm starvin'."

"I say amen to that," Tom said.

There was a good deal of glaring in response to that comment, but Anthony reached for the plate of chicken in front of him and the table fell silent as everyone began chowing down.

Amen, Jason thought, *to that.*

5

THERE WASN'T MUCH TALK AT THE TABLE DURING THE REST OF DINNER, other than people asking that rolls and pitchers of iced tea be passed. The food wasn't exactly Aberdeen Barn quality or even Roddin kitchen quality, but it *was* plentiful.

While everyone was digging into the ice cream that had been served for dessert, Mr. Gatch went to the podium. "The good news is, you already heard my welcome-home speech today," he said.

Jason might have found the comment funny if his stomach wasn't still churning and if he wasn't already sick and tired of hearing this place called home over and over again.

"You older kids know one of our traditions here at TGP is getting to know people," Mr. Gatch continued. "Tonight, you all randomly picked a table at which to sit. Note the table because that is your table for the rest of this week. Next Monday, you'll sit at a different table and stay there until the following Sunday night. And so on.

"And, every Monday, at the end of dinner, you will spend an extra few minutes at your table getting to know your tablemates. Each of you will introduce yourself, talk about yourself for about a minute—where you're from, what sport you play and your position, what your parents do, and maybe who your favorite teams or athletes might be. By Sunday, you will be expected to know the names of each of your tablemates and a little about them. If one of your coaches asks you next week who you sat with this week, you'd better know." He smiled. "There are going to be rivalries here, and there will be competition on every team. But in the end we *are* all on the TGP team—regardless of what sport you play, boy or girl."

Jason could see that he wasn't the only one at the table rolling his eyes. It was the first sign of anything resembling camaraderie he'd seen all day.

Mr. Gatch was winding up. "If you're a senior, start the introduction process at your table. If no one speaks up right away and you're a junior, you start. And so on. Let's go."

The massive room was instantly filled with noise as seniors around the room began their introductions. Apparently no one at Jason and Tom's table was a senior, because there were several seconds of awkward silence. Finally, a boy at the end with a shock of blond hair and a nose that had clearly been broken at some point spoke up.

"Looks like no seniors here," he said. "I guess I'll start. I'm

Jeremy Winslow and I'm a junior from Belfast, Maine. I'm an offensive tackle, and I play on the wedge on kickoffs. My dad's a fisherman, and my mom is the mother of six." He smiled. "That seems to be enough to keep her busy."

They went around the table that way. Six of them were football players. Two played basketball, one was a swimmer, and one played soccer.

It turned out that the hisser's name was Rudy Nesmith and he was from Ottumwa, Iowa. The only thing Jason knew about Ottumwa, Iowa, was that Radar O'Reilly, one of the characters in his father's favorite old television show, *M*A*S*H*, was from there.

Jason and Tom went last.

"Jason Roddin, New York City," he began. "I'm a freshman and I am a . . ." He paused for a second, thinking about what he was about to say. There were no coaches at the table, just other students. "I'm a receiver," he said, finally, causing both Tom and Billy Bob to give him surprised looks, "but they got me playing QB."

"Tom Jefferson, also from New York," Jason's friend said, jumping in. "No, I'm not related to the bigwig on the nickel." That got a laugh from everyone except Nesmith. "I'm Jason's quarterback, but they put me at receiver."

He shot Jason a look as if to say, *Okay, I'm in, too.*

A few minutes later they were all heading back to the dorm.

"You know this will get back to the coaches," Billy Bob said quietly as they walked out of the dining hall.

"You sure?" Jason said.

"Absolutely," Billy Bob said. "That kid Ronnie is a quarter-back, remember? Think he's not going to say something?"

"Fine with me," Tom said. "You, White Lightning?"

Jason shrugged. "Why not? What are they going to do, throw us out?"

"Only if we're lucky," Tom said. "Only if we're lucky."

· · · · ·

They didn't get that lucky.

The next day, Jason was walking out of his last class of the morning—geology—when someone he didn't recognize walked up to him and said, "Yo, are you Roddin?"

"Yes."

"Before you go to lunch, Coach Johnson wants to see you in his office."

"You mean, right now?"

"You about to go to lunch?"

"Yes."

"Then I'm guessing it means right now." The kid was a little taller than Jason, with dark skin, black hair, and equally dark eyes.

He turned to walk away.

"Hey, hold up. Who are you?" Jason asked.

The guy turned back.

"Juan del Potro. I'm on the baseball team. As part of my scholarship, I have to be a football manager in the fall. Saves my parents twenty K a year, so I put up with it."

"You sound thrilled," Jason said.

"I'm an errand boy all fall," Juan said. "But I couldn't afford to be here if I didn't do it. I'm not good enough to rate a full scholarship, only a partial. So I do it. It's that or Boston Science—which has *no* sports."

Jason nodded and gave him a dap. "Got it. Thanks."

Juan smiled. "Don't thank me, man," he said. "My guess is, you aren't being called in there to be told you had a great first day of practice." He glanced at his watch. "And you better get going. Bobo doesn't like to be kept waiting. I have no idea what this is about, but good luck. I suspect you'll need it." He turned and walked away.

There was something about him Jason liked. Maybe it was the fact that he referred to Coach Johnson as Bobo.

He pulled out his phone and sent Tom a text, then walked quickly from the academic area, across the wide lawn over to the side of campus where the athletic buildings and fields were. He was about to pull open the door to the gleaming three-story building marked TGP FOOTBALL when he heard a familiar voice behind him.

"I should have known he'd call us in together," Tom said.

"You think this is about dinner?" Jason said.

"Nah, I doubt he's going to ask us what we want for dinner," Tom joked.

Jason batted him on the back of the head as they walked up the steps in the middle of the lobby that they knew led to the coaches' offices. They had been here a year earlier when Coach Johnson had told them how much he wanted them to "be part of the Gatch family."

Chances were good this meeting wouldn't be quite as cordial.

At the top of the steps was the receptionist. Jason remembered her from their last visit at the end of seven-on-seven camp, because she was tall, African American, and stunning—not necessarily in that order.

"Mr. Roddin, Mr. Jefferson, nice to see you again," she said, giving them both a spectacular smile. She nodded to her right, where Jason knew the head coach's office was located. "You can go right in. They are waiting for you."

They? Jason gave Tom a look, wondering who else was in there.

The players walked into an outer office that had two desks—neither occupied. In front of them was a closed door with COACH JAMES JOHNSON emblazoned in gold lettering on the glass.

Jason was about to push the door open, but Tom stopped him.

"Knock," Tom whispered. "Let's not give him an excuse to start yelling before we're even inside."

Jason nodded and knocked.

"Come in!" a voice said from the other side.

Jason turned the knob and pushed the door open into a giant office, with two picture windows on the right that looked out on the practice fields. On the left were bookshelves loaded with trophies and a handful of books. Coach Johnson sat behind a huge desk. Behind him was a wall filled with plaques.

Arrayed in chairs around Coach Johnson's desk were four other men.

Jason recognized three of them: Coach Ingelsby, the offensive coordinator; Coach Reilly, the receivers coach; and Coach Cruikshank, the quarterbacks coach. Coaches Ingelsby and Reilly appeared to be trying to stare holes through Jason and Tom. Coach Cruikshank gave the boys a quick wave.

"You fellows know your O-coordinator and your position coaches," Coach Johnson said without bothering to say hello.

He nodded at the fourth man, who also appeared to be giving them the evil eye. "This is Coach George Winston. He's our strength and conditioning coach. You'll be getting to know him well."

Coach Winston showed no sign of wanting to shake hands or greet them in any way, so Jason and Tom just nodded at him. There were two empty chairs in front of the desk—with the coaches seated on either side.

"Take a load off," Coach Johnson said, pointing at the chairs.

They both sat.

Coach Johnson leaned forward in the huge, garish red executive's chair he was sitting in and put his hands on the desk. "I understand you fellas are unhappy with your position assignments. That right?"

Jason looked at Tom, who, as usual, was ready to take the lead.

"Sir, with all due respect to you and"—he nodded at the other men—"to your coaches, I don't think it's so much being unhappy as confused. I've always played quarterback, and I played quarterback most of the time in the seven-on-seven camp last summer. Jason's always been a receiver. You saw yesterday how fast he is in the sprint trials and—"

"That's enough, Jefferson," Coach Johnson said. "Correct me if I'm wrong on this—because perhaps I misunderstood something Coach Ingelsby told me, and I'm always a believer in giving my players the benefit of the doubt—but didn't you bring this up to him after practice yesterday?"

"Yes, sir, but—"

Coach Johnson put up a hand in a *stop* motion.

"And didn't he explain to you that *all* our decisions on positions at Thomas Gatch Prep are made according to what we have seen of players both live and on tape?"

This time, Tom didn't bother with the *but*, because he knew he'd be stopped. "Yes, sir," he said.

By now both boys knew where this was going.

"Now, as time goes by, we move players around. Sometimes we do it because of injuries; sometimes we do it because a player shows us he's better suited for another position. Happens all the time, in fact. So there may come a time, Jefferson, when you're moved to a different position. Heck, you might be moved to defense at some point. You, too, Roddin.

"But, regardless of whether that happens, you *will* listen to your coaches and you will *not* question their decisions." He paused to let that sink in. Then he leaned back in the chair. "You boys know how long I've been coaching football?"

"About thirty years," Jason answered, a little surprised that he could find his voice.

"Thirty-two to be exact," Coach Johnson said. "Unless I'm mistaken, that's longer than the two of you have been alive *combined*."

He pointed in the direction of the assistant coaches. "Together, these four here have another fifty years of coaching under their belts. That's more than eighty years of coaching experience. Successful coaching experience, I might add." He leaned forward again. "You think you know more football than the five of us in this room, Jefferson?"

For a moment Tom didn't answer and Jason thought perhaps he was going to tell Coach Johnson what he and his assistants could do with their eighty years of coaching experience.

Finally, though, Tom shook his head. "No, sir, I don't," he said.

Coach Johnson turned to Jason. "You, Roddin?"

"No, sir," he said.

Coach Johnson smiled. "Glad we got this straightened out once and for all. I'm sure you boys understand that none of us in here expect to hear about this again."

They both nodded—but that apparently wasn't good enough.

"You *do* understand?" Coach Johnson repeated.

"Yes, Coach," they both answered.

"Good, because the next time you *mis*understand, there won't be a clear-the-air meeting like this one. You'll be meeting with Coach Winston at five a.m. for workouts I doubt you'll enjoy very much."

At least now, Jason thought, they knew why the strength coach was there.

Coach Johnson sat back to indicate the meeting was over. The boys stood up.

"You've got about fifteen minutes to make it back to the

dining hall, grab something to eat, and hustle to your fifth-period class," Coach Johnson said. "You better get moving."

There were no handshakes or nods. The boys just turned and left. As they half walked, half ran across the campus, Jason asked Tom what he thought.

Tom shrugged. "My dad always says to not make snap judgments," he said. "Much as I'd love to call our parents and tell them to come get us, I think we have to wait and see how things go for a while longer."

"How much longer?" Jason asked.

Tom didn't slow down a step or even turn in his direction. "Let's give it a week," he said.

That didn't sound like a whole lot longer to Jason. Then again, given what the first two days had been like, it might end up feeling like forever.

6

TOM AND JASON MANAGED TO STAY OUT OF TROUBLE FOR THE REST OF
the week. The good news was that Jason liked his teachers and
found the work stimulating, if not easy.

Tom, the better student, agreed. "At the very worst, we're
getting a pretty good education for free," he said on Friday
night, sitting in the chair at Jason's desk. His roommate,
Anthony, was sitting in Billy Bob's chair, and Jason and Billy
Bob were sitting on their beds. The four of them had become fast
friends, even though Jason was struggling a little with the fact
that Billy Bob was a much better quarterback than he was.
Better than Tom? Probably not, but at least for the moment, that
was a moot point.

"Yeah, there's a reason TGP kids get into good colleges," Billy
Bob said. "Of course, some of the kids they take, like that base-
ball player who's one of our managers—what's his name again,
Jason?"

"Juan del Potro," Jason said.

"Right. From what I'm told, he's a reasonably good baseball player but a fantastic student. He's here because he'll get a scholarship to Harvard or something, and that'll look good for TGP."

"Harvard doesn't have athletic scholarships," said Tom. "None of the Ivy League schools do."

"Yeah, but they've got financial-need scholarships, and lots of good athletes tend to qualify for them," Billy Bob said. "My daddy told me when I was in fifth grade that if I ever got into Harvard he'd take out another mortgage on his house to pay for it if he had to."

One thing Jason had figured out quickly about Billy Bob was that for all his *ain't*s and *y'all*s and his distinctive good-old-boy routine, he was right there with Tom when it came to being smart.

Anthony was more like Jason: smart enough, but someone who wasn't likely to be applying for financial aid at an Ivy League school anytime soon.

Jason had become friendly with Juan during the week, talking to him in the locker room after practice while Juan was collecting dirty jerseys and other gear to give to the equipment guys for laundry and, occasionally, in the halls between classes. Jason had asked him if he and Tom could sit at his table in the dining hall the next week, and Juan had laughed.

"If you want to sit at a table with a bunch of Hispanics, sure," he'd said. "There's six of us. That leaves room for four more."

"Don't you have to sit with different guys every week?" Jason asked.

Juan shook his head. "You have to sit at a different *table* every week," he said. "There's nothing that says you have to sit with different *people*. At least no one's ever called us on it."

That surprised Jason.

"They don't care if you get to know anyone," Juan said. "That's just myth-building. The younger guys sit with different people, but after a while you just sit with your buddies."

Jason told him that Tom, Billy Bob, Anthony, and he would be joining Juan and his friends the following week.

・・・・・

The first scrimmage of the preseason was Saturday morning, and Jason was dreading it—because he doubted he would play very much. The coaches had said the depth charts would be posted in the locker room in the morning, and Jason suspected he'd be no higher than fourth on the quarterback list. He believed he was in a close battle with Frank Kessler for that fourth slot, but Frank was a sophomore and hadn't upset the coaching staff.

There was no doubt about who would be the top three on the list, only about the order. Jason believed Billy Bob had outplayed all the quarterbacks during the week with the possible exception of Jamie Dixon. At worst, he should be number two on the depth chart. Still, he was convinced Ronnie Thompson would be number two because he was a junior and because he was clearly one of Coach Ingelsby's favorites. Every time

Ronnie made any kind of reasonably good play, Ingelsby turned into a cheerleader.

There was one other thing: Billy Bob, as Jason's roommate, might be guilty by association.

"Don't really care," Billy Bob had said when the boys were hanging out after dinner that Friday night, avoiding homework. "As long as I get a chance to show them I'm pretty good, it's fine. I'm relyin' on Coach Johnson and Coach Ingelsby's morality to eventually get me the startin' job—or, worst case, number two."

"Morality?" the other three boys had said at once.

Billy Bob grinned his disarming grin. "Or should I say lack of it," he said. "They'll do about anything to win. They ain't gonna play Thompson if I'm better, 'cause they flat-out don't like to lose 'round here."

Jason couldn't argue with that. Except for one thing: If they flat-out didn't like to lose 'round here, why was the fastest receiver on the team playing quarterback? And why was someone who might be the best quarterback in the school practicing as a slotback receiver?

Sooner or later, he thought, the coaches would figure it out. Or would they?

· · · · ·

There was a crowd around the bulletin board inside the locker room door the next morning when the four friends walked in after breakfast. They waited for some space to clear, then pushed forward to get a closer look.

Jason found his name right away—it jumped off the page at him under the quarterbacks list: *7. Roddin.*

There were six other quarterbacks. Jason was last string. He knew he hadn't played all that well in practice—how could he be expected to play well at quarterback since he was a wide receiver? But he knew he'd been better than Brooks or Koepka, neither one of whom threw the ball any better than Jason did, and couldn't run it nearly as well as he did. And yet there they were, listed ahead of him on the depth chart.

As expected, Jamie Dixon was number one and—surprise—Ronnie Thompson was number two, with Billy Bob at number three and Frank Kessler at number four.

Jason was still immersed in staring at his name—as if staring at it would somehow make what he was seeing disappear—when Tom's voice brought him back to earth.

"Hey, J, you still here?"

"Yeah, yeah," Jason said, still not completely back. He shifted his gaze to the wide receivers and saw that Tom was listed as the number 5 slotback. There were five slotbacks on the team. He was also last string.

"Something's up here," Tom said. "I'm not any good as a receiver, but I'm still better than Day and Tomasulo."

Jason was back on earth now. "They're punishing us. They didn't make us show up at five o'clock to run, but they knew they were going to humiliate us this morning."

"You think we'll see the field?" Tom said.

"We'll find out later," Jason said. "But one thing's for sure: if we complain, they'll bury us even more."

"Got that right," Tom said.

. . . . .

They *did* see the field—from the sidelines. There were, according to Jason's count, eighty-two players in uniform. He knew that, because he had plenty of time to count.

He guessed that at least seventy of them—perhaps more—got onto the field during the scrimmage. He and Tom stood next to each other the entire time without getting so much as a glance from the coaches.

The only good news was that Billy Bob and Anthony, both playing with the second team offense, played very well. Billy Bob, listed as number three, took as many snaps with the second unit as Ronnie Thompson, and even got a few with the ones. As far as Anthony could tell, Billy Bob completely outplayed Thompson most of the day. It was far more difficult to judge line play, but Anthony was moved to the first unit for the last two series of the morning. That was clearly a good sign.

"This is humiliating," Jason said to Tom as the scrimmage was winding down and it was apparent they weren't going to play a single snap.

"I think that's the point," Tom said.

"What about the other guys who didn't get in?" Jason said.

"I suspect they didn't get in because they can't play," Tom said. "We can play."

"Yeah, just not at the positions we've been assigned."

"Actually, we're good enough that we should at least be getting a chance to play, even out of position," Tom said. "But that's not the issue here."

"How long do they keep doing this to us?" Jason asked.

"Good question," Tom said. "They *do* have a good deal of money invested in our scholarships."

"Maybe they want us to quit," Jason said. "Costs them nothing if we leave."

Tom nodded. "True that," he said. "Which is why we're not leaving."

"Yet," Jason said.

Tom glanced at him sideways. "Yet," he repeated. "Exactly right."

. . . . .

When the scrimmage mercifully ended, they all jogged to midfield, where Coach Johnson told them how pleased he was with the way everyone had competed. There had been a couple of injuries that had looked pretty serious and a couple of players who had to be taken off the field because of the heat, but overall the coaches were happy with what they'd seen.

"Get some rest the next couple of days," Coach Johnson said. "Pay your respects to the Lord in the morning, and then get caught up on your schoolwork. Monday, we start getting ready for DeMatha."

That was the season opener—Thomas Gatch Prep versus DeMatha High School, which was located outside Washington, D.C.

After the players had put their hands in for a breakup cheer—"Together!" was what the captains had asked for—Tom turned to Jason and said, "Pay your respects to the Lord? Is he serious?"

Jason was about to answer when he felt a hand on his shoulder. Convinced he and Tom were in trouble again, he flinched. He turned around and saw Coach Cruikshank.

"Can I see you for a minute?" he asked.

Jason actually liked Coach Cruikshank. He was different—or so it seemed—from the other coaches. He encouraged the players, only raised his voice on occasion, and usually found something positive to say. Jason had felt let down by him, though, when he'd seen the depth chart. He had to assume that each position coach decided on who fit where on the chart.

"Sure, Coach," Jason answered.

"Meet you in the locker room," Tom said, and turned in that direction.

Jason and Coach Cruikshank walked in the opposite direction. They were soon alone, with everyone else trying to get inside and out of the heat as quickly as possible.

"I know you have to be disappointed right now," Coach Cruikshank said as he and Jason stood facing each other along the sideline where Jason had already spent his morning. "I don't blame you."

Jason started to answer, but the coach interrupted.

"Let me finish and then feel free to unload. If you repeat this anywhere, you'll jeopardize my job, even though I'm going to tell you something you already know. You should have been fourth on today's depth chart and, from what I understand, Tom should have been no *worse* than third. You guys were punished today because you publicly complained about where you were playing."

"But—"

"But it's not fair. I know that. Jason, guess what, football's not always fair. TGP isn't always fair, and life isn't always fair. The good news is, you and Tom both start with a clean slate Monday. If you practice next week like you did this week, you'll both be in uniform for the DeMatha game; you might even get in the game—depending on how things go. Just do me a favor: bite your tongues, and don't get into any more trouble."

"Coach, there's still the larger issue. You guys are missing the boat not giving Tom a chance to show you what he can do at quarterback."

"And I know your speed makes you an ideal receiver," Coach Cruikshank said.

"And?"

Coach Cruikshank looked him right in the eye. "And it's not going to happen."

"Ever?"

"I never say never," Coach Cruikshank said. "Things change."

"What would have to change?" Jason said.

Coach Cruikshank smiled tightly in a way that looked like he was clamping his lips. "Try to be patient," he said after a moment. "I know that isn't easy for a high school freshman. But at this point, you don't have a choice. Neither does Tom."

"Unless we leave," Jason said.

"Don't give them what they want," Coach Cruikshank said. With that, he turned and walked away.

7

JASON DIDN'T SAY ANYTHING TO TOM, BILLY BOB, OR ANTHONY IN THE locker room or at lunch—too many ears, many of them unfriendly, were around.

They had the afternoon off, presumably to spend on schoolwork, so they retreated to Jason and Billy Bob's room—it was bigger than Tom and Anthony's—so that Jason could fill the other three in on his conversation with Coach Cruikshank. When he finished, they all sat in silence for a while.

"There's a message in there," Jason said finally, "but I've got no idea what it could be."

Tom nodded and let out a deep sigh. "You're right about the message," he said. "I think Coach C's a good guy, don't you, Jason?"

"I do," Jason said. "He's about the only coach who's been even a little bit sympathetic since we got here."

"Which is why he's trying to send you a message without jeopardizing his position with Coach Johnson," Tom said.

"Yeah, but what's the message?" Anthony said.

"I'm not sure you want to hear it," Tom said. "I'm not sure, for that matter, that I want to hear it."

"I've got a theory," Billy Bob said. "And I bet it matches your theory, Tom."

"What are you talking about?" Jason asked. He was worried about the expression he saw on his friend's face, a mix of anger and something else—sadness?

"Jason, tell me honestly, who do you think is a better quarterback, me or Ronnie Thompson?" Billy Bob asked. "You've seen us both play now for a week."

"You," Jason said. "The only reason he was with the second team today was because—"

"He's a junior and I'm a freshman, I know," Billy Bob said, finishing his sentence. "But now answer this one for me—and be straight: You've seen me for a week, you've seen Tom all your life. Which one of us is a better quarterback?"

For a moment Jason didn't answer.

"Go ahead," Billy Bob said. "The truth."

"Tom is," Jason said. "You're a little faster than he is, and your arm strength is pretty close. But he's a lot more accurate than you are."

"Am I that bad?" Billy Bob said, grinning for an instant.

"No!" Jason said. Then he smiled, too. "He's that good."

"Okay, if that's true and if we assume that the coaches 'round here know football—which I think they do—and they want to win games, why in the world is Tom playing wide receiver? Why is he playing a position where he ain't all that good?"

Jason and Anthony both started to answer, but Billy Bob interrupted.

"Hang on, not finished yet. Tom, you've seen all the receivers on the team this week, right?"

Tom nodded.

"If Jason was playin' receiver, where would he be on the depth chart?"

"He might be second for the same reason you're only third—he's a freshman," Tom said. "But he's the fastest guy on the team, and I'd guess once the games start, they'd want him on the field because he'll be our best deep threat."

"Exactly," Billy Bob said. "So let's add this up. We've got a head coach who wants to win this year more than ever because, if what I read back home is true, he could be makin' a *lot* of money next year at Alabama. We've got a coaching staff that knows if the head coach moves up, they all move up in the pecking order—one way or the other. We've got one kid who could easily be the starting quarterback, but he's at receiver, where he's probably third team. We've got another who is, without doubt, the most dangerous deep threat on the roster, who—at best—will be fourth-team quarterback but might not even be that." Billy Bob stopped to take a breath. "Somethin' don't add up here. We've got two plus two equaling five. Or six."

"So what's the catch?" Jason asked. "What's the message?"

Billy Bob looked at Anthony. "What about you, Anthony?

Old football saying is that O-linemen are the smartest guys on the team."

Anthony squinted. "If you're thinking what I'm thinking, then we've got a serious problem," he said. "I just have trouble believing it. We're almost two decades into the twenty-first century."

"What in the world are you talking about?" Jason asked.

"I think Billy Bob and Tom are saying that Coach Johnson doesn't want an African American quarterback," Anthony said.

His words hung in the air for a moment. Jason looked at Billy Bob.

"You advance to the lightning round, Anthony," Billy Bob said. "Boys, we're through the looking glass. I think we've landed smack in the 1960s."

"Maybe he's worried I wouldn't be smart enough to play quarterback," Tom said. "I might have a strong arm, but I'd probably throw the ball to the wrong guy most of the time."

"Nah, that wouldn't be it," Anthony said. "You just wouldn't be able to learn the plays."

He wasn't smiling when he said it.

· · · · ·

They talked about it for a good long while. On the one hand, it seemed impossible for someone who worked with young people—even a Southern good old boy—to be that backward. After all, Bobo's own alma mater had played African Americans at quarterback.

And yet . . .

"Do you have a reason for all this that makes more sense?" Billy Bob asked. "I'm gonna guess y'all ain't the first guys to show up here and not be happy with the position they're assigned to on the first day. You're probably not the first ones to bring it up to your coaches. But look at how they reacted."

"Like we hit a nerve," Tom said.

"Yup," Billy Bob said. "Because you did. Look, you two have led sheltered lives up there in New York."

Tom scoffed. "Not as sheltered as you might assume," he said. "You don't think Jason hasn't been given a hard time at school about always hanging out with the black kid? You don't think I haven't been in a million situations where I walk in the door and nobody looks like me—or where I make a person jump out of their white skin just walking down the street toward them at night? You don't think I haven't stepped into advanced math or history courses and gotten looks as if to say, *What are you doing here?* Hell, last year I had an advanced algebra *teacher* say, 'Young man, I think you're in the wrong room.'"

Jason was surprised by the passion in his friend's voice. He had never heard Tom speak so strongly on the subject.

"Bet the teacher apologized, didn't he?" Billy Bob said.

"He did, but . . ."

"But you're right, there are racists everywhere—unfortunately," Billy Bob said. "I reckon that, even up north, the color of your skin has led to problems that a white boy like me can't even begin to imagine. All I'm sayin' is, you can't go and broadcast your racism up there—especially if you're a public figure." He shook his head. "But where I come from, there are folks who get put on pedestals for being racists, still today. Look at that guy from South Carolina, the congressman who called President Obama a liar. If he'd done that to a white president, he'd have had to resign that night. But what happened? He gets reelected with like ninety percent of the vote—or something close to it. What's that tell you?"

"He's right," Tom said. "Guy's name is Joe Wilson. He ran unopposed in 2012 and was reelected in 2016. He'll be in Congress for life. He was actually formally rebuked by Congress, but the vote was along party lines. In other words, the Republicans thought it was okay to scream 'You lie!' at a president of the United States. Imagine what would happen if an African American congressman yelled that at President Trump."

"Heck," Billy Bob put in, "imagine what would happen if a *white* congressman yelled that at *any* president—other than Obama."

"That's pretty scary," Jason said.

"It's also scary that a prep school coach might not play a guy at quarterback because he's black," Anthony said. "I mean, seriously, I'm having trouble believing this, even though I hear what you're saying, Billy Bob. I look at pro football today, college football even more—it's almost hard to believe there was a time when black guys didn't play QB. You're talking stuff out of history books—like segregation or slavery."

"There's a lot of folks in this country who *miss* segregation and, for that matter, slavery," Billy Bob said. "Believe me. I know some of them."

"And one of them may be our coach," Jason said.

"I'm still confused about one thing," Anthony said. "They recruited you two guys. They offered you scholarships. Why would they play you at wrong positions and then, like Coach Cruikshank seemed to say, *want* you to walk away?"

Before Jason or Tom could answer, Billy Bob jumped in. "I think they honestly believed Jason and Tom were good enough to play at the positions where they've put them—and, you know what, they might be. But now they've made themselves headaches—asked too many questions. They overrecruit here at TGP on purpose. They run some people off every year, just like the colleges do. They just made a decision on Jason and Tom earlier than usual because they opened their big Yankee mouths."

"One black, one Jewish, to boot," Tom said.

"Hard to believe that matters," Billy Bob said. "But apparently it does."

"The question, then, is, What do we do about it?" Jason asked.

They all sat there looking at one another.

"First thing we've got to do is some homework," Billy Bob finally said.

"Homework?" the other three said at once.

Billy Bob smiled. "Not school homework—history homework. We need to know more about Coach Bobo."

"Like, has he *ever* had an African American quarterback here at TGP?" Tom asked.

"That's the first question," Billy Bob said. "Then we need to know more about how he grew up, who he's been friends with, who he has worked with and for, and who has worked for him."

"That's quite a research project," Jason said.

"I know," Billy Bob said. "Good thing we've got four of us to work on it."

. . . . .

By the time the afternoon was over, a plan was in place. Tom, the research wonk, would go through the school's archives—the student newspaper, anything online about TGP, yearbooks, newspaper clippings in the school library—to compile a list of all those who had played quarterback for TGP.

Billy Bob would talk to his father, who would know the names of people familiar with Coach Johnson's history at Alabama.

"Don't you think your dad will want to know what you're up to?" Jason asked.

"Oh, he'll definitely want to know," Billy Bob said. "But he won't have a problem with it. He's the editor and publisher of the *Gadsden Times*. He knows a story when he hears one."

"Does he protect his sources?" Tom asked.

"Not a lot of investigative reporting goes on down there," Billy Bob said. "But I think when the source is his son, Dad will be sure to protect him."

Anthony's job was to talk to some of the older African American players on the team about their experiences with Coach Johnson and the other coaches, and find out what they might have heard from those who had come before them.

"What you want to know is if there's ever been a sense that

he treats his white players any different from his black players," Tom said.

"Haven't seen any difference so far," Anthony said. "He doesn't talk much to any of us—white or black."

"We still haven't played a game," Billy Bob pointed out.

Jason's job was to contact people in the Virginia media who had covered Coach Johnson and TGP—the longer the better. TGP had gotten a lot of attention, both locally and nationally, because it was so much like the IMG Academy and because it had turned out nationally recruited players in both football and basketball.

"Just go online and type in Coach Johnson's name," Tom said. "That will give you a good starting point. Read the bylines and go from there."

Before they broke up to go and do some actual schoolwork— Jason was already starting to feel as if he was falling a bit behind—Billy Bob added one more word of caution.

"Not a word about this to anyone," he said. "Even if this is going on, there are probably a lot of guys who will think the coaches have it right. Regardless, we can't have anyone whispering to anyone about it. If y'all are talkin' to someone on the phone, make sure it's in a place where no one except your roommate might be listenin'. We get caught doin' this, we're all done here—whether they kick us out of school or not. Might be *better* to get kicked out of school, come to think of it."

"What happens if you've got this right?" Tom asked. "What do we do then?"

Billy Bob smiled. "We'll blow up that bridge when we come to it," he said.

When he heard that, Jason smiled, too, thinking about a movie he'd watched a few months earlier with his dad. "Ever hear of *The Bridge on the River Kwai*?" he asked the others.

"The movie?" Tom said. "Yeah, my mom loves William Holden."

For once, Billy Bob looked puzzled. "What about it?" he said.

"It's about a bunch of guys who have to blow up this bridge in the jungle during World War Two. In the end, the guy who blows it up is the guy who built it. He accidentally falls on the detonator after he's wounded."

Billy Bob grinned. "Well," he said, "let's hope we can get to the detonator if we have to—and live to tell about it."

· · · · ·

Jason was in his room Sunday morning trying to decide what to do first: conduct some online research on sports reporters who covered the TGP Patriots, or catch up on his reading for English lit—specifically, *Romeo and Juliet*, the Shakespeare play they had been assigned.

Tom had left for the library shortly after they'd gotten back from breakfast to begin his research into TGP's football history. Billy Bob and Anthony had gone to church. Jason remembered one of the forms he had filled out before coming down to school that had said that if the Protestant services offered on campus on Sunday were not deemed appropriate, transportation to churches of other denominations in the area would be supplied.

Billy Bob had told him that several busloads of TGP students were going to St. Michael's, the Catholic church on the other side of Scottsville. He and Anthony were among them.

With quiet time on his hands, Jason had just reached a compromise on what to do first: before doing work of any kind, he would read the sports section of the *Charlottesville Daily Progress*. He had just sat down in the one comfortable chair in the room with the paper on his lap when there was a knock on the door and Coach Ingelsby, the less-than-friendly offensive coordinator, stuck his head inside.

"Church check," the coach said.

Jason nodded in the direction of Billy Bob's bed.

"Billy Bob left for the bus a while ago," he said.

Coach Ingelsby pushed the door open and walked into the room. "And you?" he said.

Jason was baffled. "Coach, I'm Jewish," he said. It had never occurred to him that someone wouldn't know that.

"So Jewish people don't go to church?" Coach Ingelsby asked.

Jason didn't know whether to laugh or cry. Several wisecracks crossed his mind. He resisted them all. "Coach, if you're Jewish you go to temple, not church. And, generally speaking, you go on Friday night or Saturday morning." He decided not to mention that he and his family did neither.

Coach Ingelsby crossed his arms. "Jewish people don't believe in Jesus Christ, do they?" he said.

"Most Jews believe he existed," Jason said. "They just don't believe he was the son of God."

Coach Ingelsby stared at him in what appeared to be disbelief. "Well," he said, "I guess that's your right. But it's pretty sad."

"Sad, Coach?"

"I just feel sorry for you, missing out on salvation. Nothing personal, of course." The coach glanced at his watch. "Have to go," he said. "I've got fifteen more rooms to check before the bus leaves for the ten o'clock service."

Jason was tempted to ask Coach Ingelsby why he—or anyone else—felt the need to check on whether or not students were going to church. But he resisted. He already knew the answer: they were trying to save people.

"Nice going in the scrimmage yesterday," Coach Ingelsby said as he backed out the door.

"I didn't get in," Jason said.

"I know," the coach said with a smile, and pulled the door shut.

"Go with God, you jerk," Jason said to himself when he was alone again. He tossed the newspaper down and walked to his computer. It was time to get to work.

The newspaper—and Shakespeare—could wait.

8

JASON WAS JUST GETTING STARTED WITH HIS ONLINE SEARCH WHEN TOM pushed open the door and walked into the room with an exasperated look on his face.

"What happened?" Jason asked.

Tom collapsed in the chair where Jason had been sitting when Coach Ingelsby showed up, shook his head, and said, "I should have known."

"Known what?"

"The library is closed until two o'clock on Sundays. The sign on the door says—and I'm not making this up—GOD FIRST, STUDIES SECOND."

"Too bad you weren't here ten minutes ago," Jason said. "You missed Coach Ingelsby's church check."

"I had my own," Tom said. "I ran into him when I was coming back here. He gave me a look and said, 'Jefferson, you're not in church?' I just told him no, I wasn't. Didn't think I needed to explain further. He shook his head and actually asked me if I was Jewish, too. So I figured he'd already seen you."

"Yeah, I'm blowing my chance at salvation," Jason said.

"Well, at least Billy Bob and Anthony are in church. Maybe God will tell them how we can deal with this place."

"Not sure even *he* has the answer to that."

They both laughed. Tom decided to read the newspaper while Jason dug into the Internet. Within an hour, Jason had a list of a dozen media members: six were from newspapers; four were local-TV types (three from Richmond and one from Charlottesville); and two were radio talk show hosts (one out of Richmond, the other from Roanoke, which was about two hours southwest of Charlottesville).

"They've all got general e-mail boxes you can write to," Jason said. "Should I just send them notes?"

Tom shook his head. "Writing out of the blue, especially when we're dealing with people we don't know, probably isn't a good idea. We need to introduce ourselves on the phone. We aren't going to reach anyone on Sunday. I recommend we divide them up among the four of us—three apiece—and start calling them tomorrow."

"There are no phone numbers listed here," Jason said.

Tom sighed. "You know, for a smart kid, you sometimes aren't very smart. Look up the main number for their papers or stations online, call it, and ask for the reporter. Worst case, you get their voicemail and can leave a message saying you play football at TGP. They'll call back."

"Don't newspapers publish seven days a week?" Jason said.

"Why don't we start with the newspaper guys today and call the talk show guys tomorrow?"

Tom grinned. "So maybe you aren't as dumb as I thought."

It didn't take long to look up the phone numbers for the six newspapers in question: the *Roanoke Times*, the *Richmond Times-Dispatch*, the *Virginian-Pilot*, the *Charlottesville Daily Progress*, the *Lynchburg News & Advance*, and the *Newport News Daily Press*. They had found stories by two different writers about TGP in both the *Times-Dispatch* and the *Roanoke Times*.

Armed with the phone numbers, they decided to take a walk to find a quiet spot where they would not have to worry about someone walking in on them midconversation.

It was a hot morning, but not too humid. They headed in the direction of the athletic fields, knowing no one would be there on a Sunday morning, and settled in at a small parklike area that had several benches and was surrounded by trees. It was a popular spot for kids to congregate when the weather was good to just talk or study. Now it was empty. They each grabbed a seat on a shaded bench.

Jason had taken the *Roanoke Times*, *Lynchburg News & Advance*, and *Newport News Daily Press* phone numbers, while Tom took the others.

On his cell Jason dialed the *Times* first and asked for Bill Brill. He got voicemail—no surprise—and left a message. He dialed back and asked for Doug Doughty—voicemail again. Well, they hadn't expected much, and so far the calls had lived down to their expectations. In the background, he heard Tom leaving a message for Jerry Ratcliffe in Charlottesville.

Apparently, they weren't going to get much done today. He dialed the *Daily Press*, having no idea where Newport News actually was. The switchboard operator put him through to David Teel, and he prepared to leave the same voicemail he had left for Brill and Doughty, saying he was a football player at Thomas Gatch Prep and he was hoping to talk to them for a few minutes.

"David Teel," a voice said, causing Jason to sit up straight on the bench in surprise.

"Um, hello, Mr. Teel?" Jason said, realizing that saying the reporter's name in a questioning tone was stupidly redundant since the writer had already answered by using his name.

"Yes, this is David, what can I do for you, sir?"

It occurred to Jason that the strategy session the day before hadn't included a conversation on exactly what to say upon reaching one of the reporters. "Sorry," he said. "I actually thought I would get your voicemail."

Teel laughed. "I always come in on Sunday mornings because it's quiet and I need all the quiet I can get to write my Monday column."

"Is your house very noisy?" Jason asked, curious, though realizing the question was completely irrelevant.

"Well, I have a five-year-old daughter," Teel said.

"Got it," Jason said.

There was a pause, and Jason realized he needed to start telling Teel why he was breaking up his quiet morning.

"Oh, well," he said, "I'm sorry to bother you, but my name is Jason Roddin and I'm a freshman at Thomas Gatch Prep."

"How you enjoying TGP so far?" Teel asked.

Without knowing it, Teel had cut directly to the chase.

"Well, it's been interesting," Jason said, stalling for time so he could think about exactly what he was going to say. "I've only been here a week and I'm kind of trying to figure the place out."

"And you think I can help you figure it out in some way?" Teel said. "I don't get over there very often because I mostly cover colleges . . ."

"Yes, I know," Jason said. "But I found some stories about the TGP football and basketball teams that you've written in the past . . ."

"True," Teel said. "Not all of them complimentary." He paused a moment and then said, "Is that why you're calling me, Jason? Do you play football or basketball?"

"Football," Jason said.

"What position?"

"Well," Jason said, "that's kind of why I'm calling."

"Tell me more," David Teel said.

. . . . .

Jason's father had forced him to watch *All the President's Men* when he was eleven, and they had watched it together several times since. Jason loved the movie, the idea of two *Washington Post* journalists bringing down a corrupt president with dogged reporting. He had watched the movie often enough that he knew what *off the record* meant. Teel had to agree to not use his name or any direct quote in any article before Jason would tell him more. If Teel didn't agree and Jason told him the story, he risked the possibility of a headline that said TGP FRESHMAN CHARGES RACIAL BIAS AT SCHOOL.

"Mr. Teel, before I say anything else, I need you to let me go off the record," Jason said.

"First, it's David," Teel said. "Second, I'm impressed that a high school freshman knows what *off the record* means. And, third, since you don't know me at all, I'm willing to go off the record with the provision that if you tell me something that I think is a story, we try to work out a way for me to get it into the newspaper without putting you in jeopardy at TGP."

Jason thought about that for a moment and decided it was fair. "Okay," he said.

"Begin at the beginning," Teel said.

Jason did—without going into too much detail. He told Teel how he and Tom had decided to come to the school— leaving out all the details about their mothers' reluctance— and how Tom was an excellent quarterback and Jason an excellent wide receiver.

"Tom's got an amazingly accurate arm, but he's not that fast," Jason said. "I have a lot of speed, but don't throw the ball that well."

Teel stayed silent while Jason talked, clearly not wanting to interrupt his story.

"First day of practice, I went with the receivers, he went with the quarterbacks," Jason said. "The coaches told us we were in the wrong place. I was a quarterback, they said; Tom was a wide receiver."

Teel stopped him at that point. "Hang on," he said. "Is your friend Tom African American?"

Wow, Jason thought, *he figured that one out quickly.*

"Yes," he answered.

There was another pause at the other end of the line.

"Keep going," Teel said. "Remember, you're off the record, so tell me everything."

Jason wasn't sure he wanted to do that, but he kept going anyway. He told Teel how he and Tom had said to the coaches that they were out of position and had been informed very firmly that they weren't. He finished by telling him how neither of them had played at all in the scrimmage.

"That's when Tom and Billy Bob began wondering . . ."

"Wait a minute," Teel said. "Who's Billy Bob?"

"My roommate."

"And his name's really Billy Bob?"

"Yes, sir. He's from Alabama."

"Well, I certainly didn't think he was from D.C.," Teel said with a laugh.

Jason liked him.

"I think I know where this is going," Teel said. "And my guess is, Billy Bob's got it right. You guys think old Bobo doesn't want a black quarterback on his team."

Jason sighed. "It's just a theory," he said. "We were thinking it would at least be worth doing some research to find out how many African American quarterbacks TGP has had under Coach Johnson."

"No need for any more research," Teel said. "I can tell you the exact number—zero."

Jason wasn't completely stunned by the statistic, but he was surprised that Teel knew it with such certainty. "You sure?" he asked.

"Oh, yeah," Teel said. "It's been a subject of conversation among a few of us for a while. It isn't so much that he's never had a starter at the position—he's never had *anyone* at the position. In this day and age that's unusual, to put it in polite terms."

"Have any of you ever written about it?" Jason asked.

"No," Teel said firmly. "It's not the kind of thing you can write about without tangible proof or someone willing to go on the record and say that Bobo doesn't want a black quarterback. It isn't something that is directly provable, so you basically need someone to say, 'I *know* he won't play an African American kid at the position.' If you write that story without having it nailed down, the best-case scenario is that you become a pariah in the coaching community down here for taking on the most successful coach in the state and one of the better-known high school coaches in the country."

"What's the worst-case scenario?" Jason asked.

"That you get sued," Teel said. "You can't mess around on a story like this. Like I said, you have to have it nailed down."

"What does *nailed down* mean?" Jason said.

"Someone has to be willing to go on the record and say that they *know* Bobo won't play an African American at quarterback. Being honest, even if you and Tom were willing to do so—and end your careers before they start—that wouldn't even be enough."

"Why not?" Jason said.

"Because you have no proof," Teel said. "All you have is your opinion that Tom should be throwing the ball and you should be catching it. Bobo could shoot that down in a second: he could claim your speed makes you a double threat and forces the secondary to come up to guard against the run, and Tom's hands make him a good possession receiver and they need someone like him right now. Or he can just point to his record and say, 'Who knows more about football, me or a couple of high school freshmen?'"

Jason felt deflated. The latter had been exactly the tack Coach Johnson had taken.

"Do you think any of that's true?" he asked.

"Does Bobo know more about football than you and Tom? Absolutely," Teel said. "But I also think you're onto something."

"Why? What you just said could make perfect sense."

"Because I've known Bobo Johnson and a lot of coaches like him for a long time," Teel said. "They would like to turn back the clock four or five decades. And, with the talent he recruits every year, he isn't putting his job at risk by ignoring the potential some African American players—like Tom—have to become good quarterbacks. He can still win a lot of games. And *has* won a lot of games."

"The guys playing quarterback right now aren't as good as Tom," Jason said. "Billy Bob is the best of them, but I don't think he's as good as Tom."

"Billy Bob's a quarterback?" Teel said.

"Yes, he's third string right now, but that's just because the guy who is second string is a junior."

"The starter's going to be Jamie Dixon, right? He's supposed to be good."

"He is good. But I'm not sure he's better than Billy Bob, and I *know* he's not better than Tom. Tom is really good."

"So Tom may be better than Billy Bob, yet Billy Bob's the one who brought up the idea that maybe Bobo didn't want Tom at QB because he's black?"

"Yes."

"Billy Bob sounds like an interesting kid."

"He is," Jason said. "And a smart one, too."

"We need to talk more," Teel said. "I need to talk to Tom and to Billy Bob."

Jason was nodding, even though Teel couldn't see him. "Okay," he said. "But do you think we can prove this?"

"I have no idea," Teel said. "But it's certainly worth trying to find out if we can."

9

JASON HADN'T NOTICED THAT WHILE HE WAS TALKING TO TEEL, TOM HAD gotten up and walked off a ways, giving the two of them some space to talk. Apparently, he had also reached someone. In fact, he was still talking when Jason walked over to him after ending the call with Teel.

"Yes, sir, we'll be in touch soon," Tom was saying. "See you, I guess, on Friday night."

He ended the call a moment later.

"What was that about?" Jason asked.

"I reached a reporter named Tom Robinson at the *Virginian-Pilot*," Tom said. "He said everyone in the Virginia media knows that Bobo has never had an African American quarterback at TGP but there's no way to write about it because there's no way to prove it's anything more than coincidence."

"That's exactly what David Teel said to me. He knew just where I was going even before I told him the whole story."

Tom had been standing under a small tree while talking on the phone. Now he sat down heavily on one of the benches.

"How can it be that every reporter in the state knows about this but no one has written about it?"

"Well, it makes sense, really," Jason said, sitting down next to Tom. "If you're a reporter, you can't just say, 'Coach Johnson is a racist because he's never had an African American quarterback.' You have to be able to *prove* he's a racist before you write that he is one."

"How do you do *that*?" Tom asked.

"That's exactly the problem," Jason said. "I doubt if someone said, 'Coach Johnson, why haven't you ever had a black quarterback?' that his answer would be, 'Because I'm a racist.'"

Tom leaned back on the bench and sighed.

"Robinson said he's going to come over here for the DeMatha game on Friday. He wants to talk to us then. I wonder if Teel would come, too."

Jason shook his head. "Reporters from different newspapers working on the same story?" he said.

Tom shrugged. "I told Robinson I thought you might be talking to Teel. He said they were good friends."

Jason was a little surprised by that, but he shrugged. "Well, if that's the case, I'll find out if Teel can come on Friday as well. Two guys working on the story has to be better than one."

"We may need more than two guys," Tom said. "We may need an army of guys."

"And a navy, too," Jason said. "Let's go see if our good Christian roommates are back from church yet."

. . . . .

Billy Bob and Anthony were back, and the four of them gathered in Jason and Billy Bob's room so that Jason and Tom could update them.

"Let's say both reporters come over here Friday," Billy Bob said. "How are any of us going to talk to 'em without someone noticing? It's possible *none* of us will get in the game. Anthony's got the best shot. But, even so, why would someone other than a reporter from our hometown be interested in talking to any of us? The coaches see us talking to those guys, and they'll figure that something's goin' on."

"Why? Are we banned from speaking to the media?" Jason asked.

"No, we're not," Tom said. "At least as far as any of us knows. But Billy Bob is right. Let's say you talk to Teel and I talk to Robinson after the game outside the locker room. Some of the coaches will be bound to see us. When our pal Coach Ingelsby asks us why two reporters wanted to talk to us, what's our answer?"

"For a story on freshmen, adapting to living away from home?" Billy Bob said.

"That's not bad," Anthony added.

Tom nodded. "It's a start, but we'd have to tell them to talk to some of the other freshmen, too, to make it look good."

"What happens when there's no story about freshmen?" Jason asked.

"Maybe they can write one," Tom said, "as a cover."

That wasn't the worst idea any of them had heard, but it needed work.

Thank goodness, Jason thought, they had five more days to smooth out the rough edges.

· · · · ·

The week itself was anything but smooth. Tom and Jason continued to receive very few opportunities in practice. None of the coaches, even Coach Cruikshank, seemed at all interested in anything they were doing. Jason began to feel invisible.

The most football they played was tossing the ball around on the quad outside their dorm once in a while.

The good news was their new table in the dining room. All four of them had moved to table 6D—sixth row from the front, fourth table from the left side of the room—to join Juan del Potro and his friends. The first meal they shared, Tom noticed that he and the other new guys were all sitting across the table from the regulars.

"Donald Trump would *not* like our table," Tom said.

"You got that right, Presidente," Juan said with a grin. "He'd want a wall down the middle of it."

From the beginning, there were a lot of arguments filled with friendly insults at the table—all of them centered on what was the best sport to play: baseball, football, or soccer.

The only problem was that, according to protocol, the table

was supposed to be broken up at the end of the week. Everyone was supposed to find a new place to sit.

"I already told you: Don't worry about it," Juan said to Jason at Wednesday breakfast. "We'll sit in different seats next week, and I guarantee you no one will notice. No one around here ever does. They just announce stuff like that so they can tell parents about how open they are here and what a great place it is to meet people who are different from you."

"I get it. *Meet them*, yes," Jason said. "*Get to know them* is another story."

Still, the decision had been made that they would stick together until someone broke them up. Juan said it wouldn't happen till the end of the season—baseball season.

· · · · ·

That afternoon, the narrative of TGP's football season changed—before the team had played a single game.

Practice was just about over, but the coaches hadn't been especially happy with what they had seen from the offense, so they decided to add a couple of extra series to the afternoon's work. That didn't make anyone happy. It was hot, they were all tired, and everyone had homework to do that evening.

Coach Johnson didn't seem to care. "Ones on offense, ones on defense," he said. "Let's try to get this right."

Ones were the first-stringers, *twos* the second-stringers, and so on down the line. There wasn't a lot of call during practice for threes—like Tom—and even less for fours—like Jason.

Jamie Dixon took the ones back on the field. He was a strong, confident passer but not nearly as good at making decisions in the running game. The running game had been a problem all afternoon. The only quarterback who was even reasonably good when the ball wasn't in the air was Billy Bob.

Now Dixon barked out a play at the line—calling an audible, as he'd been instructed to do—and took the snap. He dropped back two steps as if planning to pass, then turned to pitch the ball to slotback Kendall Franklin, who was supposed to be coming from the left side to take an option pitch while running right.

But Franklin had heard the audible call wrong. Dixon turned to flip him the ball and found nobody there. He tried to plant his foot to go from reverse to forward to make something out of a broken play. But as he planted his foot, he let out a scream of pain that Jason, Tom, and Billy Bob heard clearly from the sidelines. They looked up to see Dixon collapse in a heap.

Whistles blew everywhere. No one had touched Dixon—quarterbacks wore red jerseys to indicate they shouldn't be tackled—but he was down, writhing in pain, reaching for his right knee.

Trainers came running. The practice field was completely silent, except for Dixon's moans.

"That's not just a twisted knee," Billy Bob said. "I've seen it before. He did something bad."

As if to confirm Billy Bob's theory, the team's trainer, Dave Billingsley, stood up for a moment and said, "We need a stretcher, Coach. And you better call one of the docs."

It took a couple of minutes for the managers to wheel a

stretcher onto the field. With Billingsley guiding them, four of the linemen gently lifted Dixon onto the stretcher. His teammates gathered around him to offer encouragement. He was clearly in a world of pain.

"Okay, give him some space," Coach Johnson, who looked quite pale, said finally.

"We'll get him to the hospital and do an MRI," Mr. Billingsley said to Coach Johnson. "Let you know as soon as we know."

Jason turned to Billy Bob as the stretcher was wheeled in the direction of the locker room.

"I hate to sound like a ghoul," he said. "But you better be ready to play Friday. If DeMatha's as good as the coaches claim, no way we win with Ronnie Thompson playing quarterback."

Before Billy Bob could respond, they heard the sound of Coach Johnson's whistle. He was standing at midfield.

"Everyone take a knee," he said.

"Franklin, up here," he said.

Kendall Franklin was a black kid from north Philadelphia, a sophomore with an infectious smile who liked to joke that he'd never met a white kid before he got to TGP. His smile was nowhere to be found now.

"Franklin, would you like to explain to your teammates why our starting quarterback is on his way to the hospital right now?" Coach Johnson said.

For a split second, Franklin didn't seem to understand the question. Was he being asked for a diagnosis? Then he got it.

"Because I missed a call," he said quietly. "Coach, I'm sorry, no one told me to listen for an audible. I thought we were going with the play called on the sideline before we went back in."

"You *thought*, Franklin? You *thought*? Who ever told you to think? You listen and you do what you're told to do. Next time you *think* about having a *thought*, go talk to your coach. Coach Reilly does the thinking for you. You got it? Now, what do you want to say to your teammates?"

"I'm sorry Jamie got hurt," Franklin said.

"And whose fault was it?" Coach Johnson asked.

"Mine."

"Mine *what*?"

"Mine, sir."

"Okay," Coach Johnson said, apparently satisfied that he had completely humiliated Franklin. "You stay behind to do some running, Franklin. Everyone else, that's it for today. Hit the showers."

They did a halfhearted team cheer and began walking slowly in the direction of the locker room.

Anthony was beside himself. "*His* fault?" he said. "Who kept us out here in the heat when everyone was tired? His fault?"

"Easy, big guy," Tom said.

"I'm not right?" Anthony said.

"Oh, no, you're right," Billy Bob said. "We just can't do anything about it. At least not now."

. . . . .

Word spread quickly that evening: Jamie Dixon had torn his ACL. He would need surgery. His season was over.

The next morning word spread almost as quickly: Kendall Franklin was gone. He had texted a terse message to Tom:

Enough. I'm done. Parents coming at 7 a.m. to get me. Good luck.

By the time they got to breakfast, everyone knew Franklin was gone.

"Don't blame him," Anthony said. "Bobo did everything but call him the *n*-word."

Practice that day was noticeably shorter than it had been on Wednesday. Coach Johnson gave them all a rah-rah speech about carrying on without Jamie Dixon and dedicated the season to him.

"Did he die?" Jason muttered to Tom.

Kendall Franklin's name never came up.

Friday was a long day. David Teel was also coming to the game, but on the phone he had informed the boys that he and Tom Robinson had agreed that the "what's it like to be a TGP freshman" angle wouldn't work.

"We're columnists," Teel said. "The coaches know we don't write those kinds of puffy features. They may not figure out why we're talking to you right away, but they'll know we're *not* doing that sort of piece the minute you try to sell it to them."

So an alternative was needed. It was Billy Bob who had come up with it.

"If any of us talks to the reporters after the game, there will be people everywhere," he said. "Coaches, parents, girlfriends, fans—you name it. We need to get them here *before* the game. They'll have press credentials, so that will get them past the gate and onto campus. We just tell them to meet us somewhere quiet."

"Which is where?" Jason said, impressed once again with his roommate's resourcefulness.

"What's the emptiest place in the world three hours before a football game?" Billy Bob asked.

Jason was stumped. So, apparently, was Anthony.

"The locker room!" Tom said.

"Bingo!" Billy Bob answered. "Kickoff is at seven, equipment guys get everything ready in the morning, and we're told not to come in until five because they're not back until then. We'll have the place to ourselves for at least forty-five minutes."

Just to be safe, they had asked Teel and Robinson to get there at 3:30. Their last class was over at 3:15. Seniors were allowed to have cars, and those who didn't have a game or a match or a meet were allowed to leave campus for the weekend, so Jason and Tom watched them head for the parking lot.

The four of them split into pairs and decided to walk to the stadium at five-minute intervals in case anyone was watching. Jason and Billy Bob went first. They found Teel and Robinson sitting on a bench outside the door to the locker room.

They all briefly introduced themselves. Both were, Jason guessed, about fifty. He had done enough research to know that each had been with his paper for a long time. Teel was tall and thin, looked like a guy who ran on a regular basis, wore glasses, and had a wispy mustache with hints of gray in it. Robinson was a little bigger and also had the look of someone who had been an athlete and still worked out. Both had easy smiles that made Jason feel comfortable. Probably, he figured, a good thing to have if you were trying to get people to confide in you.

"Let's go inside," Billy Bob said after the introductions. "Tom and Anthony are about five minutes behind. We figured it couldn't hurt to split up."

"Good thought," Teel said. "There tend to be a lot of eyes on alert around here."

The door was unlocked. The thinking, Jason guessed, was that the campus itself was secure—no one came in without going through the guard gate, so there was no reason to lock the locker room. The lockers themselves all had locks on them.

They walked through the locker room to the lounge area in the back. Here, there were two flat-screen televisions, several couches, and tables set up for guys who wanted to play video games or cards. There was a bar—but of course all the drinks in the refrigerator were protein shakes and Gatorade and bottled water.

"Pretty nice digs for a high school football team," Robinson said.

"The place does have some money," Teel added.

Jason was a little surprised. He figured Teel and Robinson had been here enough that they would know their way around the locker room. Teel seemed to guess his thoughts.

"They don't let the media in here," he said. "You'll see tonight after the game. We have to wait outside and grab guys as they come out."

"Unless someone is off-limits," Robinson added.

"Why would someone be off-limits?" Billy Bob asked.

"Seniors, usually," Robinson said. "If they're highly recruited, sometimes they'll keep them from the media because they don't want them 'distracted' by questions about where they're going to college."

"Occasionally they'll bring a guy who has a big game into the interview room with Bobo," Teel added. "Of course, that's usually worthless because the kid isn't going to say much interesting with the coach sitting right next to him."

"Lot of talk about stepping up, giving a hundred and ten percent, and giving all the credit to teammates, I'm guessing," Billy Bob said.

The reporters both laughed.

"There's also a lot of giving all the glory to God," Teel said. "You'll find that's big at TGP."

"We already have," Jason said.

Tom and Anthony arrived. Introductions were made, and they all sat down on the couches. They walked through the story that Teel and Robinson already knew, adding some details about the meeting Jason and Tom had been subjected to with the coaches before they'd been benched for the scrimmage.

"I guess the question," Tom finally said, "is whether we are jumping at shadows here. If not, what can we prove?"

"Second question is the hard one," Teel said. "We both agree you are *not* jumping at shadows. There's always been kind of an undertone with Bobo on this subject. Like I told you the other day, Jason, he's never had an African American quarterback. Heck, he's never had a *backup* African American quarterback."

"He's also never had an African American coordinator," Robinson added. "Even if he has a few black coaches."

"Which proves what, exactly?" Anthony said in a tone that surprised Jason a little bit.

Anthony was the classic gentle giant. He didn't talk that often, and when he did, he spoke softly. Wednesday, after Kendall Franklin's humiliation, had been an exception to that rule. But now, even in four words, there was a clear edge in his voice.

"Proves nothing," Robinson said. "You can report those facts, and Bobo will say something like 'I never noticed, I just do what's best for the football team.' He may be a racist, but he's no dummy."

"So what do we do?" Billy Bob asked.

"Well, we've got an idea," Teel said. "It's a little bit complicated on our end, and it's risky on yours. It could get you thrown out of school."

"Let's hear it," Tom said. "At this point, getting thrown out of school is the least of my worries."

"Same here," Jason said quickly.

"I'm in," Anthony said.

They all looked at Billy Bob.

He smiled. "My daddy will kill me if I get thrown out of TGP," he said. "And if it gets around my hometown that I got thrown out trying to prove that Bobo Johnson's a racist, I'll be a pariah."

Jason looked at his roomie. "What the heck is a pariah?"

Teel laughed. "I suspect you may be about to find out."

There were footsteps in the hallway. They froze. It was only 4:15. The footsteps grew louder.

Billy Bob nodded in the direction of the shower room, which was on the far side of the lounge. There was an open doorway leading to it—normally used by players coming out because the steam room was a few yards away.

They all got up as quietly and as quickly as they could and ducked into the shower room. They waited there, trying not to breathe. Someone walked into the lounge.

Jason, his heart pounding, peeked around the wall, then quickly pulled his head back. It was Coach Johnson.

What he was doing in the locker room at that hour they didn't know. What he was looking for in the lounge they absolutely didn't know. Jason was closest to the door. He peeked again. Coach Johnson was standing in the middle of the room, hands on hips as if looking for something. Jason ducked back.

A moment later they heard him walk out. They waited awhile, peeked again, and he was gone.

"Now what?" Jason whispered.

"We get out of here," Teel whispered. "Let's hope he went back to his office."

"Hope might not be enough," Billy Bob said very softly. "We might need to say a prayer."

"All the glory to God," Tom whispered back, grinning.

Then, slowly, cautiously, they walked out of the shower room.

PART 2

10

ONCE THEY HAD MADE THEIR WAY THROUGH THE LOCKER ROOM AND OUT the door, the four players and two reporters quickly separated. There was no one else around—which was a relief—but Tom understood they had already pushed the envelope far enough and had been lucky that Coach Johnson had apparently gone back to his office after leaving the lounge.

"We'll talk more tomorrow," David Teel said once they were outside.

Everyone nodded and the two reporters headed in the direction of the entrance to the stadium. The four players, with thirty minutes to kill before they were supposed to report to the locker room, walked in the direction of the campus coffee shop.

It was close to empty, with most TGP students either relaxing in their dorm rooms, bolting campus, or getting ready for games that weekend. Both soccer teams were playing the next morning, and the tennis and golf teams were on their way to early-season tournaments that would be held over the weekend.

Tom's stomach finally began to loosen up when they went to the counter to order drinks and something to eat. He had been surprised that there was no formal pregame meal for the team. He'd read plenty of stories about different coaches and their pregame philosophies when it came to eating: when to eat, what to eat, how much to eat.

He knew that once upon a time, football and basketball players had always been served steak at pregame meals. That had changed when the theory of carbo-loading had come into vogue in the 1980s. That often meant pasta and pancakes, usually served about four hours before a game began. Bob Knight, the Hall of Fame basketball coach, believed pancakes tended to sit heavily in the stomach, so his teams ate pasta only—even when playing a noon game and eating a pregame meal at eight in the morning. Every time Tom thought about trying to eat pasta at that hour he felt slightly sick.

His favorite line about pregame meals had come from Rick Barnes, the Tennessee basketball coach. "We talk to nutritionists and trainers and worry about serving them exactly the right thing," he'd said once. "Fact is, they probably play their best ball in the summer when all they're eating is fast food. I should probably just take them all to McDonald's."

Coach Johnson's philosophy was different from that. Some of the older guys had told Tom and Jason that when the team traveled, the pregame meal, served exactly four hours before kickoff, had both pasta and steak on the menu.

"He thinks real men eat steak, but he's made a big concession by serving pasta, too," Jimmy Matthews, a huge offensive tackle, had said one day in the weight room. "I just eat whatever they got."

When the team played an evening game at home, anyone on the team could go into the dining hall, where a buffet was set up until four o'clock. It wasn't mandatory, and Tom, Jason, Anthony, and Billy Bob had passed on their chance to eat in order to meet with the reporters. So they had to grab something now. Tom ordered a hamburger but skipped the fries. Jason ordered a cheeseburger, fries, a side order of garlic toast, and a milkshake.

"Aren't you afraid that's going to sit in your stomach?" Billy Bob said as he ordered.

"What difference does it make?" Jason asked. "I have as much chance of getting in the game as David Teel and Tom Robinson do."

"I don't know," Anthony said. "Teel looks like he's in pretty good shape. They might sneak him in as a wideout."

Anthony ordered three hamburgers but no fries. Tom figured Anthony could eat six hamburgers and still have room for dessert.

They sat down after glancing around to make sure no one was sitting nearby.

On the other side of the room there was one table occupied by six girls and another by a lone guy who was reading a book and had earbuds in.

"Here's the problem we have right now," Billy Bob said. "We

never got to hear the reporters' plan because Coach Johnson showed up the way he did."

Tom nodded. "I just got a text from Robinson about that," he said, looking at his phone. "He says he and Teel have an idea for how we can meet Sunday morning."

"Here?" Jason asked.

"I think so," Tom said. "He said he'd call me tomorrow morning to explain."

"Sunday morning Billy Bob and I go to church," Anthony said. "If we no-show, people will ask why."

"Not to mention my parents will find out somehow, someway, and want to kill me," Billy Bob added.

"How could they possibly find out?" Jason asked.

"Great question," Billy Bob said. "They seem to know everything I do. Sometimes I think I'm living in *The Truman Show*."

Tom remembered the movie in which a character unknowingly had his entire life secretly broadcast twenty-four hours a day as a reality TV show. Judging by the looks on their faces, Anthony and Jason knew the movie, too.

"Well, I guess we wait until tomorrow morning to find out what the plan is," Tom said.

"So the plan is to find out tomorrow how they plan for us to sit down and make a plan, right?" Jason said.

Tom thought a second. "Right," he said. "I think."

"Sounds like a plan," Billy Bob said with a grin.

· · · · ·

The game that night was a huge struggle—although it probably should not have been.

DeMatha was a national power, a team perennially ranked in the *USA Today* high school Top 25. In fact, the Stags were eighth in the preseason rankings, just two spots behind TGP.

But their star quarterback, Joey Wootten, didn't play that night. He had twisted a knee in practice that week—at least that's what Tom read online the next day in reports about the game. Tough week, it seemed, for star quarterbacks and their knees.

Without Wootten, who had already committed to play for Jim Harbaugh at Michigan the following fall, DeMatha wasn't the same team. One person who apparently hadn't gotten the word on Wootten's injury was Harbaugh. Tom spotted him sitting in the stands midway through the first quarter, with the Patriots already leading 7–0.

"Looks like Harbaugh made the trip for nothing," Tom pointed out to Jason. They were both standing languidly on the sidelines.

"Billy Bob spotted him right away," Jason said. "He's sitting two rows behind Nick Saban. Billy Bob noticed him, too."

"What's Saban doing here?" Tom asked.

"Well, according to the various scouting services, we've got eleven seniors who are big-time prospects and are still uncommitted, not to mention a bunch of juniors."

"None of them play quarterback," a voice said behind them.

It was Anthony, who hadn't yet gotten into the game either

but had been told he would get in for at least one series in the second quarter.

Ronnie Thompson had, not surprisingly, been given the starting nod at quarterback over Billy Bob. He hadn't exactly been lighting up the night with his play. TGP had scored on a twelve-yard drive after a DeMatha fumble and was now on the DeMatha 21 after Wootten's backup quarterback, Donny Ferry, had thrown an interception into the arms of Alan Inwood—who was one of the big-time prospects Jason had been referring to a moment earlier.

"You think Coach Johnson will put Billy Bob in soon?" Tom asked. He had watched Thompson overthrow open receivers on three occasions already—all throws he was certain both he and Billy Bob would have made with ease. *Heck,* he thought, *even Jason could make those throws.*

"As long as they don't show any sign of being able to move the ball on our defense, I think he sticks with Thompson," Anthony said. "But he's got to put Billy Bob in at some point. We're not beating anybody good with Thompson at QB."

"We might not be beating these guys if Joey Wootten was playing," Jason said. "Their backup is—"

He cut himself off just as Thompson overthrew Bobby Richardson so badly that the ball went right into the chest of a DeMatha cornerback, who quickly returned it from his own 5-yard line to the TGP 45.

"He's *awful,*" Tom said, disgusted.

"Hey, Jefferson," someone said, coming up from behind and

grabbing him roughly by the shoulder. "If you think you can do better, prove it in practice. If not, shut up and show some support for your teammates."

It was Coach Reilly, the receivers coach.

"If I had the—" Tom started to answer, but Anthony reached his long arm around his roommate and clapped his hand over his mouth.

"You're right, Coach," Anthony said. "We all just want to win the game, right?"

Reilly glared at Anthony. "Let him go," he said. "If he has something to say, let him say it."

Reluctantly, Anthony dropped his hand from Tom's mouth.

Tom was calmer now, but he still wanted to tell Coach Reilly he could go in the game *right now* without having taken a single snap at quarterback and play better than Thompson. He stood there, staring at the coach, saying nothing.

"Well, Jefferson? What did you want to say?" Reilly said.

"Nothing, Coach," Tom said. "Nothing. I'm sorry."

"You should be," Coach Reilly said. "Last thing we need around here are mouthy freshmen."

He turned away, and Anthony grabbed Tom again, just in case.

"I'm fine," Tom said angrily, pushing Anthony away.

"No you're not," Jason said, stepping in front of Tom—also just in case. "You want to slug him. And I don't blame you."

"Let's pick our fight in a way we can win," Billy Bob added. "Right here, right now, we've got no shot."

"Sort of like Ronnie Thompson at quarterback," Anthony said—and the tension broke.

He was, of course, right.

. . . . .

The score was tied 7–7 at halftime. In the locker room, Coach Johnson tore into the offensive line, insisting they had to give their quarterback better protection.

Coach Johnson pointed at Coach Marco Thurman, one of the four African American assistants, who served as the offensive line coach. "Coach, you need to get your boys back on track for the second half. Thompson needs more time to make good decisions."

Tom almost smirked when he heard that. Thompson had been given plenty of time. Tom thought that the guy could have been given an hour to make a decision on each play and it wouldn't make much difference.

"Why's he so obsessed with not blaming Thompson?" Tom whispered to Jason, their cleats clattering against the concrete as they headed from the locker room back to the FieldTurf playing surface.

"Because *he* made the decision to keep us on the practice field Wednesday and *he* made the decision to start Thompson tonight," Jason hissed back softly. "*He's* never wrong, remember?"

"*He's* going to have to make a decision to put Billy Bob in at some point if he wants to win this game," Tom said.

That point came midway through the third quarter. DeMatha couldn't do much against the Patriots' defense, which, Tom knew, had nine serious Division I prospects among the eleven starters, but it didn't have to—courtesy of TGP's offense.

The Stags got the ball on the TGP 8-yard line when Thompson threw behind slotback Andy Thurston—who was in the game because of Kendall Franklin's departure—and the officials ruled that he'd thrown the ball backward, making the pass a lateral and, thus, a free ball. One of the DeMatha players fell on it instantly.

Coach Johnson raged first at the officials and then at Thurston for somehow failing to catch a ball that looked to Tom as if it had been thrown two yards behind him.

"Am I nuts or was that pass completely uncatchable?" Tom said to Jason as Coach Johnson continued to poke his finger in Thurston's chest, screaming something about the slotback's "alligator arms."

"He could have Michael Phelps's arms and he couldn't have caught that ball," Jason said, referring to the swimming superstar who was six foot four but had the wingspan of someone six nine.

"It ain't never the white guy's fault 'round here, remember that, boys," Billy Bob said, helmet in hand, emphasizing his Southern twang intentionally.

Tom was about to agree when they heard Coach Cruikshank's voice cutting through the night air.

"Anderson!" he yelled. "Cut the talk and warm up. You might be in, next series."

"Yes, sir," Billy Bob said. And then to Tom he said, "Come on and play catch with me."

The two of them went behind the bench and found a football.

"I guarantee you," Billy Bob said as they began to walk away from each other, "that I'm only in if they score."

A moment later, focused on tossing the ball back and forth with Billy Bob, Tom heard a roar from the small pocket of DeMatha fans seated on the far side of the field. He looked up in time to see the DeMatha players celebrating in the end zone.

"Looks like it's your turn," Tom said to Billy Bob—happy for him but intensely jealous, too.

DeMatha was lining up for the extra point when Tom and Billy Bob both heard Coach Cruikshank's voice again.

"Anderson, you ready?" he said.

"Yes, Coach!" Billy Bob answered.

"Next series," Coach Cruikshank said. With that, he turned away.

11

ALMOST FROM THE MINUTE BILLY BOB STEPPED INTO THE HUDDLE, THE tone of the game changed. Even from the sideline, Tom was convinced that the other ten players stood up straighter when he joined them, as if knowing the finger-pointing was about to end.

On the very first play, Billy Bob took the snap, sprinted right and, at the last possible second, pitched the ball to Andy Thurston. Not only did the pitch lead Thurston just right, but the timing was equally perfect—two defenders taking Billy Bob down just as he released the ball. Thurston picked up twenty-three yards—TGP's longest gain of the night so far—rumbling across midfield to the DeMatha 48.

The crowd on the TGP side of the field came to life, the offense finally having given them something to cheer about. From there, the Patriots moved the ball steadily downfield. Twice on third down, Billy Bob faked a handoff to fullback Tad Edling and completed quick, two-step drop passes that picked up first downs.

Finally, on third down from the 1-yard line, he faked again to Edling, then followed him to the left into a huge hole. He scored standing up just as the third quarter ended. The extra point made the score 14–14.

"*That's* the way to block," Tom heard Coach Johnson say as the offense came off the field. One of the blockers on the series had been Anthony, who had gone into the game along with Billy Bob and another freshman lineman, center Billy Bryan.

"Miracle, isn't it?" Jason said to Tom.

Billy Bob came over, taking his helmet off. "Now *that* was fun," he said with a big grin.

"In case you didn't hear Coach Johnson, it was all the blocking," Tom said. They were standing far enough away from the coaches not to be overheard.

"You better believe it was the blocking," Anthony said, joining them.

"Yeah, you're right, Bryan did a great job opening up the middle," Billy Bob said.

"Who'd you run behind on the touchdown?" Anthony said, trying to suppress a grin.

"Tad Edling," Billy Bob said, which was true, although they had run right into the left tackle hole—a hole cleared by left tackle Anthony Ames.

At that moment, Tom heard a sound he hadn't heard very much in the past several days: laughter. It was coming from all four of them. It sounded pretty sweet.

. . . . .

The game wasn't decided until the final minute. It looked as if TGP would take the lead on another long drive midway through the fourth quarter, but Tad Edling fumbled a handoff that was right in his stomach on the 11-yard line. He came off apologizing profusely. No one yelled at him. This wasn't a good time for pointing fingers.

After the defense held, Billy Bob led a steady drive down the field, but again the offense stalled—this time because of a dropped pass and a ball that Billy Bob intentionally threw over everyone's head in the end zone because no one was open.

Kicker Nick Stover came in to try a thirty-two-yard field goal. Nick was the nephew of Matt Stover, who had been one of the best kickers of his era with the Baltimore Ravens. He was already being looked at by colleges—Tom knew this from Billy Bob because the two had ridden to church together the previous Sunday—and Tom had seen Nick make fifty-yarders in practice. With almost no wind in the stadium, Stover boomed the kick through the uprights for a 17–14 lead with 2:31 to play.

"The DeMatha offense hasn't done a thing all night," Jason said to Tom. "That should be enough."

Only it wasn't that simple. Afraid to get burned by a deep pass, defensive coordinator Gerry McGee went to a prevent defense—dropping all the defensive backs deep and only rushing three linemen. When Tom and Jason and their dads had gathered on Sundays to watch the Jets play, the dads had called the so-called prevent defense the "prevent victory defense" because it seemed as if whenever the Jets went to it, the other team promptly marched down the field to score.

This was no different.

Given plenty of time because there was very little pass rush and with receivers open underneath the backpedaling TGP defenders, Donny Ferry all of a sudden looked like Tom Brady. Starting from his own 24, he began moving the ball steadily downfield in chunks of six, twelve, nine, and eleven yards. He had two time-outs left, and twice, after passes down the middle, he used them to stop the clock.

With twenty-seven seconds left, Ferry completed a quick out to one of his receivers, who picked up five yards and moved the ball to the 17-yard line. But Alan Inwood made a critical play, getting the receiver down before he could step out-of-bounds to stop the clock.

With time running down and no time-outs left, Donny Ferry quickly lined his team up and spiked the ball—stopping the clock—with six seconds left.

Tom was about to comment to Jason, Billy Bob, and Anthony that DeMatha had to go for the tying field goal on third down because even on an incomplete pass, they risked having the clock run out, when he saw special-teams coach Rich Gutekunst stalking in their direction.

"Roddin!" he yelled, pointing at Jason.

Jason must have thought that Coach Gutekunst was talking to someone else, because he stood rooted to the spot, not responding.

The coach walked up to Jason and screamed, "Where's your helmet?"

"Um, on the bench," Jason said, pointing to the far end of the bench, where the helmets that hadn't been used by all the last-stringers were lined up.

"Get it!"

At that moment, as the DeMatha field goal unit was taking the field, Tom heard Coach Johnson call for time-out. That wasn't unusual. It was standard practice at every level of football to try to freeze a kicker in the final seconds by making him wait before attempting a critical field goal. It was Coach Gutekunst screaming at Jason to get his helmet that Tom didn't understand.

Jason grabbed the helmet and squeezed it onto his head as Coach Gutekunst put his hand on his shoulder.

"I know we haven't practiced this at all," the coach said. "But you're the fastest guy we've got. I want you to line up on the outside left and, as soon as you hear the snap, run right at the kicker's foot and block the kick. Have you ever blocked a kick?"

"No, sir."

"There's a first time for everything," Gutekunst said. "This kid hasn't missed a kick inside the forty in two years. Get in there and block this one."

To say that Jason looked like a deer in the headlights would have been a vast understatement. He looked more like a guy tied to the railroad tracks with a train bearing down on him.

Tom heard the referee's whistle, signaling the end of the time-out.

"Get in there!" Coach Gutekunst screamed.

Jason answered by racing onto the field and lining up wide left as he'd been told. Tom, Billy Bob, and Anthony looked at one another.

"It's actually a good idea," Billy Bob said. "Worst case, he doesn't block it. No big deal."

The ball was snapped. Tom saw Jason sprint around a DeMatha player—who made a halfhearted attempt to block him—and dive, as instructed, right in front of where the holder had placed the ball to be kicked.

The ball came off the kicker's foot and hit Jason's outstretched hands. It spun wildly to the left, losing momentum not long after it crossed the line of scrimmage. It fell harmlessly to the ground, with several players scrambling to fall on top of it.

The clock was at zero. The ball was on the ground. The game was over. Tom heard screams of celebration around him and started onto the field to be part of the welcoming committee for Jason, the sudden hero.

But Jason wasn't being welcomed by anyone. He was lying on the ground, facedown, not moving. The DeMatha kicker and holder were both kneeling next to him. Tom hustled toward his friend, with Billy Bob and Anthony right behind him.

"My foot caught him square on the chin on my follow-through," the kicker was saying. "Didn't mean it. He was just so close to the ball . . ."

He trailed off as coaches and the TGP trainers began arriving on the scene.

"We need Doc Mazzocca out here," Tom heard Dave Billingsley say. "Let's clear some space."

That led to the coaches pushing back the players from both teams who had gathered around Jason as soon as they'd seen him not get up. Tom, Billy Bob, and Anthony all moved in a little bit closer with no objection from their teammates, who knew it was their friend on the ground.

Dr. Gus Mazzocca, who watched every game from the sidelines, arrived a moment later.

"Okay, good news—he's conscious," he said loud enough for everyone to hear. "But we need the EMTs right away."

A trainer radioed for the emergency medical technicians. Tom had noticed the ambulance idling just outside the locker room before the game and knew that there was always an ambulance on-site in case of an emergency. Hearing Dr. Mazzocca call for them was a little bit frightening.

With help from the trainers, Dr. Mazzocca gently rolled Jason onto his back. Tom could see that his eyes were open as Dr. Mazzocca leaned down to talk to him.

Tom looked up as the ambulance came onto the field. He pushed past the coaches. He heard Dr. Mazzocca say, "No, Jason, don't try to sit up. There's no need. The ambulance is coming now—"

"Ambulance?" Tom heard Jason say, clear panic in his voice.

"We're going to the hospital," the doctor said. "I believe you're fine, but I want to be a hundred percent sure, not ninety-nine percent."

The trainer Dave Billingsley turned at that moment and saw Tom standing there, listening. "Get back, Jefferson," he said, not roughly, but firmly.

"Mr. Billingsley, he's my best friend. I gotta ask the doctor how he is so I can tell his parents."

Dr. Mazzocca heard him and looked up.

"The school will be calling his parents immediately to let them know of this development. Standard protocol. Give me his parents' number and I'll call or text as soon as I can with more info," he said.

Tom gave him the digits, which the doctor scribbled into a pocket notepad.

The EMTs were now wheeling a stretcher up to where Jason was lying.

"Can I talk to him, just for a second?" Tom asked. "Please?"

Dr. Mazzocca gave him an understanding smile. "For a second," he said.

Tom knelt quickly next to Jason, who smiled weakly at him.

"Did we win?" Jason asked.

"We won," Tom said. "You're the hero. I'll call your parents."

"Tell them I'm fine."

Dr. Mazzocca had his hand on Tom's shoulder.

"You need to give the EMTs some space now, son," he said. "But you can come in the ambulance. We've got room for one teammate."

"And that will be his roommate," Tom heard a voice say.

He turned to see Coach Johnson glaring down at him.

Tom tried a bluff. "I'm his roommate," he said, knowing that Billy Bob wouldn't contradict him.

"No you're not," Coach Johnson said. He turned to the other players. "Who's Rodding's roommate?"

Jeesh, Tom thought, *he just saved the game and you still don't know how to say his name?*

Billy Bob answered, "I am, Coach, but Tom's his best friend. He should ride—"

"I'll decide who rides," Coach Johnson said. "You go ahead, Anderson. You can let everyone know how he is once he gets looked at in the hospital."

Billy Bob glanced at Tom to see if he wanted him to argue more. Tom knew it would be fruitless. Making a scene here wouldn't be a good idea.

The EMTs had Jason on the stretcher. He clearly wasn't happy about it.

"I'm really okay now," he insisted. "I just need some aspirin for the headache."

The EMTs patted him lightly on the stomach and began moving him toward the ambulance.

The DeMatha kicker ran up to the stretcher. "Hey, I'm really sorry, man," he said. "I didn't mean to kick you. That was a hell of a play."

Jason held his hand up so the kid could shake it. Then, with everyone applauding—both on the field and in the stands—he was loaded into the back of the ambulance.

Billy Bob looked at Tom. "I'm sorry about this," he said.

"Don't worry," Tom said. "Go. But let me know as soon as you know."

Billy Bob nodded and followed Dr. Mazzocca into the ambulance.

Tom looked around for Coach Johnson. He wanted to ask him how he had been so certain that he and Jason weren't roommates. He finally found him, standing a few yards away, surrounded by the media, TV lights shining on him.

He had one odd but comforting thought: Maybe the coach would mispronounce Jason's name on TV.

12

THERE WERE PEOPLE EVERYWHERE ON THE FIELD AS THE AMBULANCE pulled away. David Teel appeared at Tom's shoulder. Like the reporters now surrounding Coach Johnson, he had apparently come down from the press box as soon as the game ended.

"I saw you trying to talk to him," he said. "Was he conscious?"

Tom nodded. "Yes. Talking. Asked if we won."

Teel took a deep breath and put his hand on Tom's shoulder. "That's very good news. He's probably got a concussion of some kind—almost impossible to avoid if you get hit that hard—but if he knew what was going on, that probably means it isn't too serious."

"Why'd they take him out in an ambulance, then?" Tom asked.

"Precaution," Teel said. "Nowadays they'd always rather be too careful than not careful enough. You wouldn't want to get him in the locker room and have him go into convulsion or something there. Better in the hospital."

Tom understood. Or thought he did. He was tempted to tell Teel about Coach Johnson's roommate crack but figured this wasn't the time or place.

He was starting to ask another question when he heard Coach Cruikshank's voice: "All players to the locker room—now! Come on, guys, let's get inside."

Most of the reporters were still surrounding Coach Johnson, but a few were trying to talk to players. Of course the players they wanted to talk to most—Billy Bob and Jason—were in the ambulance.

"Call me in the morning," Teel said quietly, giving Tom a quick handshake. "If there's any news on Jason tonight, text me."

Tom nodded, remembering that he needed to call the Roddins as soon as he got his hands on his phone in the locker room. He had no idea how long it would be before the doctor would call. He followed his teammates in the direction of the locker room. En route, they rubbed shoulders with a number of the DeMatha players. They hadn't left the field yet either. There were handshakes and hugs as the players from the two teams crossed paths.

"Keep moving, guys," Tom heard one of the coaches say as he shook hands with Phil Dawson.

Dawson had been in the seven-on-seven camp the previous summer with Tom and Jason, and the three had become friends. He was a quarterback and had elected to stay close to home— he was from Washington, D.C.—and was listed as DeMatha's number three quarterback, meaning he'd been the backup with Joey Wootten injured during the game that night. Tom and Jason hadn't been able to find him pregame because the coaches were zealous about keeping the players on their side of the field.

"Hey, how's Jason?" Phil said, running up to Tom, hand extended, dispensing with any greeting.

"Conscious. Talking. Think he's okay."

Phil blew air out of his mouth in relief. "That was scary. He made an amazing play, though."

"Yeah, he did."

"Hey, I saw the roster. You're listed as a receiver, and he's listed as a QB. What's that about?"

"Long story," Tom said. He was going to elaborate when he felt a hand on his shoulder.

"Come on, Jefferson," Coach Reilly said. "Locker room."

Tom shook hands with Phil again.

"Take care," Phil said.

"Will do," Tom replied.

He'd dropped behind his teammates, so he picked up the pace to a fast trot. He realized he was sweating profusely. The evening was warm, but he suspected the weather had little to do with it.

. . . . .

Once they were all inside the locker room, Coach Cruikshank told them that Coach Johnson would be in very soon and they could start getting out of uniform but should not hit the showers yet. As if on cue, Coach Johnson walked through the door and to the front of the room. There was a slightly raised platform in front of the blackboard where he had written CHAMPIONS ALWAYS START 1–0 during his pregame speech.

He held his hands up for quiet and got it quickly.

"Okay, first and foremost—that was a great win," he said. "It took everyone in uniform to beat that team—including someone who didn't get in until the last play of the game."

They all clapped and cheered with enthusiasm, except perhaps for Tom, who couldn't find it in him to cheer when—to him—the first and foremost thing should have been Jason's condition.

"Second, speaking of the last play, I'm told Roddin is fine. He's talking, he knows where he is and what happened. So that's good news."

More clapping and cheering.

"Way to go, Jason!" someone yelled.

Tom turned and saw it was Anthony.

Coach Johnson signaled for quiet again. This was his show.

"We beat a good team tonight—a very good team. But, fellas, if we want to have a chance to play for the state championship this year and if we're going to win it, we're going to have to improve a *lot* going forward. If their quarterback had played tonight, I'm not sure what would have happened—although I *do* have a lot of faith in our defense. You guys were great!"

Again, clapping and cheering.

He then handed out three game balls, all to players on the defense. Finally, he held up one last ball: "This one's for Roddin. With luck, we'll give it to him at practice on Monday."

One last round of clapping and cheering. Tom couldn't help but notice that there was no talk of a game ball for Billy Bob, who had come in at quarterback and turned the game around.

The postgame pep rally was over.

"Hey, have you called Jason's parents yet?" It was Anthony.

"Oh God, I forgot, thanks," Tom said.

He walked to his locker and pulled out his phone. He needed to walk outside to get cell service, but he knew it would be a madhouse out there.

"Back door," Anthony said, reading his mind. "Just stick a towel in the door so it doesn't lock on you."

Good thought. The back door led to a small garden area where players relaxed when the weather was good. It was surrounded by a wall, so the only way to get to it was through the locker room's back door.

He grabbed a towel and walked through the lounge where they had met with Teel and Robinson a few hours earlier. He pushed outside and stuck the towel in the door behind him. Fortunately, he was alone in the garden.

Mr. Roddin answered on the first ring. "Tom, how badly was he hurt?" he asked instantly. "We've been trying to call and text his number and yours for twenty minutes."

Tom hadn't even looked for voicemails or texts when he turned his phone on.

"Sorry, it's been crazy here," he said. "Jason is fine." He knew that was the headline. He could explain the rest once he had relieved Mr. Roddin's concerns as best he could.

He walked Jason's dad through everything that had

happened. He had to repeat his brief conversation with Jason three times, no doubt because Mr. Roddin wanted to be sure about his son's condition.

"I asked the doctor to call you as soon as he knew more," Tom said. "I gave him your numbers—home and cell."

"Do you think we need to come down there?" Mr. Roddin asked.

"I honestly don't know," Tom answered. "He could be back in his dorm room later tonight. I think you should wait and talk to the doctor and then—"

Tom heard the door being pushed open.

Coach Reilly walked outside. "Jefferson, what the hell are you doing?" he asked.

"One second," Tom said to Mr. Roddin. Then, to Coach Reilly he said, "I'm talking to Jason's dad. Updating him—"

"Let the doctor do that," Coach Reilly said sharply. "That's not your job. Get back inside—now."

Tom was truly puzzled. Why in the world would Coach Reilly have trouble with him talking to Mr. Roddin?

"Coach, Jason's my best friend—"

Coach Reilly walked over and before Tom knew what was happening, grabbed the phone from his hands. "Mr. Roddin, this is Coach Reilly at TGP. We think your son is going to be just fine. He made a great play at the end of the game. Our team doctor, Gus Mazzocca, is with him. I'm sure he'll be in touch with you very soon. Tom needs to go now—we have a team meeting." He listened for a second and nodded. "Like I said, Dr. Mazzocca will answer all those questions for you. Good to talk to you." He then hit the hang-up button and flipped the phone back to Tom. "When I tell you to hang up a call, you hang up, Jefferson," he said. "I don't know how you were raised, but when an authority figure gives you an order, you follow it. If you ever want to see the field around here, you better learn that."

With that, he turned, walked inside, and pulled the towel out of the door. Tom had to dive for the handle to keep from being locked out. He truly *hated* Coach Reilly.

Even more than he hated Thomas Gatch Prep School.

. . . . .

An hour later, Tom and Anthony were walking back to the dorm when a call from an unidentified number lit up Tom's phone.

"Hello?" he said after hitting the button to answer.

It was Billy Bob.

"What's the word?" Tom asked.

"Looks like he's fine," Billy Bob said. "They're calling it a mild concussion—whatever that means. They're going to keep him overnight, which I guess is standard procedure with any concussion. If he's okay in the morning, they'll release him."

"Then what?" Tom asked—as if Billy Bob were a doctor.

"Apparently there's a state-mandated concussion protocol he has to go through before he can get back on the field. Doctors have to check him out again twenty-four hours after he leaves the hospital and then again on Monday. If he's got no symptoms— zero—he can go back to practice. If he has any symptoms, they keep checking him every day until they're all gone. He's got to pass a bunch of tests relating to how he reacts to light and to movement and to whether he has any pain at all."

"Where are you?" Tom asked. It sounded like Billy Bob was in a car.

"I'm with Dr. Mazzocca. His wife brought their car, and they're giving me a ride back to campus. He let me use his phone. He already spoke with Mr. Roddin to explain things, and then they let Jason talk to both his parents."

"Okay," Tom said. "How'd he seem?"

"Really pretty much like himself. He's got a headache, but nothing more. He was hungry, which they said was a good sign." He paused. "Hey, I'm sorry they didn't let you go with him. They should have."

"Yeah, I know. We can talk about that more later."

"Right. I should be back in twenty minutes. Gotta hit the locker room real quick."

"Come to our room when you can," Tom said.

"Will do." Billy Bob clicked off.

Tom filled Anthony in, and the two of them walked back to the room. The dorm was quiet. A lot of the older students had left for the weekend. Others had gone out after the game. They walked slowly up the stairs.

Back in the room, they stretched out on their beds and tried to rest for a bit. But after a while they both agreed they were too worked up to nap.

Tom told Anthony about the scene with Coach Reilly.

Anthony said he wasn't surprised, although he hadn't dealt with Reilly much. He actually liked his position coach, Bill

Ogden—a former NFL lineman who, unlike a lot of the coaches, didn't seem to have anything to prove. He had played at Virginia before spending eight years in the NFL and then settling in Charlottesville. Anthony said it was pretty clear he didn't *have* to work, because he'd made a good deal of money in the NFL, but coached just for the fun of it.

The older players had explained to the younger ones that Coach Ogden had been on Mike London's staff at Virginia and, when London had been fired, Ogden was one of the coaches Bronco Mendenhall, the new coach, had invited to stay on staff. He'd turned it down.

"He hated recruiting," Anthony told Tom. "He just likes to coach."

Anthony thought that made Coach Ogden stand apart from most of the other coaches, all of whom appeared to aspire to coaching in college—or the NFL—someday. He was one of the four African American coaches among the twelve assistants.

"It's interesting," Anthony said. "The guys who are ex-players take a totally different approach than the ones who didn't play past high school."

"What do you mean?" Tom said.

"Well, I don't think Coach Ogden would ever remind anyone that he's an *authority* figure. He wouldn't need to."

"Being, like, six foot six and three hundred fifty pounds might have something to do with that," Tom said, laughing.

"Yeah, but it's more than that."

Tom nodded. "Reilly's small and was probably slow."

"Yeah, because all white guys are slow, right?" Anthony said, grinning.

"Except Jason—"

The door burst open and Billy Bob, his hair wet from the showers, walked in brandishing his phone as if it held a secret.

"Just got a text from Teel," he said, a little out of breath since he'd apparently run up the stairs. "He says Robinson's going to request an interview tomorrow with the three of us since we're Jason's best friends and Robinson's going to do a story on the game's two unlikely heroes."

"You and Jason," Tom said.

Billy Bob nodded.

"Why Robinson and not Teel?" Anthony asked—the same question Tom was about to ask.

"Apparently the coaches here don't like Teel very much. He wrote a story last year saying TGP shouldn't be allowed to play for the state championship."

Tom knew what that was about: The state high school association had voted last winter to let TGP join the statewide prep school conference. That would make the Patriots eligible to play for Virginia state championships. Other high schools had fought the move on the grounds that TGP was a national school with only a handful of students from Virginia. The high school board had apparently gone along with the proposal to let TGP play because its members knew the school would sell a lot of tickets during the playoffs—and all that revenue went to the state.

"So Robinson will make the request?"

"Yes. Then he'll pick us up and take us somewhere off campus, which is allowable on a Saturday."

"Good," Tom said. "This is too important to let go."

Billy Bob smiled. "You angling for my job, Jefferson?"

"That a problem?" Tom said.

"Wouldn't have it any other way."

They high-fived and Anthony said, "Wonder if we can order a pizza at this hour."

That sounded to Tom like a great idea.

13

IF ANYONE AT THE SCHOOL WAS SUSPICIOUS ABOUT TOM ROBINSON'S motives when he requested an interview with Tom Jefferson, Anthony Ames, and Billy Bob Anderson, they didn't show it.

All three received a text midmorning from Ed Seaman, head of the school's communications office.

Mr. Seaman had spoken to the football players on the second day of practice, explaining to them that all requests for interviews had to be cleared by him. "If someone from your hometown paper calls, that's fine—but send him to me first," Mr. Seaman had said. "I will check with your position coach to make sure your academic standing is such that you can do an interview and then we'll set it up."

It was too soon for any of the players to have any serious academic issues, and apparently Robinson's explanation that he wanted to talk to Billy Bob (as not only Jason's roommate but also the quarterback who had led both of TGP's touchdown drives), Tom (as Jason's best friend from New York), and Anthony (as Tom's roommate and thus Jason's friend) had worked with Mr. Seaman.

"Mr. Robinson will pick the three of you up in front of the locker room at noon," Mr. Seaman had written. "He has requested taking you off campus for lunch. He is to have you back here by two o'clock latest. Any problems, contact me."

Noon was the exact time that Jason was to be discharged from the hospital. Tom knew this because he'd gotten a phone call early that morning from Mr. Roddin, telling him that he and Mrs. Roddin were flying to Richmond. There, they would rent a car and make the drive to the hospital. If all went well, they'd be there well before noon and would be able to spend some time with Jason before he was discharged.

Tom reported this news to Billy Bob and Anthony as they walked from the dorm to the locker room. It was a spectacular morning, the first one since they'd arrived that wasn't so humid that the air felt too heavy to be moved aside by the simple act of walking.

"This place is kind of pretty when you ain't weighed down by ninety-degree heat and humidity," Billy Bob said. "Reminds me of Gadsden—in March."

Tom Robinson was sitting on one of the benches outside the locker room waiting for them when they arrived. They were five minutes early.

"Reporter's credo," he said, answering the question before they asked it. "Never make a source wait."

"Yeah, we're pretty tough when it comes to punctuality," Tom said, laughing.

They walked to the coaches' parking lot in the back of the building. The only car there was parked in the spot closest to the door, reserved for Bill Stiller, TGP's athletic director.

"Why in the world would Mr. Stiller be in this morning?" Anthony wondered.

"He's not in," Billy Bob said. "Someone just parked in his spot."

"That would be me," Robinson said, chirping open the doors with his key.

They headed to Charlottesville, about a twenty-minute drive with no traffic anywhere in sight, to a restaurant called the Biltmore. Teel was waiting in a booth in the back big enough to seat six—or four normal-sized people and Anthony.

They quickly updated Teel on Jason, just as they had done with Robinson in the car.

"If he's okay, why do you think his parents are coming down?" Teel asked.

"Jewish mother syndrome?" Tom said, smiling—while the others laughed. "Then again, my mom would probably do the same. But I'm guessing Mrs. Roddin flipped out when she heard the word *concussion*, and had to see her baby boy."

"Well, he set a record last night that might be tied but will never be broken," Teel said.

"What's that?" they all asked pretty much in unison.

"One play, one game saved, one concussion."

"A real stat-stuffer, my roomie," Billy Bob said.

They all ordered drinks, and then Tom told the two reporters what Coach Johnson had said about knowing he wasn't Jason's roommate.

"Did he know that Billy Bob was his roommate?" Robinson asked. "Two freshman quarterbacks rooming together wouldn't be that unusual."

Tom shook his head. "Coach Bobo said, '*Who's* his roommate?' He didn't know it was Billy Bob. He just knew it wasn't me."

"Plus, I'm an O-lineman and Tom's a receiver," Anthony said. "If they're rooming us by position, why are we together?"

"Because you *do* both play the same position," Billy Bob said. "Black person."

Teel nodded. "You guys know of any African American player with a white roommate?"

They looked at one another.

"Not off the top of my head," Tom finally said. "But there's about eighty guys on the team—about half black and half white. We don't know all the rooming assignments."

"Well, we need to know them," Robinson said. "I'm betting there's not a single interracial room."

"And I'll bet if we track down some ex-players, there won't be any white guys who had black roommates," Teel added.

"You really think so?" Billy Bob said.

"Tell me you aren't beginning to see a pattern here," Teel answered.

"Okay, but how?" Anthony said. "How do we get the rooming list?"

"I would think that's not a national security issue," Teel said, "even at TGP."

"Everything is a national security issue at TGP," Billy Bob said. "We just walk in and ask for a rooming list, someone's going to want to know why."

"Maybe it's on the school website—the one that only TGP students, faculty, and staff can get on to," Anthony said.

"We can check," Tom said. "I'm betting against it, though. But I do have an idea how we can get the list without asking anyone in any kind of authority."

They all looked at him.

"Juan del Potro's roommate, Jimmy Gomez. He's the floor monitor on the fifth floor of our dorm. He's a basketball player, but he rooms with Juan because there are an odd number of baseball players. He and Juan are pals, and since he's a senior, he got to choose a roommate."

"Let me guess," Billy Bob said. "As the floor monitor, Jimmy has a list of all the rooming assignments for the fifth floor."

"How do you know all this?" Robinson asked.

"We've been sitting at the same table with them all week. Jimmy was telling me on Friday that he's in charge of the dorm this weekend. Each of the six floor monitors has to stay on campus one weekend out of six to make sure the guys who are around don't run amok with parties and stuff. Underage alcohol, drugs, or—worst of all—girls in the rooms."

"You're telling me there are never girls in the rooms?" Teel asked—clearly shocked.

"Have you seen some of the volleyball players?" Tom asked with a dreamy smile.

"Of course there are girls in the boys' rooms all the time—and vice versa in the girls' dorms. They're just not *supposed* to be there," Anthony clarified. "Anyway, I'm betting that when a guy is in charge for the weekend, he's got the rooming list for the entire dorm in case of an emergency. And the entire football team lives in our dorm."

"You think Jimmy would give you the list?" Teel asked.

"I think he'd give it to us in a heartbeat," Tom said.

Teel and Robinson looked at each other and then at the three boys.

Robinson spoke first. "If you guys get a rooming list, and Teel and I can track down some former players—which we can, I'm sure—then we can start to build a pretty strong circumstantial case."

"We can definitely find some guys," Teel added. "There are several at Virginia, a few more at Virginia Tech, and others at Richmond and Old Dominion. Probably twelve to fifteen in all, right there."

Tom frowned. "But isn't a circumstantial case always considered shaky? Don't you need a smoking gun?"

Teel shook his head. "A circumstantial case might not hold up in a court of law, but in the court of public opinion it'll hold up just fine—if it's strong enough. This isn't 'beyond a reasonable doubt' stuff. This is making a case people will believe."

He looked at Tom with a smile. "How do you know so much about circumstantial evidence?"

"I watch *Blue Bloods* a lot," Tom said, a bit sheepishly. "Erin's always arguing with her father and her brother about only having circumstantial evidence."

"Who's Erin?" Robinson asked.

All three boys stared at the reporter in disbelief. "Bridget Moynahan," they said, almost at once. "Supermodel? Used to date Tom Brady?"

"So," Teel said, "I'm betting you guys agree with her side of the argument all the time, right?"

"Right!" they answered.

"Well, the good news is that we aren't going up against anyone who looks like Bridget Moynahan," Robinson said.

"Okay," Teel said, bringing them all back from Hollywood to Charlottesville. "You guys will try to get the rooming list. Tom and I will try to contact some former TGP players. We'll circle back no later than the game against South Hill on Friday and see where we are."

"You guys coming to the game?" Billy Bob said.

"No." Teel shook his head. "You'll kill South Hill. That's a walkover game before you start conference play in a week. We both have to cover UVA, anyway. But let's be in touch to see if we need to get together next weekend." He looked at his watch. "Okay, we better spend a few minutes asking you what happened last night, because if we don't produce stories about it, your coaches are going to want to know what you've been doing with us for two hours."

They all cracked up, and Teel and Robinson both took out notebooks and digital recorders.

· · · · ·

Billy Bob did most of the retelling since he had played such a key role in the comeback. Anthony, who had played in several series, filled in with some detail. Tom didn't come into the story until the last play of the game. Then Billy Bob picked up again with detail about the ride to the hospital. It was agreed there would be no mention of Coach Johnson's insistence that Billy Bob, not Tom, go in the ambulance.

They made the drive back to campus with Robinson, who dropped them off in the coaches' parking lot. By now, there were a half-dozen cars there.

"Guess the coaches are breaking down the tape," Robinson said.

"They have to do it today," Tom said. "Coach Johnson doesn't like anyone working on Sunday."

"Amen to that," Robinson said.

The three boys walked back across campus, agreeing that Tom would try to find Jimmy Gomez as soon as possible to talk to him alone about getting the rooming lists.

"Jason should be back by now," Tom said as they climbed the steps. "I'm surprised he hasn't texted me."

"Well, let's all go to our room and see if he's there," Billy Bob said. "He might still be out with his parents."

"Good point," Tom said. "Maybe that's why he hasn't texted."

Billy Bob put his key in the door and then knocked—just in case the Roddins were in there with Jason.

"Come in," they heard Jason say—a sound that made them all light up with smiles.

Billy Bob pushed the door open and they walked in. Their smiles quickly turned to looks of stunned surprise.

Jason was sitting on his bed, legs outstretched, looking no worse for the wear. His dad was sitting on Jason's desk chair and his mom was sitting on the edge of Billy Bob's bed.

But the three of them weren't alone. There were two other visitors in the room: Alan and Elaine Jefferson.

"Tom!" Elaine Jefferson said, jumping from the edge of Jason's bed to give her son a hug.

"Mom?" Tom said, confused, surprised, and a little bit concerned.

His father stood up, hands in his pockets. "Aren't you going to introduce us to your friends?" he said.

"Sure," Tom said, still trying to figure out just what was going on.

Introductions were made. Finally, the three boys turned to Jason—who hadn't said a word yet.

"How you feeling there, hero-guy?" Billy Bob said.

"My head's spinning," Jason said, "but it has nothing to do with the concussion."

Tom knew exactly how he felt.

14

"IT'S A BEAUTIFUL DAY," MR. RODDIN SAID. "WHY DON'T WE GO FOR A walk? None of us have seen the whole place."

Billy Bob and Anthony had left as quickly as possible, heading, they said, to the campus coffee shop—even though both had just eaten lunch.

"I feel like a milkshake," Anthony had said—believable, since he was always hungry.

"Me too," Billy Bob said—not as believable, but enough to allow the two of them to escape from the room.

"Is it okay for Jason to be walking around?" Tom asked after their friends had left.

Jason stood up from the bed. "No dizziness," he said. "Good sign. And yes, the doctor told me that walking is good. I could use some fresh air."

The two boys looked at each other, Tom hoping Jason

would give him some kind of signal to let him know what was going on. There was nothing. Maybe he didn't know either.

They walked outside and strolled around for a while, making small talk about how pretty the campus was.

"Bigger than I envisioned," Mrs. Jefferson said. "This feels more like a small college campus than a boarding school."

"Not that small a college campus, actually," Jason's mom added.

Tom and Jason gave them a mini guided tour, pointing out the various buildings before walking, almost inevitably it seemed, in the direction of the athletic facilities.

"Very quiet today," Mr. Jefferson said. They had stopped in a comfortable, shaded area in the back of the enormous gym—which seated five thousand people for basketball games. There were chairs and tables—all of them empty—so they all sat at one of the tables, Tom dragging extra chairs from other tables for the mothers.

"So," Mr. Roddin said. "Who wants to begin?"

"Exactly what is it we're beginning?" Tom asked.

The four parents looked at one another. It was Tom's mother who spoke next.

"We're beginning a conversation about you boys coming home."

Tom looked at Jason, who said nothing.

Mrs. Roddin was right behind her friend. "We made a deal when we agreed to let you two come down here: one and done." She looked at Jason. "It took *one* play to land you in the hospital."

"Mom, it was no big deal. I could have gone home last night. They only kept me there as a precaution."

"That's usually what happens the first time," Mr. Roddin said. "Maybe even the second. Eventually, though, the repeated hits affect your brain."

"Dad, are *you* turning on us?" Jason said, his eyes wide.

"I wouldn't call it turning on you," Mr. Roddin said. "But I think Alan and I both understand the concerns your mothers have. More now than before."

Tom wasn't sure how to feel about the conversation taking place in front of him. Part of him wanted to say, *Give me thirty minutes to pack and let's get going.* Another part of him was thinking, *If we leave now, we'll never get to the truth about Coach Johnson.* That bothered him.

He decided to stall—to try to find out more information before taking a position.

"Dad, Mr. Roddin, if we go home now, it's going to be really hard to get on a team anywhere," he said. "Everyone's already started their seasons. You can't just show up a week or two into the season and say, 'Here I am, let me play.'"

"We aren't talking about you coming back to play football," Tom's father said. "We're talking about you coming home and going to school."

"And not playing football?" Jason said.

"Of course not playing football," Mrs. Roddin said. "We had a deal."

Tom and Jason both looked at the two fathers for support. None was forthcoming.

"I haven't had a concussion," Tom said—knowing how weak the argument was as soon as it was out of his mouth.

"*You* haven't been in a game yet," his mother said. "Next week they might have you diving at some kicker's foot, and then you guys will be two for two."

"Not likely," Tom's dad said. "My boy's too slow."

That crack lightened the mood—briefly.

"We're not going back," Jason said finally, as if the decision were his to make. "Look, I had a mild injury that got a lot more attention than normal because it was at the end of the game. I'm fine. The doctors said I should be able to practice before the end of the week if I pass all the concussion protocols, which I will." He paused, then took it further. "Tom and I have something to prove here—a lot to prove—more even than you know or think. This is a very good school academically. Even Tom's having to work hard, and he makes everything look easy. Give it one more chance."

"What do you mean, a lot to prove?" Mr. Roddin said, going to a place Tom didn't think either of them wanted to go—yet.

"We're not playing at all," Jason said, thinking fast. "We should be playing, and I don't just mean trying to block kicks."

"That reminds me," Jason's dad said. "The news reports about your block identified you as a backup quarterback. What's that about?"

Uh-oh, Tom thought. As the old song went, they had trouble in River City. Amazingly, Jason appeared to be ready for the question.

"When you're deep depth around here—which we both are right now—they look at you at other positions so that, later in your career, if you aren't a starter at what should be your best position, they might play you as a backup at a couple positions."

"That's about the dumbest thing I've ever heard," Tom's dad said.

"Maybe," Jason said. "But I know there are colleges that do it, too, so it isn't as dumb as it sounds. But we don't want to quit after two weeks—for any reason."

Tom jumped in. "Jason's right," he said. "Look, Dad, we aren't crazy about all our coaches for a bunch of reasons. But we both suspect that's what they do to freshmen: they test you. They want you to prove your toughness, physically *and* mentally. This is all part of it."

"And you feel some sort of need to prove yourself to these people?" Tom's mom said. "Why?"

Tom turned to his mother and said, meaning it, "Good question, Mom. I know this sounds corny, but I think if you get in the habit of running away anytime a situation is difficult, you tend to keep doing it because it becomes instinct." He then looked directly at Mr. Roddin. "How would that work out for a cop?" he asked.

Mr. Roddin smiled. "Not very well," he answered softly. "Alan, your kid really is too smart."

Alan Jefferson sighed. "I hear you, son," he said finally. "But we got our way when you first came down here. Now I think it's up to the moms."

There was a long silence. Tom still wasn't sure what answer he was hoping to hear. He suspected Jason felt the same way.

"Can you go to your coaches and ask them *not* to put you in to block kicks anymore?" Julie Roddin said, finally breaking the silence.

Jason shook his head. "No, Mom, I can't do that." He smiled. "But I *will* promise not to get too close to the kicker's foot the next time they ask me to do it."

The fathers laughed.

Elaine Jefferson spoke up. "Julie, I can't believe I'm saying this, but I think Tom's right. This *is* a very good school, one we couldn't possibly afford if we had to pay for it. And even though I'm much less crazy about football than I was before this happened, I do like the idea that they're facing up to a challenge. They're fourteen and, because they're good athletes, they've had a pretty smooth ride until now. Dealing with a couple of bumps isn't a bad thing." She looked at Tom. "As long as it doesn't get *too* bumpy."

All eyes now turned to Julie Roddin. She sighed.

"If Elaine's in, well, I guess I'm in, too. If the vote was two–two, I'd insist they come home, since, like Alan said, we moms have the final say this time around. But, Elaine, if you really feel that way, that makes the vote three to one, and I'm not going to try to overrule the majority. I'm not happy about it, but I'll go along—for now." She turned to her son. "Jason, are you *sure* you want to stay? I'm not getting any vibe from either of you that you like it here."

Jason nodded. "No, Mom, I'm not sure I want to stay. Not even close. But I think Tom's right—we need to give this a little bit longer."

Left unsaid, Tom knew, was the most important reason they wanted to stay: to find out whether they were right about Coach Johnson and then try to prove it.

Alan Jefferson stood up.

"Okay then, if you're going to stay, how about showing us around the rest of this place?"

. . . . .

After the tour, which even included the empty locker room—the parents were amazed by how large and posh it was—the boys were treated to dinner. Freshmen weren't normally allowed to leave campus on weekends, unless their parents were visiting.

Tom and Jason begged for a return trip to the Aberdeen Barn and got it—in part because the parents were staying at the Courtyard Marriott right next door. Their flight out of Richmond to go home was early the next morning. Tom, Jason, and Tom's dad introduced Tom's mom and the Roddins to Martha Washington, who actually remembered them.

"How are things at TGP?" she asked. "I saw where you guys won a close one last night."

"Thanks to my buddy here," Tom said. "He blocked the last field goal attempt."

Martha looked at Jason. "That was you?" she said. "I read in the paper you were hurt. You okay?"

"Fine," Jason said with a smile. "But very hungry."

"We can fix that," Martha said, leading them to a table.

A few minutes later, the manager came over to introduce himself. "Doug Newburg," he said. "It's a pleasure to have you back—Martha told me you stopped here on your way to school a couple weeks ago." He turned to Jason. "Is this the heroic Mr. Roddin?" he asked.

"Jason, yep," the boy said.

"Well, as it happens, my wife and I are longtime season-ticket holders over at Gatch," he said. "UVA, too, although we've seen a lot more wins at Gatch than at Scott Stadium recently."

Tom knew that was accurate: Virginia had struggled in recent years in football, even at home.

"So I'd like to buy you all dinner tonight as thanks for saving the day—or the night—yesterday."

"That's not necessary," Mr. Roddin said.

"I know it's not," Mr. Newburg said. "But it would be my pleasure."

He shook hands all around again, turned, and walked away.

"Wow," Mr. Jefferson said. "That's quite a gesture."

"Yeah," Tom said. "Imagine if we ever get to *really* play. We can come in here and eat for free every night."

Jason was grinning. "The life of a star athlete, I guess," he said. He patted Tom on the shoulder. "Someday, son, you'll find out what it's like."

Tom snorted. "Oh, White Lightning, I'm just happy to bask in your reflected light."

Everyone laughed. They'd come a long way in a few hours.

15

REALITY SET IN AGAIN SUNDAY.

Since neither Tom nor Jason had cracked a book on Saturday, they had plenty of homework to do. With the library closed, Tom came down to Jason's room so they could hang out together while Billy Bob and Anthony were in church.

Tom knew that Juan del Potro and Jimmy Gomez both went to church, so a trip to see Jimmy about the rooming list would have to wait until they got back. He was antsy, wanting to get moving. He was struggling to focus on trying to memorize a list of igneous rocks for a geology quiz he had to take the next day.

Bored out of his mind, he walked over to Jason, who had claimed he was writing an essay analyzing *Catcher in the Rye* for his English class. But there was nothing about Holden Caulfield on his computer screen. Instead, Tom saw a newspaper headline: FRESHMAN SAVES THE DAY—AND TGP. It was the *Charlottesville Daily Progress*'s story on Friday night's game.

They had both gone online earlier to read Teel's and Robinson's stories from the Saturday lunchtime interviews. The stories were similar, but Robinson's had one twist that caught Tom's eye—a quote from Coach Johnson.

"It was just a gut feeling," the head coach had said. "Roddin ran a very fast forty in our preseason time trials, and I thought we might get lucky even though he hadn't practiced much with special teams."

Jason had read the line and grunted. "Much? How about zero?"

"And you weren't just 'very fast' in the forty, you were the *fastest* in the forty," Tom had added.

That, though, wasn't the most intriguing aspect of the quote. Tom remembered the sequence leading up to the kick pretty well. TGP had called time to try to freeze the kicker. Coach Gutekunst had come out of nowhere to grab Jason and send him into the game. Tom had no memory of seeing him anywhere near Coach Johnson. So whose idea was it to send Jason into the game? In his quote, Coach Johnson was making it clear to Robinson it had been his idea. In fact, that same quote had appeared in other newspaper coverage of the game, too. Teel had chosen to leave it out.

"Reading your press clippings again?" Tom asked now, grinning.

"I needed a break from Holden," Jason said with a smile. "So . . ."

"You're wallowing in your newfound glory," Tom said. "I get it."

He did get it, although he had to admit he was a tiny bit jealous. At breakfast that morning, even with the dining hall half empty, there had been a parade to the table of kids congratulating Jason and asking how he felt. A number of them had been girls. Tom and Jason had felt pretty invisible so far when it came to the girls at the school. Billy Bob called it "freshman syndrome."

"None of the girls, especially the really good-looking ones, are goin' anywhere near a freshman," Billy Bob had said. "We're beneath them."

Jason hadn't been beneath anyone that morning. Tom suspected the same would now be true of Billy Bob, who'd been absent from breakfast because he'd opted to sleep in prior to church.

While Jason continued to revel in being a hero, Tom walked down the hallway to the bathroom. Naturally, he ran almost smack into Coach Ingelsby, making his weekly church-check rounds.

"No worship again today for you, Jefferson?" the coach said, his voice as unpleasant as ever.

Tom was over being told how to live his life and was emboldened by the fact that he knew the door to go back home was pretty much wide open. "No offense, Coach," he answered. "But how or when I practice my religion, whatever it may be, is really my business alone."

He and Coach Ingelsby were now face-to-face in the hallway.

"You've got quite a mouth on you, don't you, Jefferson?" the coach said. "Too bad your parents didn't use that time you weren't in church to teach you manners."

Tom was sorely tempted to haul off and hit Ingelsby. But he suspected that was exactly what the smarmy coach wanted. And if he did something like that, he would no longer have the option to stay or go—he'd be gone.

Instead, he shrugged and said, "It must be nice to have all of life's answers, Coach."

"You aren't apt to find many answers sitting in your room on Sunday morning, are you?" Coach Ingelsby said. "See you at practice tomorrow." He maneuvered around Tom and kept walking.

There was a bit of menace in his last sentence. Tom suspected this little encounter wasn't over yet. He decided to swallow any further responses. He looked at his watch. It was almost noon. Juan and Jimmy should be back soon. That thought put a smile on his face.

· · · · ·

Billy Bob and Anthony showed up in the room after church. They all went to lunch and then returned to Billy Bob and Jason's room.

There, they decided that Tom should go see Jimmy Gomez alone. He and Juan had been at lunch, but the dining hall was no place to open up the conversation about roommates and race.

"If we all go, or even if two of us go, it makes it a bigger deal," Billy Bob said.

"What's my excuse for wanting the list—if he asks?" Tom said.

"Tell him you're just checking a hunch about something," Billy Bob said. "I doubt he'll give you a hard time about it."

They agreed. They also agreed that Tom should just walk upstairs and knock on the door rather than calling Juan on his cell to see if his roomie was around.

"The more casual this looks, the better," Anthony said.

Even though Juan and Jimmy were good guys—and probably would be allies if they knew what the four freshmen were up to—Tom was taking deep breaths as he climbed the steps to the fifth floor and knocked on the door marked GOMEZ/DEL POTRO.

Juan opened the door almost right away. "Hey, Presidente, what's up?" he asked.

Tom could see Jimmy sitting at his computer.

"Actually, I wanted to ask Jimmy something," he said.

"Come on in," Juan said, holding the door open.

Jimmy Gomez had struck Tom from the beginning as almost incurably polite—even formal. Now he stood up from his computer and crossed the room to shake hands with Tom— whom he'd seen at lunch twenty minutes earlier. He was very tall, about six foot five, and, according to Juan, was being heavily recruited by several big-time college basketball schools because he could shoot and had excellent grades.

"Everything okay, Tom?" he asked.

"Fine, fine," Tom said, realizing he sounded nervous.

Jimmy pointed at an extra chair, sitting near the window. "Have a seat. Tell me what's up."

Tom sat, as did Jimmy and Juan—both at their desks.

"I was just wondering something," Tom said. He paused.

Jimmy and Juan waited.

"I was wondering, being a floor monitor and all, if you had rooming lists."

"Of course I do," Jimmy said, a puzzled look crossing his handsome features.

Tom didn't feel like he was an expert on what made most guys good-looking or not, but he knew Jimmy was movie-star handsome. His girlfriend, Maria Ramos, was captain of the volleyball team—six feet tall and drop-dead gorgeous.

"You mean for the floor?" Juan said.

"Actually, I meant for the whole dorm," Tom said.

Another puzzled look from Jimmy. "I don't have them right here, right now, but I certainly have access to them," he said. "When the other monitors get back later today, all I have to do is ask for their lists and they'll give them to me. Why do you need them?"

"Just a hunch about something, no big deal," Tom said. "I guess I figured you'd have them since you're in charge this weekend."

Jimmy smiled. "I should, actually," he said. "But it's my first weekend in charge. I have a list of everyone's cell numbers but didn't even think about the rooming list."

Juan leaned forward in his chair. "What's your hunch, Presidente?"

Tom wasn't really ready for that one, but he came up with an answer pretty quickly. "Can I wait to tell you till after I know whether I'm right?" he said, hoping that would suffice.

The two roommates looked at each other and seemed to shrug at the same moment.

"Fair enough," Jimmy said, "if you *promise* to tell us then. You've got me curious."

Tom breathed a mental sigh of relief. "Yeah, that's fine," he said. "Promise."

"I should have 'em for you tonight," Jimmy said.

"Perfect," Tom said. He stood up to leave, figuring he shouldn't push his luck. They all shook hands as if an important meeting had just ended. Which, Tom figured, was true.

"You're full of surprises aren't you, Presidente?" Juan said as they walked to the door.

"Time will tell," Tom said, managing a smile. "Time will tell."

• • • • •

Jimmy Gomez was as good as his word.

Everyone in the school was required to be back on campus for dinner—at six o'clock sharp—on Sundays. At eight o'clock, Jimmy knocked on Tom and Anthony's door.

"I printed them by floor," he said, holding out a stack of paper to Tom. "Not sure what you're looking for, but it may take some time. It's not broken down by class or anything, just a list of each guy's age, sport, and room assignment."

"All I need," Tom said. "Thanks."

"Remember your promise," Jimmy said with a smile.

"Count on it," Tom said.

He waved the list at Anthony and sent a text to Jason and Billy Bob. Two minutes later, the four of them were gathered around Tom's desk.

"Eight pages in all," Tom said. "Let's take two pages each. Football players only. Mark who's of color, who's not."

"That's fine," Billy Bob said. "But there are goin' to be some guys we don't know, so we won't know if they are black, brown, white, or blue."

"So we just mark what we know and put in a question mark if we aren't sure," Tom said.

"Won't be hard to figure it out," Anthony said. "In case you haven't noticed, most of the white guys sit together in the dining hall, and most of the black guys do, too."

Jason nodded. "Yeah, we're kind of the exception at our table—Jewish American, African American, Hispanic American."

"You forgot redneck American," Billy Bob said.

"And redneck American," Jason added. "You know something else I noticed at practice the other day? There's not one Asian or Hispanic dude on the whole football team."

"True," Billy Bob said.

"Bobo may have ideas about that, too," Tom said.

The boys got busy. Every once in a while someone would call out a name to see if the other three knew who he was and whether he was black or white. Some they knew, some they didn't.

When they were finished, they added up the numbers. Of the original eighty-two players on the TGP team, they had been able to identify, with confidence, sixty on the list by race (including themselves, of course). That left them with twenty-two question marks.

Six of the players (all seniors) had single rooms. That left seventy-six players who were divided into thirty-eight double rooms. Five of the six guys in the singles were white; the sixth— Tony Jones—was a question mark.

Of the other twenty-one question marks, eleven were in rooms where the boys had been able to identify the other occupant. Ten more question marks were divided into five rooms, with two question marks apiece.

That meant they knew with certainty the racial identity of the occupants in the remaining twenty-two rooms: twelve rooms had two white guys in them, and ten had two African Americans—if they included the double room that was now occupied solely by Jameis Almonte, the onetime roommate of the player who had left the school, Kendall Franklin.

"So far, not a single mixed room," Tom said when they had finished. "But we can't be sure of anything until we figure out the last sixteen rooms. That's still a lot."

"Yeah, but if I put the over/under number at one room with

a black guy and a white guy, would you take the over or the under?" Anthony asked.

They all looked at one another.

And then they nodded, reading one another's thoughts.

The under was clearly the better bet.

16

TO NO ONE'S SURPRISE, IT TURNED OUT THAT THE UNDER WAS THE RIGHT call.

It took a few days to pin down the IDs on the remaining players. Not wanting to raise any eyebrows, they spread out their research. Some of the work of putting faces to names was easy—walking casually through the locker room before and after practice and taking note of guys standing in front of their lockers.

In other cases, they had to ask specific questions. Most of the players they didn't know were upperclassmen, since most of their classes were with the other freshmen. So there were times when they'd just say to someone they knew: "Who's that?" pointing at a player in the hallway between classes or on line in the dining room.

"Ted Harvey," would come the answer. And another name would be checked off the list.

The most awkward moment came when Billy Bob asked a kid he knew from Alabama, a junior wide receiver named Robert Alonzo, to point out his roommate to him.

"He points in the direction of a locker where there's an African American guy standing who I don't know," Billy Bob recounted, "and he says 'It's Joey Allen.' For a split second I thought we finally had a black-and-white room. So I nod where I thought he was pointing and, since the guy was huge, I said, 'Oh, so you room with a lineman, huh?' He looked at me like I was insane and said, 'You mean Willie White? No, dummy, I was pointin' at Joey—right there.'"

Billy Bob then explained that Allen had been walking *past* White when Tommy pointed. "I just said, 'Oh, yeah sorry, easy mistake to make, I guess.' He gave me a look and said, 'Not if your IQ's over a hundred. You see any black guys and white guys rooming together around this place?' He walked off laughing like that was the funniest thing he'd ever heard."

"Probably was," Anthony said.

· · · · ·

By Wednesday night they'd gathered back in Tom and Anthony's room to go over the list. They now had all eighty-one remaining players sorted. Of the thirty-eight double rooms, there were nineteen rooms with two white guys and nineteen with two black guys (still including Jameis Almonte and Kendall Franklin, since that was the original room assignment).

And it turned out that the one question mark among the

players in single rooms, Tony Jones, was black; he was a star linebacker who was being recruited by every top program in the country.

"Some of the guys told me he was talking about transferring for his senior year," Anthony said when Jones's name came up. "All of a sudden, the school found him one of the singles."

"That's interesting," Tom said. "But more important, we found what we thought we'd find: every double room has either two black or two white players in it. Our case is still just circumstantial, but it's a lot stronger."

It was Jason who played devil's advocate. "We've only proved what Robert Alonzo and everybody else already knows. It's not like we can march into Coach Johnson's office and say, 'Hey, Bobo, we know you haven't got a single biracial double room among the players on your team, and this proves you are a racist SOB.' Coach Johnson is just going to smile and say, 'Is that true? I had no idea. The admissions people handle the room assignments. We just give them the names of our players and ask that they all be allowed to room together because we like our players to become close away from the field. How they handle those assignments is up to them.'"

Billy Bob nodded. "They can come up with some kind of explanation for every individual thing. They can say that the white quarterback thing is coincidence, that they didn't know about rooming assignments, and that Coach Johnson knowing Tom wasn't Jason's roommate was because he'd heard they'd complained about not being put together."

"So we need something else," Jason said. "A smoking gun."

"How do we get it, though?" Anthony said.

"It's worth thinking about," Tom said. "But for now, our next move is to figure out a way to meet with Teel and Robinson again, and see if they've found anything out."

"Well, they're not coming to the game Friday night, and we aren't allowed off campus without a good reason on Saturday and Sunday," Billy Bob said. "So we need to come up with something."

"Think there's any way to convince them to come Friday?" Jason asked.

Tom shook his head. "If South Hill is as bad as they say and they show up, won't the coaches want to know why?"

"Maybe they want to see if Jason will be the hero again?" Billy Bob said.

"If I am, the entire team will probably be on lockdown all weekend," Jason said. "Coach will not be happy."

They all nodded. He was right.

· · · · ·

Tom texted Teel anyway to tell him they needed to talk. He said nothing about their research, paranoid enough by now to think his phone might get confiscated at some point if they got much further with the investigation. No sense giving the coaches or the school any written evidence of what they were up to.

"Of course, the fact that you're texting with a reporter at all would probably convict you if it ever got to that," Jason pointed out as they were walking off the practice field on Thursday.

Tom knew Jason was right, but he wasn't that concerned. Part of him *wanted* a confrontation of some kind with the coaches. As the week had gone on and he continued to get very few "reps"—as the coaches called plays—in practice, he'd found himself having more and more regret about not jumping at the chance to go home the previous Saturday.

Another part of him, though, he had to admit, was being a little jealous about Jason's new status with the team. Jason had gone from being as invisible as Tom, day in and day out, to being a full-fledged hero. When he'd walked into the locker room before practice on Monday, almost everyone in the room had stopped to clap for him, and then they'd crowded around to congratulate him and ask him how he was feeling.

The answer was fine. Dr. Mazzocca had taken him into the training room for his concussion protocol test before he was allowed to join everyone else on the field. Soon after they finished stretching, Jason came jogging onto the field—in uniform.

He reported to Dave Billingsley, the trainer, and Tom saw Mr. Billingsley pat him on the back, point him to where the quarterbacks were gathering, and then walk over to report to Coach Johnson.

As Jason jogged past the circle of wide receivers he slowed for a second and said to Tom, "Passed with flying colors. My brain's still intact."

"Still?" Tom couldn't resist saying—earning him a glare from Coach Reilly, who couldn't hear what was being said but clearly didn't see any reason for *any* conversation at all.

When they scrimmaged that day, Jason was the number three

quarterback, even getting a few reps with the second-stringers. Billy Bob was still taking more snaps with the twos than with the ones, which annoyed him and confused everyone else.

"Coach Johnson just doesn't want to admit he was wrong starting Ronnie Thompson last week," Billy Bob said on Wednesday when the depth chart for Friday's game was posted in the locker room. Thompson was again listed as the starting quarterback.

"You're right," Tom said. "He knows he can get away with playing Thompson this week. If, by some chance, they make it a game, you come to the rescue again."

Billy Bob gave Tom his Billy Bob grin. "And I can't even claim race is involved, can I?"

They both laughed—one of Tom's few laughs during the week.

On Thursday night, after he'd gotten into the relatively brief Thursday scrimmage—most of Thursday practice being devoted to special teams—for a grand total of two plays, Tom went to Juan and Jimmy's room to keep his promise by explaining to them why he'd asked for the rooming list.

"You're kidding," Juan said. "You didn't have to go to all that trouble. All you had to do was ask us. You think there's some secret reason why we're roomies? You think there's some secret reason why there's always an even number of Hispanics on the baseball team?"

Jimmy took it a step further. "We've got two Asians on the basketball team this year—one from China, one from Korea.

The Chinese kid can really play—every big-time school out there is recruiting him. The Korean kid can barely dribble with one hand. But TGP recruited him . . ."

"So that the Chinese kid would have an Asian roommate," Juan finished.

They both nodded.

"If that's the case, then it isn't just Coach Johnson—it's the entire school," Tom said.

"It's not the entire school," Jimmy said. "It only takes a few bad apples. Especially when they are big apples."

"You've researched Coach Johnson's background, right?" Juan said as Tom nodded. "Have you googled our beloved founder, Mr. Gatch, at all?"

They hadn't. It had never occurred to Tom or to his other three friends that the issue might go beyond the football team. They knew Mr. Gatch was from the South—he didn't have a deep accent, but you could hear it when he spoke—but that didn't necessarily mean anything. Billy Bob was as Southern as they came, and so were a lot of the other kids he'd met at TGP who clearly couldn't care less about skin color. One of the things Tom had figured out growing up as an athlete was that race pretty much disappeared when you were playing ball. Not always. But most of the time.

He remembered a quote from the great basketball coach Red Auerbach, who was the first coach in professional sports to start an all-black lineup back in the 1960s.

"I can't stand black players," Auerbach had said. "I also can't stand white players, red players, or green players—if they *can't play*. They all look the same to me until they get on the court. Then I decide who I like and who I don't like."

Tom's father had given him a book about Auerbach to read a couple of years earlier. Reading it, he had learned that Auerbach had made Bill Russell the first black coach of a major professional sports team when he'd handed the Celtics over to him in 1966. It was hard to believe that more than fifty years later, race could still be a factor in who got coaching jobs—or who played quarterback.

Or who roomed with whom.

"So what am I missing about Mr. Gatch?" he asked Juan.

"He's from Louisiana," Jimmy said.

"So?"

"There's more," Jimmy said. "Go and google Gatch; then we'll talk again."

"Why so mysterious?" Tom asked.

"Not being mysterious," Jimmy said. "But it's easier for you to read about it than for me to try to explain it."

Tom sighed. Every time he thought they had answered a question, new ones popped up. He headed back to his room to look into Mr. Thomas A. Gatch.

· · · · ·

There really wasn't anything shocking—at least that Tom could find—in the biography of Mr. Gatch.

His Wikipedia page was brief and had obviously been

written by the school's communications department. It was glowing, talking about his career as a teacher, then as an administrator, and then as a "player management representative" (in English that meant he'd been a sports agent) before his "groundbreaking decision" to found TGP. In truth, Tom thought, it was hardly groundbreaking: IMG Academy and others had already fostered the concept—for better or worse.

Remembering what Jimmy had said about Mr. Gatch coming from Louisiana, Tom started looking at websites from there for more information. There appeared to be nothing. Finally, having gone to the website of the state's largest newspaper, the *New Orleans Times-Picayune*, Tom found something. It was a one-paragraph mention, buried deep within a story headlined PREP SCHOOL PERSONNEL. The seventh item in the story, after mentions of football coach hirings and firings in the area and a couple of paragraphs about new department heads, came under the heading "Metairie Christian Names New Head-of-School":

Thomas A. Gatch, 35, has been named to replace Harold D. Samples as head-of-school at Metairie Christian School. Gatch is the headmaster of the Louisiana Boys School in Baton Rouge and was formerly head of the English department there.

The date was August 1, 1985. Tom quickly did the math in his head and was a little surprised to learn that Mr. Gatch was sixty-seven years old. He'd have guessed closer to sixty.

A few minutes later, Tom found Mr. Gatch mentioned in a

second clip. This one was considerably longer and bore the head-line HIGH SCHOOL HEAD-OF-SCHOOL DEFENDS DUKE INVITATION.

The story was dated December 2, 1989. It only took a couple of paragraphs to figure out what Jimmy and Juan had been talking about:

> **Thomas A. Gatch, the head of Metairie Christian School, said yesterday he will not back away from the invitation he has extended to former Ku Klux Klan grand wizard David E. Duke—now a member of the Louisiana State Legislature—to come and speak at the school.**
>
> **Duke, who was once a member of the Nazi Party, won a special election earlier this year, running as a Republican. Gatch insisted again yesterday that Duke's invitation to speak to the 335 students at Metairie was not an endorsement of his politics.**
>
> **"He's an elected official who has a political point of view that the students can learn from—regardless of how they feel about that point of view," Gatch said. "You don't always learn by listening to people whose views are inside the box. I've known Mr. Duke for a long time. I don't have to agree with his views to respect him as a communicator."**

The story went on to mention that Gatch and Duke had been at Louisiana State University together.

There were no more specifics.

Tom found another clip—from two days later—announcing that Gatch had reversed himself and withdrawn the invitation to Duke "under pressure from the school's board of trustees."

Tom found one more clip, dated a month later, announcing that Gatch was resigning from his job at Metairie Christian to "pursue other opportunities."

The trail ended there. Tom sat back in his chair. Anthony was asleep, snoring softly.

The man who had founded TGP had apparently known a Ku Klux Klan grand wizard who was also a onetime member of the Nazi Party. And he had apparently been fired for inviting him to come speak to his students at the school where he was head-of-school.

"Wow," he said softly to himself. "What now?"

17

TOM DIDN'T REALLY HAVE A CHANCE TO SHARE HIS NEWFOUND information with the others until after classes on Friday. The day just started too early for any sort of group talk, and he wasn't going to bring it up with people nearby in the dining hall or in the classroom.

As they were sitting down at breakfast, Jimmy Gomez did ask him if he'd found anything, and Tom said he had. Jimmy just smiled. Tom had questions for him and for Juan del Potro, too, as in: Why hadn't they said something earlier?

For the first time since Tom and Jason had arrived at school, TGP had been hit that morning with a real rainstorm, the all-day kind—no thunder or lightning, just relentless, miserable rain. Once he and Anthony were back in their room after their last class, Tom texted Jason, asking that he and Billy Bob come up to their room. He did the same with Juan, but Juan texted back that he and Jimmy were "blowing out of here" for the weekend.

Tom remembered that Juan was dating a freshman at UVA and had mentioned going to see her this weekend. Since he was a senior, he could have a car to make the short drive to Charlottesville.

Juan did briefly mention Mr. Gatch—indirectly—in his return text:

Jimmy says we can talk more when we get back Sunday. About 5.

Tom wasn't a hundred percent sure he could wait until then, but he had no choice. Teel and Robinson had both texted that they couldn't get over to the school for the game that night or Saturday but maybe could figure something out for Sunday.

When Jason and Billy Bob arrived, Tom filled everyone in on what he'd found in his Google search on Mr. Gatch.

"I can't believe that Teel and Robinson wouldn't mention it to us," Tom said after summing up his findings. "I mean, that's a huge piece of the puzzle, isn't it?"

"It could be," Billy Bob said. "But it's also entirely possible they don't know about Mr. Gatch's past."

"It was in the New Orleans newspaper," Tom said, slightly exasperated.

"More than twenty-five years ago," Jason pointed out. "I mean, honestly, I've never heard of this Duke guy. Have you?"

"I have," Anthony said. "When Trump was running for president, the guy endorsed him."

Billy Bob snapped his fingers. "Yeah, I remember now. Duke

said Trump was the best candidate; Trump said he wasn't sure he wanted an endorsement from Duke. Something like that."

Tom felt like they were getting off-topic. "Look, doesn't matter. What does matter is that Mr. Gatch was associated in some way with a guy who was once a self-declared Nazi and later was a KKK big shot. I mean, my God!"

"Slow down, Tom," Jason said. "You might be jumping at shadows here. The article you found says they went to college together and knew each other. That doesn't mean they have the same beliefs, does it?"

"What about Gatch inviting Duke to speak at his school?" Anthony said.

"That's disturbing—maybe," Jason said. "But I'm sure Mr. Gatch can make the case that it's good for kids to hear *all* viewpoints."

"Might be interesting to find out who else he had speak at the school while he was there," Billy Bob said.

"Remember, though, that Mr. Gatch backed down and Duke never actually spoke," Jason said. "But Billy Bob's right."

"So what's next?" Tom asked.

They all looked at one another.

Tom finally sighed. "I guess there's not much more we can do until Sunday," he said. "I feel like we're running in sand. Every time we think we've figured something out, we don't seem to have made much progress."

"Not entirely," Jason said. "We may not know what we're onto right now, but it does feel as if we're onto *something*."

Billy Bob stood up. "I gotta go lie down for a little bit," he said. "We *do* have a game to play tonight."

Tom had almost forgotten. Which, he thought, was understandable. Billy Bob would certainly play tonight, as would Anthony. Even Jason would get in on special teams; he'd been designated as the outside rusher on all kicks—field goals, extra points, and punts—after his heroics the week before. Meanwhile, Tom would almost certainly watch from the sidelines.

Which would give him even more time to stew about the mysteries of Thomas Gatch Prep.

· · · · ·

The rain had stopped by kickoff, although the air was muggy—and buggy—on the sidelines. Standing there with nothing to do but watch, Tom almost wished it was still raining, if only to cool things off a little bit.

The crowd was sparse compared to a week earlier, when the ten-thousand-seat stadium had been almost sold out. Tom wasn't sure if it was the weather or the opponent—he figured both—but the stadium was half full at best.

It turned out that Teel and Robinson had been right about South Hill High School. The Hilltoppers were smaller, slower, and weaker than TGP at just about every position. They had one big-time player, a wide receiver named Freddy Johnston, who ended up with seventeen catches for the night and provided his team with just about all of its offense.

TGP's offensive line dominated the game, pushing the South Hill defense backward on almost every play. Given all sorts of time and space, Ronnie Thompson suddenly became a star quarterback. He threw the ball only on occasion, usually after the Patriots had ripped off five straight solid runs and South Hill crowded the line of scrimmage.

By halftime, the offense had put together three long scoring drives and had scored on two short drives set up by South Hill turnovers. The score was 35–10 and, as he walked to the locker room, having not yet put a foot on the field, Tom could see that some of the crowd was clearly heading to their cars already. He wished he could leave, too.

In spite of the big lead, Coach Johnson was hardly upbeat at halftime.

"Honestly, fellas, we should score on just about every play against these guys," he said, pacing up and down in front of his players. "I'm not really concerned about scoring this second half; I'm concerned about execution." He paused. "O-line, I know you guys will think picking up eight, nine, ten yards each play means you're doing your job. But if you can't hold your blocks longer than that against *this* defense, what happens next week when we play Culpeper at their place? Those eight-yard gains will be two-yard gains, if we're lucky.

"Defense, I understand that Johnston is really, really tough to defend. I'm going to get together with the coaches right now to come up with a way to at least slow him down. But we've got to do that. We're going to face a lot of good receivers in conference play."

He went on with a few more details. As Tom listened, it occurred to him that every point was right on target. Bobo Johnson could coach. Of that there was no doubt.

The one starter who didn't get singled out for any criticism was Ronnie Thompson. There hadn't been anything wrong with Thompson's play, but if the O-line should have been opening bigger holes, Thompson probably should have been picking up more yardage, given the holes they *had* created. It was pretty clear—at least to Tom—that Thompson was Coach Johnson's guy. He wondered why.

The second half wasn't much different from the first. Coach Johnson began to play second- and third-stringers late in the third quarter when the margin was extended to 49–10. Anthony, who had been alternating series at right tackle with starter Wyatt Wilson, was told at the end of the third quarter that his night was over.

On the next series, Billy Bob finally got into the game, playing with second- and third-stringers and with orders to keep the ball strictly on the ground. He settled for fullback handoffs and the occasional pitch to a slotback. Even at that, TGP still tacked on another touchdown.

With the score 56–10 and the stands just about empty, Tom got a surprise when Coach Cruikshank walked over to where he was standing with Jason—who hadn't blocked another kick, in large part because there wasn't any real need for the desperate move he'd made the previous week, but also because a blocker was assigned to him on every punt and on the two South Hill place kicks.

"What do you think, Roddin? Wanna go in and finish up?" the coach asked.

Billy Bob, who was also standing there, looked a little bit surprised, but said nothing.

Jason glanced at Billy Bob, then nodded. "Sure, Coach," he said. "As long as Billy Bob doesn't mind."

"Anderson doesn't have a vote in this," Coach Cruikshank said—though he was smiling when he said it. "Go on—run the fullback dive, and try to stay out of trouble."

Jason went in with 2:11 on the clock. He handed off to third-string fullback Emerson Snell three times and, on third and three, Snell just barely picked up the first down. At that point, the coaches ordered "victory formation," since only one more play was needed to run out the clock. Jason took the snap with the entire backfield lined up deep behind him and dropped to one knee. He flipped the ball to the referee and jogged to the sideline to join Tom, Billy Bob, and Anthony for the postgame handshakes.

"After that performance, you might start next week," Tom joked.

"Probably play ahead of me," Billy Bob said—not smiling.

"Well, you're *all* playing a lot more than I am," Tom said. He *was* smiling, even if he didn't mean it.

. . . . .

The locker room was subdued, with very little celebrating, because the players understood the win didn't mean very much.

Coach Johnson told them, "The season begins Monday at practice."

The game against Culpeper Prep the next Friday would be the first of eight straight games in the Virginia 5-A Prep School League—the VPSL in jock vernacular.

Since this was TPG's first year in the league, it was also the first year it would be eligible to win a state title. But it would have to win the league to qualify for the playoffs.

The media contingent was tiny compared to the week before. Tom, Jason, Billy Bob, and Anthony walked past the handful of reporters without anyone so much as glancing in their direction.

"Guess your fifteen minutes are over," Tom said.

"Fifteen minutes?" Jason asked.

"Andy Warhol, famous artist," Tom said. "He once said that in the future everyone will have fifteen minutes of fame. Looks like your time is up."

"Guess so," Jason said, laughing.

"Yeah," Billy Bob added. "If only you'd blocked their field goal, we could have won fifty-six to seven, and then they'd have been all over you."

Tom was about to point out that it would be some sort of record to block two field goals in two attempts when his phone started buzzing. Figuring it was his parents checking in, he pulled it from his pocket. It was David Teel.

"Did you get in at all?" the reporter asked when Tom answered.

"Nope," Tom said. "But Jason got four snaps at quarterback."

"How much did Billy Bob and Anthony play?"

"Anthony a lot—every other series until the starters got pulled. Billy Bob, not so much."

The others were looking at Tom quizzically. He held up a finger and indicated they should all keep walking.

"Yeah, figures," Teel said. "Bobo isn't going to admit he's playing the wrong quarterback until he has no choice."

"Which could be next week," Tom said.

"True that," Teel said. "Listen, Robinson's come up with a pretty good idea for us to see you on Sunday without raising suspicion."

"What's that?"

"He's going to write a story about a week in the life of a sudden hero. How was last week different for Jason at TGP as opposed to the first two weeks?"

"Very," Tom said, not realizing the question was rhetorical until he'd already responded.

"Yeah, exactly. So Robinson's going to need to talk to Jason, to his roommate, and to his closest friends to do the story."

"What about you?"

"No," Teel said. "Robinson and I can't keep writing the same story. I'll meet you guys at lunch like last week, but they don't need to know I'm involved at all."

"They like Tom Robinson."

"They dislike him less than they dislike me. They don't like any of us."

"So what do we do?"

"Nothing. Robinson will make the request tomorrow and point out it needs to be Sunday because he's covering UVA tomorrow. I would imagine it won't be a problem. They like puffy-sounding pieces. He'll pick you up the same as last week. He'll borrow my SUV so there'll be room for Anthony."

"Good," Tom said. "We've got a lot to talk about."

"I don't doubt it," Teel said. "Stay out of trouble the next couple of days."

He hung up. Tom caught up to the other three and reported what Teel had said.

"So," Jason said, laughing, "I guess my fifteen minutes aren't quite over yet."

"Don't get carried away with yourself," Tom said, giving him a look.

"Not much chance of that," Jason said.

Tom knew that was true. Although it occurred to him that if they continued with their investigation they might all be in for a lot more than fifteen minutes of fame.

Or infamy.

PART 3

18

JASON WOKE UP THE NEXT MORNING TO FIND AN E-MAIL FROM ED Seaman, the TGP communications director, telling him that Tom Robinson had requested an interview with him for Sunday to talk about his "week as a hero."

"As always, it is up to you whether to accept the invitation," Mr. Seaman wrote. "He has also requested that Mr. Anderson and your friends Jefferson and Ames join you for a group interview. He can pick you up at one o'clock since, of course, we don't allow nonfamily onto the campus on Sunday until then."

Of course we don't, Jason thought. He e-mailed back that he'd be glad to talk to Mr. Robinson. He was tempted to ask why Billy Bob rated being called "Mr." and Tom and Anthony didn't, but he resisted. His dad had a saying: "Choose your battles." This wasn't one he wanted or needed to fight. There were bigger ones ahead.

They passed a quiet Saturday, catching up on studies, staying inside for the most part because it was raining again. The campus felt empty with so many of the upperclassmen gone for the weekend.

Jason wished there was a way to talk to Jimmy Gomez and Juan del Potro before their meeting with the reporters to find out if they knew more about Mr. Gatch's relationship with David Duke. He had accused Tom of jumping at shadows, but somehow he couldn't get those same shadows out of his own mind.

. . . . .

On Sunday, Jason, Tom, Billy Bob, and Anthony skipped lunch in the dining hall since they were going to be eating with Teel and Robinson. Billy Bob and Anthony had changed from their jacket-and-tie church clothes to T-shirts and shorts. The rain had stopped, but it was another warm, dreary late-summer day in central Virginia.

Robinson was waiting for them on the same bench where they had met eight days earlier. Everyone quickly piled into Teel's car. None of the coaches were working today—or at least none of their cars were there. Again the reporter's car was the only one in the lot.

They small-talked en route to Charlottesville, Robinson filling them in on Virginia's overtime loss to Richmond.

"Not a good start for a new coaching staff to lose at home to a I-AA team," Robinson said. "They were beaten soundly."

"Don't they call I-AA something else now?" Tom asked.

He and Jason were in the backseat. Anthony, in deference to his size, was up front, and Billy Bob was in the way back.

"Yeah, FCS, which stands for Football Championship Subdivision," Robinson said. "Typical NCAA. They don't want anyone to imply that somehow there are different levels of college football—even though there clearly are."

"So what do they call Division I now?" Jason asked.

Tom knew that one. "FBS," he said. "Football *Bowl* Subdivision. Since the power schools play bowl games, they call it that as opposed to FCS, which has an actual championship tournament."

"Sounds pretty silly to me," Anthony said.

"You got that right," Robinson said.

When they arrived, they found Teel holding the same booth in the back that they'd used on their previous trip to the Biltmore.

"I got here early because I figured it would be crowded," Teel said. "And it was packed. I just now sat down."

They ordered quickly since it was already one-thirty and the boys, having skipped lunch at school, were starving. Except for Anthony. He'd eaten in the dining hall but was ready, willing, and able to eat again.

"So where do we begin?" Teel asked.

Tom was the keeper of the rooming lists. He pulled them out and went over the numbers.

"Well, we found pretty much the same thing," Teel said. "We talked to"—he glanced down at his notebook—"a total of twenty-three TGP graduates: eighteen football players and five basketball players. None of them ever roomed with someone of a different race."

"So where do we think that leaves us?" Robinson said, looking at Teel. "What's our next move?"

Tom cleared his throat. Jason knew what was coming.

"You guys ever hear of David Duke?" Tom asked.

The reporters looked baffled for a second. Then Teel said, "The KKK guy?"

Tom nodded.

"What about him?" Robinson said. "Don't tell me that bozo has got some connection to Bobo."

"No, not that we know of," Tom said. "But the former grand wizard was, at least once upon a time, some kind of acquaintance of the proud founder of Thomas Gatch Prep."

Teel and Robinson looked slightly stunned.

Teel turned to Robinson and said, "You remember the famous line from Watergate, when the *Washington Post* city editor—"

"Barry Sussman," Tom said, apparently knowing where his reporter friend was going.

"Who's Barry Sussman?" Jason asked.

"He was Bob Woodward and Carl Bernstein's original editor when the Watergate break-in happened forty-five years ago," Robinson said. "At one point, after Woodward and Bernstein had broken one of the first big stories connecting the Nixon White House to the break-in, Sussman looked at them and said, 'We've never had a story like this. Just never.'"

He reopened his notebook.

"Tell us more, Tom," he said. "Tell us everything."

· · · · ·

It didn't take Tom long to retell what he had found in the New Orleans paper.

It was all news to Teel and Robinson.

"You've never heard anything about this?" Tom asked, truly surprised.

"Nothing," Robinson said. "Not a word."

"Of course, it isn't the kind of thing you go looking for," Teel said. "We don't vet heads-of-schools all that closely to begin with. It isn't as if they're running for office."

"What's *vet* mean?" Anthony asked.

"It means you check someone's background," Teel said. "When someone applies for a job, they're vetted. When someone runs for office, they're vetted in even more detail."

"Don't they put that stuff in their application for a job?" Jason said, still curious.

"They do, but history shows that job applicants aren't always honest," Robinson said. "A guy named George O'Leary was hired as Notre Dame's football coach years ago. After they hired him, they found out he'd lied on his résumé about playing college football."

"What difference did that make if he was a good coach?" Anthony asked.

"None," said Robinson. "In fact, O'Leary ended up getting hired at Central Florida a couple of years later and was very successful. But the issue was that he had lied."

"Central Florida didn't seem to care, did it?" Billy Bob asked.

Teel smiled. "Winning games makes up for most sins in sports," he said.

"Witness our coach," Tom said.

"Not to mention, perhaps, your school's founder," Teel added.

By the time they'd finished the hamburgers and french fries they all ordered, their updated plan was in place. Teel and Robinson were going to look further into Mr. Gatch's background to see if there was anyone still at LSU who remembered him—even though he'd graduated more than forty years ago, meaning that was a long shot. More relevant might be talking to people at Metairie Christian: there were bound to be at least a few people still there who had worked with him.

"Might even be worth trying to talk to David Duke," Teel said.

"It's worth a try," Robinson said. "Long shot, but this whole story started out as a long shot."

"What do you mean?" Anthony asked.

It was Tom who answered. "It's the twenty-first century in America, and we're talking about a high school sports story that might include the words *Ku Klux Klan* and *Nazi Party*," he said. "That's a long shot."

Jason smiled. As usual, his buddy was exactly right. He hadn't even mentioned that the story with those words centered on a coach named Bobo.

The waitress returned and they all ordered dessert.

"Before we go," Billy Bob said, "you guys better ask us some questions about the heroic Jason Roddin."

"Almost forgot," Robinson said. He pulled his notebook back out.

Jason couldn't help but laugh. "You guys gotta admit, this isn't your typical day," he said.

"How so?" Robinson said.

"One minute you're talking about tracking down a guy in the Ku Klux Klan, the next you're interviewing Jason Roddin and friends."

· · · · ·

Tom Robinson's story in the next day's *Virginian-Pilot* was glowing enough that Jason received considerable ribbing about it when he walked into the locker room before practice. Ever helpful, Billy Bob had sent the entire team a link to the story as soon as it was posted on the Internet.

When Jason and Tom arrived on the practice field, they found Coach Gutekunst waiting for them—actually, he was waiting for Jason.

"Ever return kicks, Roddin?" the coach asked, throwing an arm around Jason and guiding him away from Tom.

"No, sir," Jason said.

The seven-on-seven camp hadn't included any special-teams work. The only kicks Jason had ever returned were in Riverside Park, playing touch football growing up. He'd been good at it— if only because he was faster than everyone else.

"Well, starting today, when we get to the special-teams phase of practice, you're going to alternate with Solo and Quinn returning punts."

Ray Solo was the team's punt returner. Matt Quinn was his backup and usually stood seven yards in front of Solo in case of a short kick. Both were backup wide receivers without much speed, but with excellent hands.

"We want to see how well you can catch a punt," Coach Gutekunst said. "Coach Ingelsby remembered you had decent hands as a receiver when you were here for seven-on-seven. Given your speed, you might be able to help us." He paused, then added, "We aren't going to rush you into anything. Solo and Quinn are reliable. They don't fumble, which, honestly, is the most important thing for a punt returner. But if you can catch a punt with eleven guys bearing down on you, well, with your speed you might be able to help."

Jason wasn't so sure about the "eleven guys bearing down on you" part, but he figured anything that might get him on the field for something other than trying to block field goals or hand-ing off during mop-up time was worth attempting. Then he thought of Tom, who had yet to see the field at all.

"Whatever you say, Coach," he said. "I'll give it a shot."

He jogged over to join everyone else just as they were all lining up to stretch.

"What was that all about?" Tom asked.

"They want to see if I can return punts," Jason said. "Coach Ingelsby remembered from the seven-on-seven camp that I could catch the ball pretty well."

Tom grunted. "Did he remember who was throwing you the ball most of the time?"

Jason glanced at Tom to see if he was smiling. He wasn't.

"Maybe I should remind them."

"Lot of good that will do," Tom said.

Then, to Jason's surprise, his friend did smile.

"What?" Jason asked.

"Nothing," Tom said. Then he added, "Maybe Tom Robinson's story next week can be THE LEGEND CONTINUES."

He was still smiling when he said it, but Jason sensed he wasn't being funny.

The whistle blew. Jason got into position, but his mind wasn't on the coach bellowing instructions at them to bend left—now, right! It was on his best friend. He was clearly frustrated and unhappy. But could he also be jealous?

Impossible, he thought. Or hoped.

19

COACH GUTEKUNST WAS AS GOOD AS HIS WORD ABOUT NOT RUSHING Jason into the art of punt returning.

On Monday and Tuesday he was asked to catch the ball and then run a few steps with no one trying to tackle him. It wasn't until Wednesday that he actually attempted to catch a punt with people running at him. Each returner was asked to catch six punts in a row. After Ray and Matt had finished their turns, Jason took their place.

"Just fair-catch the first one," Coach Gutekunst told him. "Remember, look up at the ball, take a quick glance at the rush, then find the ball again in the air."

Jason tried, but when he looked down and then back up again, he had trouble refinding the ball. It sailed over his head. The second time, he found the ball in time to get to it, then dropped it after putting his arm into the air to signal for the fair catch.

"Let's just try to get the fair catch down today," Coach Gutekunst said. "We can worry about dealing with a return tomorrow—maybe."

Jason ended up catching the last two punts—catching the fifth one cleanly, then bobbling the sixth one before holding on. He had a long way to go. He was about to say something to Coach Gutekunst when he heard Coach Johnson's whistle. There was only so much time to spend on third-string punt returners.

"Not quite there yet, huh?" Tom said as he jogged to the sideline while the starters lined up to scrimmage for a few series.

"You saw it," Jason said. "Nowhere close."

Tom put his hand on his shoulder. "You'll get it," he said. "Just be patient with yourself."

Jason appreciated the encouraging words—especially from Tom. He'd been quieter than usual during the week, clearly brooding about his status with the team. About the only time he'd perked up was when he got a text from Teel that simply said,

Making some progress.

Teel and Robinson weren't coming to the game Friday night, because they had to travel with Virginia to a game at Indiana. Jason thought it must be pretty cool traveling around the country to go to games—and get paid for it. Maybe, he thought, if football didn't work out for him, he'd become a sportswriter.

. . . . .

He voiced that thought at lunch on Thursday, his stomach already twisting at the thought of trying to catch punts again at practice that afternoon.

"It's a dying profession," Tom said. "Papers are folding, and there's so much stuff floating around the Internet that guys are begging for work."

"How do you know all this stuff?" Jason asked.

Tom smiled. "Because I had the same thought as you. Did a little research. The money now is all in TV. Look at all the sportswriters who are on the major channels. *That's* how you get rich."

"You mean like Tony Kornheiser and Michael Wilbon?" Jason said, thinking of the hosts of his favorite ESPN show, *Pardon the Interruption*.

"Them and a lot of others," Billy Bob said. "Where I live, Paul Finebaum's a big star on TV and radio. He started in newspapers, too."

"So why can't I do that?" Jason asked.

"You can," said Juan del Potro, who'd been listening. "You just have to get in line with every other single guy—and girl—who is into sports. They all want to be on TV if they aren't good enough to be pro athletes."

"Yeah, and when the pro athletes retire, they all want a TV gig, too," Anthony said. "And you're behind every one of them in that line."

"Some want to be coaches," Jason said.

"Only if they can't get a TV job," Anthony said.

Everyone laughed. Jason didn't think it was so funny.

· · · · ·

That afternoon, Jason finally caught *and* returned a punt. The problem was, he returned it backward.

The special-teams segment of practice was always longer on Thursdays, so he was given ten chances instead of six.

After he had gone five-for-nine making fair catches, including fielding the last two smoothly, Coach Gutekunst asked, "Ready to try one for real?"

Jason wasn't certain that he was, but he wasn't about to say no. "Absolutely," he said, hoping his voice wasn't quavering.

The teams lined up, and punter Todd May, who was being recruited by just about every major college in the country, spiraled a high kick in Jason's direction. Jason picked it up in the air and realized he needed to back up to catch it. He retreated, not bothering to take his eyes off it for fear he'd lose track of it. He caught it cleanly and, just as he did, someone slammed into him. He fell backward, losing control of the ball as he hit the ground. Someone else came in, scooped it up, and trotted into the end zone.

"We're gonna say the ground caused the fumble," Coach Gutekunst said as Jason's tackler helped him to his feet. "So, technically, you caught it and got tackled for about a five-yard loss. In a real game, that was one you'd fair-catch. We'll work more next week."

Oh joy, Jason thought. He was starting to be a little jealous of Tom, standing safely on the sideline, his body very much in one piece. Jason wasn't so sure about his.

．．．．．

The game against Culpeper Prep on Friday was a cross between the DeMatha game and the South Hill game. The players boarded two buses—one for the offense, one for the defense—for the trip to Culpeper. It was only about sixty-five miles from the outskirts of Scottsville to the outskirts of Culpeper, but a lot of the road was two-lane, so it took about an hour and a half to get there.

Culpeper's stadium was considerably smaller than TGP's and considerably older. Coach Johnson didn't believe in leaving players behind on road trips, so all eighty-one TGP players, even the six who were injured and wouldn't play, had made the trip. The visiting locker room had only sixty lockers in it, so almost all of the freshmen had to leave their clothes on benches that sat in the corner of the room after changing into their uniforms.

The stadium, which Jason figured probably seated about four thousand people when full, was perhaps two-thirds full at kickoff, almost half the crowd appearing to be TGP fans.

It was a beautiful late-September evening, the temperature probably around seventy at kickoff with almost no humidity. Both teams were 2–0, and each knew that this was a key game—even if it was only the conference opener. The Culpeper Cornstalks had finished second in the league behind Roanoke Christian a year earlier. Those two teams and TGP had been labeled the preseason favorites—TGP being the unknown quantity since this was its first year in the league.

Not surprisingly, the game was intense from the beginning—rife with penalties, the two teams nervous, tight, and amped.

The halftime score was 7–7, each touchdown scored by the defense on an interception return.

Both quarterbacks looked overmatched against the other team's defense. Once again, Coach Johnson placed most of the blame on the O-line when the team came back into the locker room.

Sitting next to Anthony in the back row, Jason heard him whisper, "This is getting old, man. Can't he see he's playing the wrong quarterback?"

The coaches went off to meet. The captains—center Conor Foley and linebacker Ford Bennett—got up and, for a few minutes, exhorted their teammates to do better. When the coaches came back into the room, Coach Cruikshank signaled Billy Bob to wait a minute as the players returned to the field.

Jason lingered a little bit, slowing his pace so he could hear the conversation.

"If we don't make something happen first series, you'll be in for the second one," he heard Coach Cruikshank say. "Get ready."

Cruikshank then ran ahead to join the other coaches.

"What does 'make something happen' mean?" Jason asked Billy Bob, who had picked up his pace enough to join him in the tunnel.

"I hope it means that if we don't score I'm in," Billy Bob answered. "But we'll see."

They saw right away. The Patriots took the opening kickoff of the second half and quickly went three-and-out, Ronnie

Thompson overthrowing a wide-open Ray Solo on third-and-four. Solo almost made a spectacular one-handed catch but couldn't hang on to the ball as he hit the ground.

Culpeper had already changed quarterbacks. The starter—Terry Holland, according to the roster sheet Tom had grabbed before the game and shown to Jason—was out. Dave Brady, like Billy Bob a freshman, was his replacement.

Brady quickly took Culpeper down the field to a go-ahead touchdown, finding receivers on short routes, using a three-step drop on most plays.

"Guess Coach Johnson's not the only one stubborn about playing a freshman quarterback," Tom said as Brady scored from one yard out, running behind his fullback.

"I think he may be about to get less stubborn," Jason said, putting his helmet on to go in for the extra point. Once again, there was a blocker lined up wide on his side, meaning that when Jason went after the extra point there was a blocker gunning for him. As a result, he had to go way outside to try to get to the kicker, and didn't come close. He had a feeling his kick-blocking days were over. Teams had scouted him based on the block against DeMatha.

He jogged to the sideline and saw Billy Bob putting on his helmet.

"Turns out 'don't make something happen' means letting them score," he said, grinning through the bar on the helmet.

Once again, the offense clicked with Billy Bob at quarterback. His strength, Jason noticed, was his ability to make quick decisions—whether running an option or dropping to pass. TGP quickly matched Culpeper's touchdown drive and then, when one of the Cornstalks' backs bobbled a pitch at his own 23, Bennett fell on top of it. Five plays later, Billy Bob faked a pitch to Matt Quinn, cut inside the defenders who had bought the outside fake, and scored from the 6 for a 21–14 lead as the third quarter ended.

Brady got Culpeper moving again, but on a third-and-six from the TGP 23 he was buried as he dropped to pass by a cornerback blitz. The eleven-yard loss put his team out of field goal range. The punt was downed on the 1-yard line.

As Billy Bob prepared to go back on the field, Coach Johnson grabbed his arm.

"Nothing fancy," the coach said. "Fullback dive on first down, and then look to me. Even if we pick up almost nothing, May will kick us out of there."

Billy Bob nodded. Then, as he pulled his helmet on, Jason was convinced he winked in the direction of where he and Tom were standing.

"Uh-oh, he's up to something," Tom said. He'd seen the wink, too.

Billy Bob brought the team to the line and began barking signals. When Jason heard him call "Black!" he gasped. *Black* was the signal to listen for an audible. Unless the word *White* was coming soon to tell the other players he was bluffing, Jason knew that Billy Bob was about to ignore Coach Johnson's order.

He didn't call *White*. Instead, he took the snap, turned as if to hand the ball to fullback Danny Nobis, and quickly pulled the ball out of his stomach as Nobis was buried at the goal line by about half the Culpeper team.

Still holding the ball, Billy Bob dropped into the end zone. At least nine Culpeper players had been lined up in the box, all within two yards of the line of scrimmage to stuff the fullback dive they knew was coming. Billy Bob bounced on his toes and released a long, beautiful spiral down the field.

Terrell Davidson, the second-fastest player on the team— behind only Jason—had taken off on a streak pattern, which was the play Billy Bob had audibled to a split second earlier. No one from Culpeper had gone with him, everyone buying the fake. The ball dropped perfectly into Davidson's hands at about the 40-yard line, and he was gone. The only person on the field within twenty yards of him as he ran the last fifty yards was the back judge, who sprinted as best he could to stay close to him in case he should somehow fumble before he got to the goal line.

He didn't. The bench emptied to celebrate in the end zone, which did give the back judge something to do: throw a flag for excessive celebration. No one in a TGP uniform cared much. The ninety-nine-yard touchdown pass was a backbreaker, and everyone in the stadium knew it.

Billy Bob came to the bench, accepting high fives from everyone. Until he got to Coach Johnson.

"When I called the fullback dive, did I tell you that you could audible?" the coach demanded.

"Well, no, Coach, but—"

"No buts, Anderson!" Coach Johnson was screaming now. "Except for this: you can *sit* your butt down the rest of the night. I have no idea who you played for in middle school, but when you are told specifically to run a play, you run that play! Understand?"

"Yes, sir."

"Good. And just to be sure you don't forget, you can report to Coach Cruikshank at five o'clock tomorrow morning to do a little running."

He turned to Coach Cruikshank, who looked almost as stunned as Billy Bob.

"Coach, I'm sorry you're going to have an early wake-up," Coach Johnson said, "but maybe it will help you do a better job teaching your position players some discipline."

Coach Cruikshank said nothing. Instead, he put an arm around Billy Bob's neck and guided him back to the bench while the TGP fans were cheering the extra point that made the score 28–14. Jason followed the coach and his roomie and stood a few feet away while Coach Cruikshank knelt in front of Billy Bob to talk to him. Billy Bob had gone from being mobbed coming off the field to radioactive after Coach Johnson's tirade. No one, other than Jason, wanted to be anywhere within earshot of the coach and the player.

"We'll talk about this in the morning," Coach Cruikshank said softly. "Coach has to make sure all of us know who's in charge."

"Like we don't already know?" Billy Bob said, anger and hurt in his voice.

Coach Cruikshank put a finger to his lips. "Not now," he said. Then he dropped his voice a little bit lower and added, "Great call. Great play. Leave it at that."

He patted Billy Bob on the shoulder, stood up, and walked away. Jason sat down next to him.

"He's right, you know," Jason said.

"About what?" Billy Bob said.

"Great call. Great play."

"Leave it at that," Billy Bob said, his wide Southern smile returning, if only for a moment.

20

BENCHING BILLY BOB HAD NO EFFECT ON THE OUTCOME OF THE GAME.
The ninety-nine-yard touchdown pass had broken Culpeper's
spirit, and the home team showed little life on offense during
the remainder of the fourth quarter. Even with Ronnie Thompson back in the game, the Patriots were able to pick up enough
first downs on the ground to keep the clock moving, although
they didn't score again. TGP won by the same 28–14 margin
that Billy Bob had created with his unauthorized audible.

Walking off the field with Billy Bob and Tom, Jason couldn't
help but point out one statistic. "Three drives with Billy Bob,
three touchdowns," he said. "Rest of the game with Thompson—"

"Zip, I know," Tom said. "You know what, though? All Johnson cares about is this stat: three-and-oh, one-and-oh."

That was TGP's record: 3–0 overall, and 1–0 in conference
play.

Mr. Gatch came into the locker room and made a big

production of presenting the game ball to Coach Johnson in honor of the school's first conference victory.

Coach Johnson then gave a game ball to John Graves, the cornerback whose interception return had provided the team's only first-half touchdown, and to Terrell Davidson, the wide receiver who had caught six passes—including Billy Bob's last pass of the night.

As they stood in the crowded little corner where they had to change back into their street clothes, Billy Bob's sense of humor returned.

"Now we know for sure Johnson's a racist," he whispered, loud enough only for Jason, Tom, and Anthony to hear.

"We do?" Jason said.

"Yeah," Billy Bob said. "He gave a game ball to the black wide receiver, but *nothing* to the white quarterback."

They laughed so hard at that one that heads turned in their direction.

There was one issue before they left. Not surprisingly, several media members had asked to speak to Billy Bob. Equally unsurprising, they had been turned down. Ed Seaman, the communications director, who looked and sounded like the perfect Southern gentleman, turned up in their corner as they were all putting their shoes on.

"Anderson, there's some folks out there who are gonna want to chat with you," he said. "You just tell 'em polite as can be that Coach doesn't want you talkin' tonight. If they try to ask why, just tell 'em they should ask Coach."

Billy Bob, sitting on one of the benches, stood up and smiled.

"Whatever Coach wants, Mr. Seaman," he said. "I'm here to serve."

If Mr. Seaman picked up on the sarcasm in that answer, he didn't show it.

Sure enough, when the four freshmen walked into the cool night air, there were a couple of TV camera crews and a handful of others with notebooks and tape recorders waiting. Jason knew that Coach Johnson always spoke to the media while the players were showering and changing, so he wondered why Coach Johnson hadn't already told them that Billy Bob was off-limits.

Jason waited for Billy Bob to do as he had been told by Seaman. He, Tom, and Anthony surrounded Billy Bob to provide him a path to the bus.

"Can't tonight, fellas," Billy Bob said. "Really sorry. Coach's orders."

They were walking fast now, Anthony leading the way, Tom trailing, and Jason by Billy Bob's side. Two off-duty state troopers always accompanied Coach Johnson to and from the field and the bus, but they were nowhere to be found.

One of the reporters yelled, "Seriously, Anderson? Not even for a minute?"

Billy Bob looked back over his shoulder and smiled. "Got a very early wake-up in the morning," he said. "Need my beauty sleep."

No one seemed to have an answer for that one.

Once the friends were safely on the bus Jason said to Billy Bob, "You know, if they show that last answer on TV or even on the Internet somewhere, you'll probably be in more trouble."

"Heck with it," Billy Bob said. He held his thumb and fore-finger about a quarter-inch apart. "I came this close to stopping and talking."

"Don't blame you," Tom said, sitting across the aisle. "But I also don't envy you. I have a feeling Jason's right."

. . . . .

Jason was right. He was sleeping when Billy Bob crept back into the room at a little after six the next morning. Jason heard the door open and rolled onto his side to see Billy Bob collapse onto his bed.

"So it went well, then?" he said.

Billy Bob groaned. "Want the good news or the bad news?" he said, his voice an exhausted croak.

"Start with the bad."

"I have to run four more days this week. Ten times up and down the steps of the stadium, just like this morning."

"What's the good news?" Jason asked, a little bit baffled.

"I get tomorrow off. Because it's Sunday."

"That *is* good news," Jason said. He was now wide awake. "What got you the extra four days? The crack to the TV guys?"

"Bingo," Billy Bob said. "First thing Coach Cruikshank said was, 'You couldn't just keep your mouth shut and get this over with for both of us?' I knew exactly what he was saying, and I feel bad for him. But four more days, really?"

"Guess Coach doesn't think he's gonna need you rested for Danville."

"Did you check last night's scores yet? They lost to Roanoke, forty-seven to fourteen."

"Roanoke's supposed to be good."

"Not that good."

"By the way, how many rows of seats on the west side of the stadium? I assume you ran that side since it's clearly got more seats than the east side."

"Boy, your brain is functioning full power early today, isn't it?" He smiled wanly. "Forty-seven."

"Sure?"

"Never been more certain of anything in my life."

"So there's more good news, then. You now know something almost no one else on the team knows. Something to be proud of, my friend."

Billy Bob sighed. "I'm taking a shower. My whole body feels like it's going to fall off."

"Interesting visual," Jason said.

"Shut up," Billy Bob said.

Jason searched his usually upbeat friend's face for a smile. There wasn't even a hint of one.

· · · · ·

Billy Bob decided to sleep through breakfast. When Tom and Anthony knocked on the door, Jason opened it a crack and put a finger to his lips.

"Sleeping child inside," he whispered, slipping out to join them.

"How bad?" they both asked.

"Worse than bad. Ten times up and down the steps this morning *and*, for his comment to the TV folks last night, more of the same for four mornings this week."

"Let me guess," Tom said. "He gets tomorrow morning off."

"Go with God, my friend. You are correct. And to answer your other question for the morning, there are forty-seven rows of steps on the west side of the stadium."

"Guess he had plenty of opportunity to pin that number down," Anthony said.

"If the question ever comes up on 'Final Jeopardy,' he's a lock winner," Jason said. "Meanwhile, any word from our newspaper pals?"

Tom nodded, holding up his phone. "They're both home tonight. They're fresh out of excuses to get us off campus, but they say they have a lot more info on Mr. Gatch. They don't want to talk about it by text or e-mail."

"So what do we do?" Jason asked.

"We hope to hear from them tomorrow morning. Meantime . . ."

"We wait," Jason said.

"I was going to say we eat, but that works, too," Tom answered. "And you might want to bring something back for your wounded roommate."

"He's not wounded."

"Yes he is," Anthony said. "He's wounded thinking about what next week's going to be like. He can sleep after he runs

210

today. Not so starting Monday. He'll be lucky if he has time to shower and get to breakfast before class."

"I guess he could always start earlier," Jason said.

"Great roommate you are," Tom said.

They walked into the dining room grinning but, as Jason pointed out to Billy Bob later, feeling bad about it. But not *that* bad.

．．．．．

"They both think we need to hold off a week because if they keep showing up here, someone's going to get suspicious."

Tom was sitting in Jason's room on Sunday morning, looking at the text he'd just gotten from David Teel. Billy Bob and Anthony were at church.

"But they cover TGP and we're three and oh," Jason said. "Why shouldn't they be here?"

Tom shook his head. "They don't cover us *that* much. They're lead columnists at their papers. Virginia, Virginia Tech, and Old Dominion are all much more important to them. Richmond and VCU during basketball season."

"This isn't basketball season," Jason said, a little bit irritated. He wasn't feeling very patient. He wanted to know what Teel and Robinson had learned about Mr. Gatch. He understood their reluctance to put anything in a text or an e-mail. But why not a phone call? Apparently it wasn't quite as important to them as it was to him. He felt like he was stuck inside some kind of straitjacket.

It was worse, he knew, for Tom. As good a quarterback as Billy Bob was, Jason knew that Tom was better. He was just as fast as Billy Bob, could throw the ball at least as far, and was more accurate. And yet, every day in practice, he got to run a few pass patterns, was almost never thrown the ball, and then stood with his helmet under his arm throughout most of the scrimmages.

Then, during games, he got to watch Ronnie Thompson start and play, at least until things got desperate and Coach Johnson was forced to send Billy Bob into the game. Tom was a better quarterback than Thompson playing *lefty*.

And now, they knew—or at least suspected—that they were playing for both a coach and a school founder who were textbook racists straight out of another era. But the two reporters whose help they desperately needed to prove that to the world were taking their sweet time getting to the story.

He swore out loud, using a word his mother didn't especially like. His father used it, but only when he was really upset about something and at the risk of incurring his mother's wrath. "Robert," she would say—calling her husband by his full name— "save that kind of language for the squad room!"

Tom looked up, surprised. It wasn't as if Jason didn't use profanity on occasion, but it didn't usually come while he was sitting on his bed thinking.

"What?" Tom asked.

Jason shrugged. "It's just making me crazy sitting around here doing nothing—not able to accomplish anything. We shouldn't be here. We should have gone home when we had the chance."

"We can call our parents right now," Tom said. "If we tell

them what's been going on, they'll be down here to pick us up before dark."

Jason thought about that for a minute. Tom was right. But it was now mid-September. School was well under way in New York, and so was football season. At the very least, they had to suck it up until the end of the semester. And, once again, the thought that they *had* to expose Mr. Gatch and Coach Johnson went through his mind.

"No," he said finally. "We have to stick it out. We've got to prove that these guys are as messed up as we think. Did Teel say anything about when we might be able to talk to them again?"

Tom nodded. "UVA is at home this week, and Virginia Tech is playing a I-AA team—"

"You mean an FCS team."

"Whatever. Point is, maybe they will come over Friday night for our game and find us afterward. Even if people see them talking to us, they can just say they were catching up since they've both written about you and talked to me the last couple of weeks. It won't look all that suspicious."

"Yeah and maybe Billy Bob will be allowed to talk to the media this week."

Tom smiled. "Wouldn't count on it."

"You're right," Jason said. "He might be too tired to talk, anyway."

"Think he'll play Friday?"

Jason shook his head. "Only if we get behind."

21

THEY DIDN'T GET BEHIND. DANVILLE PREP WASN'T AS WEAK AS SOUTH Hill had been, but it wasn't as good as Culpeper. TGP was too strong on defense for the Rally Cats, who had as many turnovers—two—as first downs in the first half.

The two turnovers led to short touchdown drives and, soon after that, fullback Danny Nobis burst through the bunched-up Danville defense on a third-and-one and, with no one deep, raced seventy-one yards for a third touchdown. That made the score 21–0 at halftime. Nobis only played in short-yardage situations because, the joke went, he was timed in the 100 on a sundial. But no one from Danville could catch him.

A third turnover, this one a fumble on a quarterback sack inside the 10-yard line, led to a fourth touchdown that made it 28–0 midway through the third quarter.

Coach Johnson substituted liberally in the fourth quarter—except at quarterback, where Ronnie Thompson took every snap.

"He's not going to put me in ahead of you because that would lead to questions he doesn't want from the media," Jason said to Billy Bob as the fourth quarter dragged on. "But you aren't playing, either—"

"Because he's not needed tonight," Tom put in, finishing Jason's sentence accurately.

Billy Bob shrugged. "Honestly, as long as I don't have to get up and run again in the morning, I don't care," he said. He smiled when he said it, but he clearly wasn't happy. Jason didn't blame him.

The final was 28–0.

In the locker room, Coach Johnson said there would be two game balls handed out. The first, he said, would go to defensive coordinator Andy Fallon, for being the "mastermind" behind the shutout and the four turnovers the defense had accumulated. Everyone liked Coach Fallon. He'd been a high school coach his entire career and apparently was asked questions on occasion like "So what was Red Grange really like?" because he'd been around so long.

Still, Jason couldn't help but wonder how the guys on the defense—the ones who had actually created the four turnovers and pitched the shutout—felt about that decision. Everyone cheered as Coach Johnson tossed a ball to Coach Fallon, who held it up and said, "No up-downs for the defense on Monday!"

That drew lusty cheers from the defenders. Up-downs were a dreaded pre-practice conditioning drill, except when they were used as punishment. On the first whistle, while running in place, you hit the ground on your stomach and then jumped up. Then you did it again and again and again. It was not uncommon for players to get sick before the drill was over—especially in the preseason August heat.

"We'll talk about that Monday, Coach," Bobo said, flashing a rare smile. "Second game ball"—he paused and held a ball over his head—"goes to Ronnie Thompson, for a perfect game behind center tonight! Way to go, Ronnie!"

He tossed the ball to Thompson, who was so stunned that he almost dropped it.

He wasn't the only one who was stunned. It took a moment for the standard cheer given to game-ball winners to start. It was as if everyone was waiting to hear Coach Johnson say, *Just kidding*. Only when he actually tossed the ball to Thompson did the cheer—not exactly a lusty one—go up.

It was nothing personal. It was just that everyone in the room knew that if Billy Bob had been playing quarterback that night, the final would have been more like 56–0. Jason couldn't help but think it might have been even more one-sided than that if Tom ever got to play.

"It's like the emperor's new clothes," Jason whispered to Tom, remembering the old fairy tale in which the emperor had insisted his new clothes were beautiful when, in truth, they didn't exist.

"Yeah, but where's the little kid to shout, 'He's naked!'?" Tom said.

They both stifled a laugh.

Coach Ingelsby, the sullen-faced offensive coordinator, appeared as if by magic behind them. "Something funny, gentlemen?" he asked in a sneering voice.

"Nothing at all, Coach," Tom said quickly.

Coach Ingelsby didn't respond. He just stood directly behind them as Coach Johnson finished up.

"Boys, we're four-and-oh and two-and-oh and that's all good," he said. "But we're into the grinding part of the season now. Everyone's a little bit tired and banged up. Midterms aren't that far off. We've got to keep focusing and refocusing. It's important that you catch up on your schoolwork over the weekend so that you're ready to go from minute one at practice on Monday." He dropped to one knee. "Now let's give thanks."

Everyone else in the room knelt, too. Jason felt awkward at these team-prayer moments but knew he would feel more awkward if he remained standing. He bowed his head and said nothing as Coach Johnson prayed.

"We thank you, Lord, for the great execution of our defense and the wonderful pad level from our O-line."

Jason resisted the urge to look at Tom because he knew they'd both start cracking up at the notion that God paid any attention to TGP's defensive execution or pad level. When Coach Johnson finally wrapped up with "Amen," everyone stood.

"Nice of you two to kneel along with your teammates," Coach Ingelsby said.

"I believe in showing respect for *all* religions, Coach," Jason said, knowing his voice probably had more steel in it than was prudent. "Mine and others."

Coach Ingelsby stared at him for a moment, then walked off.

"And amen to that," Tom said when the coach was out of earshot.

"I might dislike him more than any of them," Jason said.

"That takes in a lot of ground, doesn't it?" Tom suggested.

"Amen, brother," Jason said. "Amen."

· · · · ·

Coach Johnson had been right about one thing: it was a grinding time—both in school and on the practice field. Midterms were a couple of weeks away, but there were quizzes to take and papers to finish. That left little time to do much more than study, eat, sleep, and go to practice. Their reporter friends offered no relief, texting that they'd gotten tied up.

"I guess I should be glad I'm not up running every morning this week," Billy Bob said on Wednesday night while they were at dinner. "I'd probably flunk out."

"We'd all flunk out," Tom said.

Jason, though, knew his friend was breezing academically.

Wednesday had been a big day at practice for Jason. He had successfully caught two punts without fumbling while being rushed, and on the second one had actually picked up some yardage—three yards to be exact. The first time, he had thought he saw some daylight if he ran wide right, but someone had missed a block and he'd run about twenty yards to the right while picking up exactly zero yards going forward.

"First rule of punt returning," Coach Gutekunst had said, "is always run forward first. You start running sideways, the best thing that happens most of the time is you go nowhere.

The worst thing that happens is one of your blockers gets called for holding or clipping. We'll try it again tomorrow."

It occurred to Jason that if they wanted him to catch punts because of his speed, having him run straight ahead sort of defeated that purpose. He decided not to debate the issue. He actually like Coach Gutekunst and, until he got to the point where he could routinely catch a punt and start running with it, there wasn't much point in debating *where* he should run.

· · · · ·

The last tests and quizzes of the week were always on Thursday. The older players explained this wasn't a coincidence. TGP's teams—football, soccer, volleyball, tennis, and golf—almost always had a game or a match or a tournament on Fridays, throughout the year. Without tests or quizzes on Friday, teams that had to travel could leave in plenty of time and everyone could get some rest the night before.

Jason, Billy Bob, Tom, and Anthony were relaxing in Jason and Billy Bob's room that Thursday night, joking about the fact that Anthony was probably the only one in the group who really needed his rest. After all, Tom was still zero-for-the-field in games, Jason might get in for a few plays on special teams, and Billy Bob was very much in Coach Johnson's doghouse. During practice that week, Billy Bob and Jason had actually split the second-team snaps at quarterback.

"Yeah, but if the game's close, you think he's putting me in?"

Jason said when Billy Bob brought up the possibility that he and Tom had an exactly equal chance—zero—to get into the game the next night.

"He might take a loss just to prove his point," Billy Bob said.

"Well, it won't be the next two weeks," Tom said. "Lynchburg and James Madison are both supposed to be pretty bad."

Jason was about to respond when there was a knock on the door. They all yelled, "Come in!" and looked up to see Juan del Potro and Jimmy Gomez standing there.

"What's up?" Tom said.

"This," Juan said, handing what looked like a printout to Jason.

It was a story that had apparently appeared in the *Birmingham News* that day.

"I put Gatch and Johnson on Google Alerts just for the heck of it," Juan said. "Read it aloud for everyone."

Jason complied.

With offensive coordinator Brian Daboll almost certain to receive multiple offers at season's end to become a head coach again, people are starting to toss the names of possible successors around even as Alabama prepares to open conference play this weekend against Mississippi.

The name mentioned most often is that of Georgia graduate James "Bobo" Johnson, who has been wildly successful the last eleven years as the head coach at Thomas Gatch Prep, the prestigious athletic/academic academy in central Virginia.

"Prestigious?" Tom said. "When did this place become prestigious?"

Everyone quickly shushed him. Jason continued.

Johnson's team is currently 4–0 and has a bevy of big-time recruits on the roster. At least six of his seniors are reportedly being recruited by Nick Saban and his staff this fall, and the Crimson Tide is apparently scouting another half-dozen TGP juniors with great interest.

In a possible twist to the story, Johnson's boss, TGP founder Thomas Gatch, is reportedly negotiating to sell the school to one of several sports management companies that are bidding to purchase it. The prep school, which Gatch started eighteen years ago, is a copycat of the IMG Academy in Florida. IMG, the world's largest management company, purchased Nick Bollettieri's tennis academy in 1987 and has since built it into an athletic and academic monolith and has made huge profits—charging most students $70,000 a year to attend.

Apparently several powerful management companies see the potential for that kind of profit in Gatch's relatively new operation. Sources in Tuscaloosa say that Johnson's hiring could be part of a major package deal: Johnson would become the O-coordinator at a salary north of $1 million a year; Gatch, who stands to make millions if he sells his school, would be hired as vice president for development—a newly created position—and

most, if not all, of the seniors being recruited by 'Bama would likely end up in Tuscaloosa.

"You can stop there," Juan said. "The rest is just background fluff on what brilliant guys Johnson and Gatch are."

"Well, if they pull something like this off, they're certainly going to look pretty smart," Tom said.

"Forget smart," Billy Bob said. "Rich is better than smart."

"Yeah," Anthony said. "We're all smart, but we're a long way from rich."

"So what does it all add up to?" Jason said. "I mean, to us?"

"Nothing," Juan said. "And everything. It doesn't change anything going on with the team day-to-day, but I'd say it does make it that much more important that you guys figure out a way to prove that Gatch and Johnson are what we think they are."

"Because if we don't, they're both gonna be very rich, very soon—apparently," Tom said.

"If going to Alabama means they're both gone from here, is that a bad thing?" Anthony said. "New guy running the school, new coaches—might be the best thing that ever happened to us."

They thought about that for a minute.

"Of course," Anthony added, "there's no guarantee. Those management companies only care about making money. Who knows what they'd do if they took over?"

"Exactly right," Billy Bob said. "I read a book once where the writer was talking about agents and he said, 'The only time you know for sure that they're lyin' is when their lips are moving.'"

"Sounds like they'd be perfect business partners for Gatch,"

Jason said. "The question is, do we just sit back and watch while these guys walk out of here with millions when we're all pretty certain they're lowlifes?"

"Racist lowlifes," Anthony added.

They all looked at one another.

"We have to let Teel and Robinson know that there's no more time to waste," Tom said.

He pulled out his phone and began writing a text.

22

MUCH TO EVERYONE'S CHAGRIN, THERE WASN'T MUCH TEEL AND
Robinson could do at that moment. Both Virginia and Virginia
Tech were starting Atlantic Coast Conference play on the road—
Virginia Tech that night at Miami, Virginia on Saturday at North
Carolina State—and they had to focus on those stories since far
more of their readers were interested in that than a possible con-
troversy, no matter how incendiary, at Thomas Gatch Prep.

The following week the two colleges had their home openers
in conference play, and Teel and Robinson had to be all over
those games, too. The TGP story would have to be put on hold,
at least for a while.

That made for a long two weeks. TGP was in the midst of
what amounted to two straight bye weeks, with games against
teams that would finish at or near the bottom of the conference:
Lynchburg Academy and James Madison Prep, which was
located in Harrisonburg, near the college of the same name.

Neither game was close. The Patriots beat Lynchburg 31–7, a late touchdown angering Coach Johnson, who, hoping for another shutout, had left the defensive starters in during the fourth quarter.

A week later, the TGP players got their shutout against Madison Prep, although the offense sputtered through most of a 17–0 win.

Billy Bob never saw the field either night. He wasn't needed. Anthony was now firmly established as a starter. Jason continued— without anything close to success—to try to block placekicks.

After the win at James Madison, Coach Johnson acted as if they'd lost the game. He still never mentioned the mediocre— to put it kindly—play of his quarterback.

"You'll play next week," Jason said to Billy Bob as they dressed.

"You think?"

Jason nodded. "Middleburg is six-and-oh, four-and-oh just like we are. They apparently have a really good quarterback. Ronnie Thompson can't win that game."

Tom was listening. "Yeah, that'll be a real game," he said. "Meantime, we've got to figure a way to talk to Teel and Robinson. Maybe they'll be around next weekend."

"About time," Anthony said.

"Yeah," Jason added. "Past time."

. . . . .

Middleburg Prep was in northern Virginia, a reasonably long bus trip from TGP. The town was in what was referred to as "horse country"—an area about fifty miles from downtown Washington, D.C., that was filled with sprawling estates.

The bus ride to the school was supposed to take a little more than two hours, but, according to the coaches, traffic on a Friday was a potential issue. As a result, the team left at noon and drove not to the school, but to a place called the Salamander Resort.

Jason and Tom had stayed at some nice hotels with their parents on vacation. Jason was especially fond of the Marriott Long Wharf, right on the Boston Harbor. Tom had told him about a trip to Naples, Florida, when his dad had been able to cash in points from his many long nights on the road, and they had stayed at a Ritz-Carlton.

But neither of them had seen anything quite as swanky as the Salamander Resort.

"Place just kind of breathes money, doesn't it?" Tom whispered to Jason as they walked down a long hallway to a dining room for their pregame meal.

The itinerary they'd been handed after getting on the bus said they'd eat their pregame meal upon arrival at two-thirty, and then they'd take the keys they had all been given as they walked into the lobby and go to their rooms to rest for a couple of hours. The bus would leave for the field at five. After the game, they'd come back to the Salamander and, rather than make the drive home that late, they'd spend the night. After breakfast in the morning, they'd head back to TGP.

When Jason and Billy Bob reached their room—which was

about three times the size of their dorm room at school—Billy Bob shook his head.

"They must have gotten some kind of deal to pay for fifty rooms in this place," he said as he plopped on the bed.

"What do you think a room goes for here?" Jason asked.

Billy Bob shrugged. "More than the Fairfield Inn in Gadsden," he said. "I'll guess four hundred."

Jason thought that might be low. "Even if it's five hundred, that's still only about twenty-five grand. That's less than one-half of one kid's annual tuition. They can handle it."

"Long as they have to handle it and not me," Billy Bob said, laughing.

Because the team was spending the night at the Salamander, the original plan to talk to Teel and Robinson had changed. Rather than be rushed and worried about people noticing them talking, Teel and Robinson were going to pick them up at the hotel thirty minutes after the team returned there.

This idea had been hatched during a pre-breakfast phone call between Tom and Teel. Tom had decided to go for an early run since there were no classes post-tests that morning. Everyone had a free day—except for those on varsity teams.

Tom had run to the far side of campus. From there, with no one around, he'd called Teel. That was when Teel had told him what he and Robinson wanted to do. The boys would leave their rooms and exit through a back door of the hotel and then circle to the parking lot, where Teel and Robinson would be waiting in their cars. From there, Teel and Robinson had scouted a place that was a couple of miles away from the hotel that stayed open late on Friday night.

"He said we should leave by twos, not all together," Tom had reported. "Maybe five minutes apart."

"What if there are coaches in the lobby?" Billy Bob had asked.

"Just say you can't sleep and you're going for a walk," Tom said. "Teel says there's a lot of places to walk in the back of the resort."

"How in the world does he know that?" Jason asked.

"Apparently the ACC held their preseason football media days up there a few years ago," Tom said.

"Nice life those guys live," Billy Bob said, about two seconds before Jason could say it.

"Well," he said, "at least for one night, we'll be living it, too."

· · · · ·

Middleburg Prep, according to the all-knowing Tom Jefferson, had traditionally finished near the bottom of the Virginia Prep School Conference.

"Lotta rich white kids," he said. "They've never really recruited much like the other schools do."

Technically, high schools were not supposed to recruit. But it was a little bit like jay-walking in New York City. Everybody did it, and no one got ticketed for it.

That had changed in the past two years, though, after Middleburg hired a former University of Maryland assistant coach named Bill Hamer as their new coach. Hamer was known, according to Tom's research, as a great recruiter. A year earlier, Middleburg had gone 4–3 in conference play—the first time it had ever had a winning record against its prep school rivals.

The Colts were also 6–0 and 4–0 coming into the game, which would explain why Coach Johnson had said all week, "You older guys, this is *not* the Middleburg team you've played in the past."

For once, he wasn't exaggerating. Middleburg had a quarterback named Drew Whitlock, whom the D.C.-area media had labeled "the Flash." He *was* a blur on most plays, getting to the edges so fast he almost didn't need blockers. With Whitlock carrying the ball on nine of eleven plays, the Colts scored on their first possession to lead 7–0 and then, after TGP's offense had stalled near midfield, Whitlock had taken off on first down from his own 12-yard line and had simply outrun the entire TGP defense to the goal line.

Seven minutes into the game, the Patriots trailed 14–0.

"He can't wait until the second half to put Billy Bob in tonight," Jason said softly to Tom after returning to the sidelines following another futile attempt at blocking an extra point.

In response, Tom just nodded in the direction of the coaches—Johnson, Ingelsby, and Cruikshank, who were talking intently to one another up near the 50-yard line. Coach Cruikshank was clearly animated, gesturing with his hands and raising his voice—though not loud enough for Jason and Tom to hear.

Finally, Coach Johnson pointed a finger directly at Coach

Cruikshank and leaned into him. A moment later, Coach Cruikshank shook his head in apparent disgust and walked away.

"How's your lipreading?" Jason asked Tom.

"Don't need to read lips," Tom said. "Coach Cruikshank wanted Billy Bob in the game *now*, and Coach Johnson said no."

"And a few extra words for emphasis," Jason said.

A moment later, Billy Bob strolled up, a smile on his face. He had been standing a few yards away from the heated conversation.

"So what happened?" Jason asked.

"Let me quote the esteemed Coach James 'Bobo' Johnson for you boys," he said. " 'He'll go in the *blanking* game when I say he goes in the *blanking* game. When you get a head coaching job, Cruikshank, you can have the *blanking* final word. But *blanking* not until then.' "

"Well, at least he made himself clear," Tom said.

They heard a roar go up from the crowd. Ray Solo had fumbled the kickoff, and Middleburg had recovered.

"You better be ready," Tom said. "They score again, and he's not going to have a *blanking* choice."

Except that Coach Johnson did, it seemed, have a choice.

The Colts needed only three plays to punch the ball into the end zone. Whitlock carried on every play. Even though the TGP defense *knew* he was going to keep the ball, no one could catch him.

After the extra point there was no sign of Coach Cruikshank trying to convince Coach Johnson to change quarterbacks again and, at least as far as Jason could see, no one had come close to Billy Bob to even suggest he get warmed up.

· · · · ·

By halftime, the Flash had scored his fourth touchdown of the night and, when he led his team down the field in the final minute to the 15-yard line to set up a buzzer-beating field goal, the halftime margin was a stunning 31–0. A chant of "Overrated!" came from the Middleburg crowd, alluding to the fact that TGP had been ranked fifth that week in the *USA Today* national high school poll.

"It's almost like Coach Johnson doesn't care if we win the game," said Anthony, who had played most of the first half, as they trudged slowly to the locker room.

"If we want to win a state championship, we can't do it without winning the conference," Jason said. "We lose tonight, that's gonna be tough to do."

"And if he wants that Alabama job, losing a hundred to nothing can't help him, can it?" Tom added.

"Maybe he's already got the job," Billy Bob said. "Where I come from, stories don't usually leak unless someone wants them to leak."

There was no chance to discuss that further, because they were all now inside the locker room and Coach Johnson was standing in the front, hands on hips. Behind him was a whiteboard on which he had simply written "1–0, 7–0." That had become his weekly message: Go 1–0 every Friday and then add up the wins as you went along. It wasn't looking as if 8–0 was going to be on the board next week.

"I honestly don't know what to say to you, boys," Coach Johnson began when everyone had settled down. "Talent is fine, fellas, but what about pride? Have you got no pride?" The questions hung in the air for a moment. "Look, this isn't all on you players. Coach Ingelsby, Coach Fallon, you both need to regroup during halftime, because what we're doing out there scheme-wise clearly isn't working. Captains, you've got five minutes with your teammates. You see what you can come up with while we coaches do the same."

He walked out, followed by the coaches, for their halftime get-together. Jason didn't think the two coordinators were likely to come up with any new schemes in five minutes—unless one of those schemes included changing quarterbacks. Poor Ronnie Thompson sat in the front row, head down, staring at the floor. He knew better than anyone in the room that the offensive scheme was not the problem.

The captains did what they could, which wasn't much. They took turns telling everyone that this was a test of their toughness; that if Middleburg could score thirty-one points in a half, TGP could score even more points in a half; and that what they needed wasn't a change in the schemes, but a change in their attitudes.

The coaches returned a few minutes later to tell them that all eleven defensive players should focus on Whitlock and force him to give up the ball.

"*That's* what they figured out?" Billy Bob grumbled as they all began heading back to the field. "That's like saying, 'If you don't let that Brady guy throw the ball, New England won't score much.'"

The defense *did* make Whitlock give the ball up more often in the second half, but it didn't do a lot of good. His decision making on when to pitch the ball was almost perfect. Meanwhile, the TGP offense continued to sputter. By the end of the third quarter, the score was a humiliating 45–0.

At that point, Coach Hamer took Whitlock and a lot of his starters out of the game, seeing no need to further humiliate TGP. Coach Johnson made no move to switch quarterbacks.

"You would think by this point he'd take Thompson out, if only to spare him further embarrassment," Tom said.

"He doesn't worry about embarrassing people," Billy Bob said. "He only worries about proving he's in charge. This was all about sending me a message."

"For one act of so-called defiance?" Jason said. "At the expense of the team?"

"What do you think?" Billy Bob said.

"Forget I brought it up," Jason responded.

The final was 45–0. TGP never came close to scoring, except in the final minute, when a second- or third-string Middleburg running back fumbled on his own 14-yard line. TGP ran four plays from there—two runs and two passes—and never picked up a yard. The last play, a heave into the end zone by Ronnie Thompson that came near no one, summed up the entire evening pretty well.

They shook hands with the jubilant Middleburg players and trudged to the locker room.

"Well, that was about as bad as it can get," Coach Johnson said. "At least I hope so. As of Monday, we're back to square one. There are no starters on this team anymore. Every job is wide open. Let's take a knee."

There were no thanks during the prayer for great pad level. Instead, Coach Johnson said, "Lord, let these young men learn from the mistakes they made tonight."

There was, Jason noted, no mention in the prayer that he—Coach Johnson—might have made any mistakes.

"Think he means it about the starting jobs?" Tom asked.

"I guess we'll find out Monday," Jason said. "But we've still got a lot to do tonight."

23

THE BUSES PULLED UP TO THE FRONT DOOR OF THE SALAMANDER AT A little after ten. There had been no lingering at the stadium. Players had gotten on the buses still in uniform for the short ride back, having been told to wait to shower at the resort.

Coach Johnson had stayed behind to talk to the media. No one else from TGP was allowed to talk to the swarm of reporters. Jason suspected few of the reporters would object since at least part of the reason for the large turnout had to be the story about Coach Johnson leaving for Alabama. If Mr. Gatch had made the trip north, no one had seen him.

At 10:25, just as he was putting his shoes back on, Jason got a text from Teel:

Far side of parking lot, to the right if facing front of resort, in 10 minutes.

Jason showed it to Billy Bob, who nodded. He then forwarded the text to Tom, just to make sure he and Anthony knew. A note came back quickly:

Already heard. Ready to go.

At 10:30, Jason and Billy Bob slipped quietly out of their room. Tom and Anthony were to wait until 10:35. They had found a stairway at the far end of the hall that would let them avoid the lobby. They made it down the four flights of stairs and came out on the side of the building. It was very dark, but only a few steps to reach the parking lot. They paused when they got to the parking lot, dimly lit this far from the lobby. Almost immediately, they saw car lights flashing in their direction.

Billy Bob saw them first. "Right there," he said, and they hustled in the direction of the lights.

Teel was in the driver's seat. He nodded behind him at a car parked a few yards away. "Robinson's there waiting on Tom and Anthony."

He wheeled out of the parking lot and drove carefully down the long driveway. It was no more than a mile or so to downtown Middleburg. Teel found a spot on what looked like Main Street, and they walked into a place called the French Hound.

It was crowded, but Teel had apparently made a reservation and they were led to a table in the back.

"They don't normally take reservations, especially this late on a Friday," Teel explained when they sat down. "Cost me a few bucks."

"Worth it," Jason said.

The place wasn't that loud, but having some extra space and being near the back of the room was a good idea.

"So," Billy Bob said, "how was Coach Johnson?"

Before Teel could answer, the waiter showed up with menus and asked if they wanted to order something to drink or wait for the rest of their party. They all asked for iced tea.

At first glance, the menu looked a little upscale for Jason, but he spotted steak-frites, which he knew meant steak and french fries. There was pizza, too. He would be fine.

"You were saying," Jason said to Teel. "Coach Johnson?"

Teel smiled. "It was kind of funny because most of the guys there who don't normally cover high school ball no doubt were prepared to ask if there was truth to the Birmingham story," he said. "Instead, the first question was whether he thought a loss like this would affect his chances of getting the Alabama job."

"How'd he take that?" Billy Bob asked.

Teel shrugged. "Like you'd expect: 'My only focus is on coaching this team and clearly we all have a lot of work to do after tonight.' Then someone asked if the story was true and he said something like, 'No one at Alabama has contacted me.'"

"That surprise you?" Jason asked.

"No," Teel said, shaking his head. "First contact in a situation like this would be with his agent. So, technically, he's not lying. By the way, Billy Bob, I did ask why you didn't get into the game."

"What'd he say?" Billy Bob said.

"That he thought the team's best chance to move the

football was Ronnie Thompson at quarterback and the failure of the offense wasn't Thompson's fault."

"He's right," Billy Bob said. "It was a team effort."

"I also asked him if you not playing the last month had anything to do with you calling an audible on the one-yard line at Culpeper."

"Whoo boy," Billy Bob said. "How'd *that* go?"

"Again, as you'd expect. He said if a player on his team is disciplined in any way it is a team matter that he won't discuss in public."

Robinson, Tom, and Anthony arrived at that moment. The waiter came back and took their drink orders.

Teel, with Robinson filling in some details, repeated what had happened during Coach Johnson's talk with the media. The drinks arrived, everyone ordered, and Teel said, "Given that it's almost eleven and you guys probably shouldn't be out for too long, let's get down to business."

That was fine with Jason. He'd been waiting a long time to find out what Teel and Robinson had learned. Even so, he wasn't prepared for Teel's opening statement.

"Tom Gatch is a card-carrying member of the Ku Klux Klan."

The four players stared at Teel, then looked at Robinson for confirmation. He just nodded.

"Can't be true," Anthony finally said. "It's 2017."

"Not in some places," Teel said. "Not to Tom Gatch. Coach Johnson is Barack Obama compared to Gatch."

"Seriously?" they all chorused.

"Frighteningly seriously," Teel said. "Let me explain."

· · · · ·

Teel and Robinson had split their reporting on the TGP founder and head-of-school. Robinson had focused on learning more about the Ku Klux Klan itself; Teel had tried to find people who could tell him if Gatch had any real connection to the group.

"A lot of people think the Klan no longer exists," Robinson said. "And it's true that its membership is only a tiny fraction of what it once was: into the millions eighty or ninety years ago, probably less than ten thousand today. It's hard, though, to get a handle on actual numbers because it's a super-secret organization and it doesn't exactly have membership lists lying around. Or actual membership cards. David Duke was an exception.

"Most people will never admit to any Klan involvement—for obvious reasons. But they do still have occasional rallies, and there has been violence involving people protesting against them in the recent past. Plus, Louisiana is one of the states where Klan groups are likely still active."

He turned to Teel, who picked up the story from there.

"I found a guy, Bobby Meyer, who works for the *Times-Picayune*," Teel said. "He tried to follow up on the Gatch–Duke connection after the incident at Metairie Christian. He got pulled from the story when Gatch left to go work as a sports agent, but he made some progress."

"Like what?" Tom asked.

Teel held up a hand as their food was being delivered. "Hang on, I'll get to it."

Once the waiter departed, he picked up the story.

"It turns out that Duke and Gatch didn't just know each other at LSU. They were both members of a KKK chapter located in Baton Rouge. According to this guy, Gatch got forced out of Metairie Christian not because of his connection to Duke, but because everyone suddenly noticed that the school had dropped to one African American teacher during Gatch's tenure and only twelve African American students: eight on the football team, four on the basketball team."

"How'd Meyer find all this out?" Billy Bob asked.

"He was able to get the names of the teachers who'd left the school after Gatch took over," Teel said. "One of them—a white guy—had also known Gatch at LSU. Apparently, Gatch's KKK involvement wasn't a secret back then."

"So why haven't you two made all this public yet?" Tom asked, a little exasperated.

Teel and Robinson both shrugged. "One guy saying he heard someone was in the KKK—even on the record—isn't enough. Even getting some of the ex-teachers to say they left Metairie because they thought Gatch was a racist isn't enough."

"What *is* enough?" Jason asked.

"A verifiable document," Teel said. "Or a public statement."

They all looked at him as if he were crazy.

"Let me spell it out," Teel said. "You guys have gotta get Mr. Gatch to write something to you or to say something to you in public that is undeniably racist."

"Why in the world would he say something like that?" Anthony said. "He'd have to be insane."

"Doesn't being in the KKK tell you he's already insane to begin with?" Robinson said.

"Different kind of insanity, no?" Billy Bob said.

"Yes," Teel agreed. "You guys ever see a movie called *A Few Good Men*?"

All four football players began yelling, "You can't handle the truth!"—Jack Nicholson's signature line from the movie. In the climactic scene, Tom Cruise, as the Navy lawyer defending two Marines accused of murder, had baited Nicholson's character into admitting that he had ordered the accused Marines to perform a "Code Red"—an often violent form of Marine hazing—on the victim.

Jason, who remembered watching the movie on TV with his parents, laughed and began channeling Cruise's character, paraphrasing the pre-courtroom scene when it had been suggested to him that he get Nicholson to admit he'd ordered the Code Red. "Well, that's just perfect," Jason "Cruise" said. "I mean, no problem. We'll just march into Mr. Gatch's office on Monday and tell him he needs to confess to us—four freshman football players—that he's a card-carrying KKK member and that Coach Johnson is, thank God, also a racist. Soon as we're done with that, we should have time before lunch to find a cure for cancer."

Robinson laughed without mirth. "No one said it would be easy, but—"

He stopped in midsentence. Jason, who had been finishing off his french fries, looked up in the direction where the reporter was staring and saw why he had broken off his sentence.

Walking toward them, with a smirk written across his face,

241

was Coach Ingelsby. Right behind him were Coach Reilly, Coach Gutekunst, and Coach Cruikshank.

Coach Reilly also appeared to be smirking. Coach Cruikshank looked stricken. Coach Gutekunst had his head down as if he couldn't watch what was about to happen.

"Well, what do we have here?" Coach Ingelsby said as he reached the table. "Boys, you must have gotten permission from someone to leave the resort. I assume you did that, right?"

Tom was the quickest thinker in the group. "Coach, no one said anything about needing permission to leave the resort," he said. "There's no curfew, since—"

"Since no one had a car, not even the seniors, much less a bunch of freshmen," Coach Ingelsby broke in. "And it was a *given* that no one was going to go out. Except I guess we forgot about your pals in the media." He then looked at Teel and Robinson. "I assume you two got clearance from Ed Seaman to be spending time with these four players, right?"

This time it was Teel who had an answer. "We're not interviewing anyone right now, Don," he said. "You know we both wrote about these guys during the first couple weeks of the season. We thought it would be nice to buy them a postgame meal as thanks for the time they've given us."

That, thought Jason, *was pretty smooth.*

Coach Ingelsby didn't see it that way. "Good try, Teel, but you know better than that," he said. "You and Robinson aren't exactly rookie reporters. You know our rules." He turned to Robinson. "Him, I expect this kind of thing from," he said, nodding in Teel's direction. "I'm disappointed in you."

"I'll try not to lose sleep over it," Robinson answered, causing Jason and the others to stifle laughs.

Coach Reilly jumped in. "I don't know what all of you are up to, but we'll find out," he said. "You two guys are supposed to be big-time columnists. Why the sudden fascination with four high school freshmen—only one of whom is a starter right now?" He pointed a finger at Tom. "Jefferson, have you even seen the field yet for a single play?"

"I've seen it quite a bit," Tom said. "From the sideline."

Before any of the coaches could respond to Tom's wisecrack, Teel jumped back in.

"Which raises a question: How in the world could you guys not get Billy Bob Anderson here in the game tonight when it was clear your offense was going nowhere with Ronnie Thompson at QB and Anderson had already bailed you out twice this season?"

"How many games have you ever coached, Teel?" Ingelsby said.

Now it was Teel's turn to look disgusted. "Oh, please, Don, do better than that. I don't need to have coached to see who your best quarterback is."

Coach Ingelsby apparently didn't have a wise-guy answer for that one. "Rather than ruin our dinner," he said, "I'm going to very firmly suggest to the four of you that you get your chauffeurs here to get you back to the resort right now. In fact, I'm going to call Coach Winston and have him meet you in the lobby at"—he looked at his watch—"eleven forty-five. That gives you seventeen minutes. Which is very generous of me." His smirk widened. "Oh, and all four of you can report to Coach Johnson's office before breakfast on Monday. We'll expect you at seven."

Jason wanted to argue but figured it was pointless.

"We'll get 'em back right away, Don," Robinson said. "No need to call Winston to check on them."

"I'm not doing it because I need to," Coach Ingelsby said. "I'm doing it because I want to."

He turned, pulled out his cell phone, and walked away. The other coaches—without another word—followed. But only to a booth a few yards away.

The boys' dinner with the reporters was over.

24

NOT SURPRISINGLY, WORD GOT AROUND REGARDING THE LATE-NIGHT visit to the French Hound, and there was a good deal of needling about it on the bus trip home.

"You guys gonna get some new running shoes? You're probably going to need them," was one crack.

"Hope you're going to make a lot of money when those guys write your book—you'll need it when you get kicked out of here."

Most of the comments were good-natured, although the most repeated one was in reference to their timing. "We lose forty-five to nothing, and you go out with a couple of reporters? Are you trying to make us even *more* miserable on Monday?"

That wasn't a major concern for the soon-to-be-forgotten foursome (or so they were figuring) over the weekend. Jason and Tom were again wondering if it was time to just call their parents and go home. At least that way they'd avoid another lecture and, no doubt, quite a few reps up and down the stadium steps.

But mid-October was no time to try to get into another school—anywhere.

"It's also possible we'll have no choice," Billy Bob said as they sat and talked on Saturday afternoon.

It was a spectacular fall day, the leaves starting to turn, and they'd walked to their favorite corner of the campus after lunch.

"It's a private school," Billy Bob went on. "They *can* just kick us out because they don't like us."

"Which they don't," Tom put in.

"I don't think they'll do that," Jason said. "Anthony's basically a starter at this point, and like it or not, they're gonna need Billy Bob to play quarterback to have any chance to win the conference."

"Winning the conference might not be possible even if we don't get booted," Anthony reasoned. "If Middleburg wins out, we have no chance."

"They still have to play Roanoke," Jason answered. "They lose to them and we beat Roanoke, it could be a three-way tie."

"*If* we don't lose to anyone the rest of the way," Anthony said.

"Which gets back to the original point," Tom said. "At the very least, TGP needs you two guys. Jason might be able to help on special teams. I'm just deadweight at this point."

"Let's assume we don't get kicked out," Jason said. "We need a plan."

They sat and talked for the next hour, coming up in the end with nothing. Jason was ready to call it quits and suggest they go to the campus coffee shop for a snack when they saw a group of girls walking back from the soccer stadium, having just played a game.

"How'd you guys do?" Anthony yelled in their direction.

One of them was a tall, striking African American girl whom Jason recognized immediately because he'd stared at her every time she walked past their table in the dining hall. She paused and peered over at them.

"We won," she said. She put her hand on her forehead to shade her eyes from the sun. "Anthony, is that you?"

"Yeah," he said, waving.

She turned and said something to several of her friends, and they all began walking in their direction.

"That's Zoey Desheen, isn't it?" Tom said.

"Yup," Anthony said.

"She knows you?"

Anthony smiled triumphantly. "I somehow tested into sophomore English, remember? We're in the same class."

Zoey had brought three friends with her. Even though it was a cool afternoon, they were all dressed in shorts, T-shirts, and flip-flops. Zoey was at least five foot ten and stunning. The other three weren't quite as stunning but were plenty attractive.

Boys and girls didn't interact much on campus. The girls had their own dorm, and even though there didn't appear to be a formal rule against it, none of the dining room tables were coed. The only place where there was any real interaction was in class, and that was relatively minimal. Very few of the upper-class girls had much time for freshmen. Plus, it wasn't like being a jock made you special in a school where everyone, girls included, was a jock. Jason had gotten a brief flurry of attention after his blocked kick, but it had faded pretty quickly.

"I thought we'd already determined your fifteen minutes of fame were over," Tom had commented after Jason had tried to start a conversation walking out of class one morning with Andrea McIntosh, a blond-haired, blue-eyed volleyball player, and Andrea had disappeared like a puff of smoke.

"Thanks for the encouragement, Bull's-eye," Jason had said.

Now the girls walked over, sat down, and began asking questions about what in the world had happened to the football team at Middleburg.

"They had a great quarterback, and Coach Johnson wouldn't put Billy Bob into the game," Anthony said. "It was pretty much that simple."

One of the girls, Hope—Jason couldn't remember her last name, but she had mesmerizing green eyes—crinkled her nose. "I've seen you play," she said to Billy Bob. "You're way better than Ronnie Thompson. Why won't he play you?"

"Billy Bob was a bad boy," Tom said. "He didn't follow orders."

"Oh, not good," said Toni Andrews, who Jason knew was the soccer team's goalie. "Everyone in the school knows you don't mess around with Bobo. The older guys talk about 'The

Bobo Rules' all the time, and that he's judge, jury, and—when need be—executioner."

"How long have you been here?" Billy Bob said.

"I'm a senior," Toni answered. She looked away for a moment, and then returned her focus to the boys. "Well, maybe Bobo will get that job in Alabama and you guys will get a new start."

"Not if they give Ingelsby the job," Zoey said. "My friend Willie White says he's worse than Bobo, but Gatch thinks Ingelsby is the next Bill Belichick."

"Well, he does have Belichick's personality," Jason said.

"Oh no, he's worse than that," Billy Bob said. "People say Belichick has a sneaky sense of humor. Plus, I think he's a little better coach than Ingelsby."

"So's my cat," Tom said.

They all laughed. The girls lingered a little while longer. It was the most pleasant twenty minutes Jason could remember since they'd arrived at school eight weeks—and a lifetime—ago.

As they stood to leave, Zoey looked directly at Billy Bob and said, "You guys coming to the dance next Saturday?"

Jason remembered seeing posters around campus for the midsemester dance, but he hadn't given it any thought.

"Absolutely," Billy Bob said, looking right back at Zoey. "All you guys going?"

They all said they would be there.

"It's one of those deals where the new kids get to know each other a little," Toni said. "Some of the seniors won't go, but a lot of us will. It's kind of dorky and old-fashioned, but it's fun."

"Lot of stuff around here is dorky and old-fashioned," Tom said.

"True enough," Zoey said. "But we'll make sure you guys have a good time." She was looking right at Billy Bob when she said it.

"In that case," Anthony said. "I think we'll all be there, too."

The girls waved goodbye. Jason looked around to see if his three friends had the same silly grin he suspected he had on his own face.

They did.

. . . . .

When they all came out of their trance, Billy Bob received a good deal of teasing about Zoey's final question.

"She practically asked you out right there!" Anthony said.

"And was looking right at you when she promised a good time," Jason added.

"Zip it," Billy Bob said. "There's not a guy on this campus she can't go out with. Why me?"

Even so, he was a bright shade of red.

"Well, you *should* be the starting quarterback on the football team," Tom said.

"Actually, based on what my roomie says, *you* should probably be the starting QB," Billy Bob snapped back.

"Okay then, *I'll* go out with her," Tom said.

Anthony shook his head. "Appears she has eyes for somebody else, from what I just saw."

"Pretty sure she was just being nice," Billy Bob said, still grinning in spite of himself.

No one disagreed with him on that.

. . . . .

The ribbing of Billy Bob continued that night in the dining hall—with Juan del Potro and Jimmy Gomez also contributing after they'd been clued in about the events of the afternoon.

"You're probably right, Billy Bob," Juan said finally. "Zoey's not going out with some redneck freshman from Alabama when she can date anyone in the school. She was just being nice to you since you got yourself benched."

Tom could tell that Juan was trying to get a rise out of Billy Bob. Not surprisingly, it worked.

"So you don't think she'll go out with me, huh, Juan?" Billy Bob said, smiling but with some fire in his eyes.

"Not a chance," Juan said. "Look at her. Look at you."

"How much?" Billy Bob said.

"Ten bucks," Juan said.

Billy Bob almost gagged. "Ten bucks? You want me to put myself on the line with the best-looking girl in the school for ten bucks?"

"How much, then?" Juan asked.

"Loser has to bring the winner breakfast in bed for a week," Billy Bob said. "*That's* worth it."

There were strict rules against food in the dorm, but they were usually ignored and the people who worked in the dining hall tended to look the other way when people carried food out the door.

"Done," del Potro said. "But you gotta go and ask her now."

"What do I ask exactly?" Billy Bob said.

"Ask her to go with you to the dance as your date."

Billy Bob reached into his pocket for a comb, smoothed his blond curls, and stood up.

"Eat, drink, and be merry," Jason said. "Because in about five minutes, you die."

"Love it when you quote the Bible, roomie," Billy Bob said.

Jason had no idea that he'd quoted the Bible.

Billy Bob walked over to the table where Zoey sat, surrounded by nine other girls. Zoey stood up and Billy Bob started talking. Tom could tell he was talking, because his hands were going in fourteen different directions—a sure sign of nerves. They saw Zoey smile—you could see her smile from across state lines. They talked for another minute or so—Billy Bob's hands in his pockets. Then he turned and came back to the table.

The look on Billy Bob's face when he sat down made asking him how it had gone almost moot.

"I like my breakfast at about seven-thirty," he said to Juan.

"Seriously?" Juan said. "She really said yes?"

Billy Bob shook his head. "No," he said. "What she actually said was, 'I'd love to.' I even asked her if she and her friends might want to hang out with us tonight in the coffee shop."

Tom's heart skipped several beats. "And?" he said.

Billy Bob shook his head. "Easy, big fella, sorry," he said. "They're all going to hang out in their common room tonight, girls only, and watch the U.S. women's team play some kind of friends match."

"Friendly," Jason corrected.

"Whatever," Billy Bob said. "Only thing I know about soccer is that no one ever scores."

"So she said yes *and* no, then," Juan said, clearly trying to salvage something.

Jason was a bit baffled, too.

"She said *yes* to me, *no* to you guys," Billy Bob said. "That's the bottom line. Eggs over easy. Make sure the bacon's crisp."

· · · · ·

Tom was trying not to fall asleep the next morning reading a geology textbook when his phone buzzed. It was a text from Jason.

BB says Zoey asked if she & friends cld rain-check at coffee shop @ 3. U up 4 it?

That was one of the dumbest questions Tom had ever been asked.

R U kidding? Meet in yr room @ 2:55.

Jason replied,

Anthony too, right?

Anthony had gone to church with Billy Bob and the bus wasn't back yet, but Tom had no doubt he'd be in. He responded to Jason—

For sure.

—then decided it was time to close his eyes lying on his bed rather than sitting up trying to stare down a list of metamorphic rocks.

A few hours later, when they walked into the coffee shop, they found Zoey sitting at a corner table with the three girls who had been with her the day before.

When they walked over to the table, Zoey formally introduced them since she hadn't the day before. Heather Watson was pretty: not as tall as Zoey, African American with a warm, friendly smile. Tom had seen Heather in the hallways, but it was Toni he remembered most vividly. She was blond-haired and blue-eyed and *very* tall. He breathed a sigh of relief when the two girls didn't stand up during introductions. Zoey also introduced Hope, the one with the green eyes, whose last name was Kaufman, and the four boys grabbed chairs and sat down.

Zoey took control of the conversation. "Billy Bob and I were talking on the way to church today, and we thought it'd be fun for all you guys to actually meet one another," she said. "I mean, Billy Bob asked me to the dance and, even though it's all pretty informal, I thought it might make it a little easier on you guys if you actually knew some girls when you get there."

"Boys, especially you freshmen, tend to be shy," Toni said. "And girls like me tend to end up standing in the corner."

"Are you kidding?" Tom blurted out. "You? Impossible."

She smiled at him. "I'm six-two," she said.

"Or six-four if you wear heels," Heather said, laughing.

"You know a lot of guys who want to dance with someone who is six-two?" Toni went on.

"Well, count me in," Tom said, unsure where his sudden courage was coming from.

"Okay then, it's a date," Toni said, shooting a dazzling smile at Tom.

"Hang on," Anthony said. "I'm six-three *without* heels."

"Yeah, but I think Tom's cute," Toni said.

"I'll happily dance with you," Hope said to Anthony. "As long as you don't step on me with those big feet."

"Only size fourteens," Anthony said. "And I'm an excellent dancer."

"Well," Jason said, looking at Heather. "Guess that leaves you and me. What do you say?"

"Dance with White Lightning?" Heather said. "What girl could turn that down?"

They all started laughing and talking at once.

It was Billy Bob who brought them back to reality. "Four interracial couples on the dance floor at TGP," he said. "This could be a first for the school."

"Oh, please," Zoey said. "Nobody's even going to notice."

Maybe, Tom thought. *Or maybe not.*

25

WITH ALL THE TALK ABOUT THE DANCE, THE BOYS HAD ALMOST FORGOTTEN that when they got to practice on Monday they were going to be dealing with a coaching staff that wasn't the least bit happy about the 45–0 beatdown the TGP team had experienced at Middleburg on Friday.

Surprisingly, they had heard nothing over the weekend about their punishment for being caught at the French Hound after the game with Teel and Robinson. They had shown up at the football offices, as ordered, at seven on Monday morning and found no one around.

"Maybe Coach Ingelsby didn't want to make Coach Johnson even madder than he already was," Jason speculated as they walked, relieved, to breakfast.

"Or maybe they're going to nail us with it in front of the whole team when we get to practice this afternoon," said Billy Bob, who had decided to pass on breakfast-in-bed because he preferred having Juan owe him something for letting him off the hook.

Billy Bob's theory sounded more likely to Tom. It wasn't as if Coach Ingelsby was a forgiving person. Most of the other players had heard about what had happened and fully expected the "Hungry Four"—as they'd been dubbed, because they were always hungry for punishment—to get what was coming to them at practice.

"Hammer drop yet?" was the question all four of them heard throughout the day Monday.

It hadn't. And, surprisingly, it didn't.

When the players arrived in the locker room they were told to stay put after getting into their practice gear. It was raining outside, the kind of all-day rain that could ruin one's mood after a 45–0 *win*, and even though it was still mid-October, it was also quite cold. Both factors contributed to the dark feelings inside when Coach Johnson and the staff walked in a few minutes later and brought everyone to attention by a sharp whistle blast that rebounded off the walls.

"Take a seat," Coach Johnson said.

The whole team complied.

The coach stood in the front of the room, hands on his hips, as if deciding where to begin. "With the way it's raining outside, it makes absolutely no sense to practice outdoors today," he said. "I know we would all be more comfortable in the bubble."

TGP had an indoor practice bubble used throughout the winter by spring sports teams and in bad weather by teams that were in-season. Needless to say, the football team had priority.

Everyone in the room breathed a sigh of relief at their reprieve from the bad weather. It didn't last long.

"Having said that," Coach Johnson continued, "I don't think anyone in this room deserves or needs to be comfortable this afternoon. After looking at the tape of your performance on Friday, I feel a little bit guilty: the coaching staff had you prepared to play and all of you"—he paused and looked around the room for effect—"all of you failed to show up. So we will practice outdoors, and the coaches will get soaked, too. Collateral damage."

Another pause. Tom couldn't believe that Johnson wasn't taking *any* of the blame for Friday's debacle. Then again, he could believe it. What he really couldn't believe was that he and his friends hadn't been called out yet for Friday's restaurant incident. Maybe, he thought, Coach Ingelsby was a little better guy than he'd believed.

Coach Johnson was still talking.

"What's more, as I mentioned after the game, we have all decided that, as of today, there are no starters on this team. None of you deserve to be called a starter after Friday. So, for the next few days, we're going to mix and match players on each unit and see who rises to the top. Try to imagine that it's August again and you are all trying to prove yourselves, because that's what you are going to need to do if you want to see the field against Powhite on Friday." He stopped again and paced up and down for a moment. "I've been a football coach for twenty-six years. I've been the head coach here for eleven. I have *never* felt as let down as I did by this team on Friday," he said finally. "Ultimately, I'm the man in charge. I hired the coaches and we recruited all of you to play. I get the credit when we play well, so I'll publicly take the blame when we play poorly." He paused and glared at them all. "But I will tell you one thing. I do not plan to *ever* have the feeling again that I had Friday. I don't accept failure. If I were you boys, I'd make damn certain it never happens again. Because if it does, practicing in the rain will be the *least* of your problems." He paused a final time to let his words sink in. "All right, let's go."

Tom wondered if Coach Johnson expected the players to jump to their feet and knock down the locker-room door to get to the practice field. If he did, he had to be disappointed. What he got was everyone standing up and walking slowly to the door, their cleats clattering on the concrete as they clumped out into the rain.

"Well, at least he said he was ultimately responsible," Anthony said.

"Not quite," Billy Bob said. "He said he'd publicly take the blame."

"What are you getting at?" Jason asked as they began to jog in response to shouts from Coach Ingelsby.

"Let me guess," Tom said with a grim expression. "Coach Johnson will take the blame *publicly*, but there's no telling what he'll do in *private*."

They lined up to stretch, the captains leading them. The mood on the practice field was as black as the skies overhead.

. . . . .

The coaches kept their promise to give everyone a chance in practice for the first three days of the week. No coach said a word about punishment for the Hungry Four.

During practices, even Tom got some scrimmage reps and during the workouts actually caught a couple of passes—not coincidentally when Billy Bob was at quarterback.

After his first catch on Tuesday, a slant-in that Billy Bob overthrew slightly and Tom dove to catch, he heard Coach Reilly's voice behind him.

"Stay on your feet when you make a catch, Jefferson."

Tom resisted the urge to say that Rob Gronkowski would have had to dive to catch that ball. When he came to the sideline, Jason and Anthony were waiting.

"Thought sure Coach Reilly was going to stop the scrimmage to present you with the ball," Jason said. "Your first catch ever at TGP."

"Not true," Tom said hotly. "I caught a few in preseason."

"Yeah, thrown by Jason," Anthony said. "Which may explain why he's fourth string right now."

"Hey, we're all starters, remember?" Jason said.

. . . . .

On Thursday, they arrived in the locker room to find a new depth chart on the wall. It wasn't that different from the old depth chart. There had been a few swaps—Anthony, for example, who had been playing most of the minutes at right tackle, was now officially listed as the starter—but for the most part little had changed.

Including at quarterback. Ronnie Thompson was listed as the starter. Billy Bob and Frank Kessler were listed as "co" number twos, and Jason was number four. He was, however, listed as the number two punt returner. He wondered how Matt Quinn felt about that.

For once, Billy Bob's sense of humor failed him as he and Tom glanced at the new chart. Tom was right where he'd been all fall—fourth team Z receiver. The wideouts were listed as Y and Z.

"What a bunch of idiots," Billy Bob said, tapping the chart and glancing around to make sure no coaches were listening. "The two best quarterbacks on this team are you and me. And this is what they come up with."

"I promise you if we get behind tomorrow, Coach Johnson won't screw around," Tom said. "He'll get you in. He has to. We lose twice, we're definitely out of the playoffs. And, unless he's got a signed contract at Alabama, that can't help his chances for that million-dollar job down there."

"Tell you one thing," Billy Bob said. "He doesn't get the Alabama job, I'm not back here next year no matter what else happens—on or off the field."

Tom grinned. "You dying to play for Ingelsby? Odds are, he'd get the job."

Billy Bob's smile returned. "You a Stars Wars fan?"

"Yeah, why?"

"Never tell me the odds."

That ended the Han Solo talk for the day.

．．．．．

This time though, Tom had it right.

Powhite, a school near Richmond, was a midpack conference team. The Spartans were 5–2 coming into the game and 3–2 in the conference, yet that Friday they took a quick 7–0 lead when Ronnie Thompson threw an interception deep in TGP territory, leading to a short touchdown drive.

After the kickoff, TGP went three-and-out. As soon as the punt team went onto the field, Tom saw Coach Cruikshank walking toward where he and Billy Bob were standing.

"Anderson, you ready to go?" he asked, as if he and Billy Bob were late for dinner.

"Been ready, Coach," Billy Bob answered, causing Coach Cruikshank to give him a brief sideways look and put his hand on Billy Bob's neck. "I don't care if we've got a dive play called and you see eleven men lined up in the box," he said. "You do *not* audible. Got it?"

"Got it."

Coach Cruikshank smiled for a brief moment. "You audible and two things will happen: you'll never play here again, and I'll be looking for work."

He walked away.

"He's not such a bad guy," Billy Bob said.

"Everything's relative," Tom answered.

Just as in the first two games in which he'd relieved Ronnie Thompson, Billy Bob turned the game around. The reasons were simple: Thompson was an adequate runner; Billy Bob was a good one. Thompson was a lousy passer; Billy Bob was a very good one.

"He's not as good as you," Jason said to Tom, after Billy Bob threw a perfect pass to Bo Reynolds on a slant for a fifteen-yard gain. "But he's pretty good."

He was certainly good enough. The Patriots scored touchdowns on their first three drives after Billy Bob entered the game. From the sidelines, you could see the entire offense's body language perk up the minute he jogged into the huddle.

At halftime it was 21–7. Powhite pieced together a drive to start the second half, helped by a blown coverage in the secondary. Mitch Knox, the cornerback who had been completely fooled by a play-fake, was instantly yanked and Coach Johnson berated him at length as he came to the sideline.

"How can you be so dumb?" he said. "How can we have recruited someone so dumb? I should fire the coaches who recruited you right now. Son, if you get into college someplace, I hope they've got a team of tutors to work with you. Now go sit down and see if you can learn some football by watching."

Mitch slunk to the bench, took his helmet off, and sat staring at the ground. No one went near him. He'd been a starter for two years and had made a mistake almost anyone could make.

"Do you think there's any chance he talks to a white kid that way?" Jason asked Tom.

"Good question," Tom said. He was pretty sure he knew the answer.

. . . . .

The game stayed close until midway into the fourth quarter. The teams traded field goals to make it 24–17. Powhite began moving the ball again but stalled at the TGP 38-yard line. Too far away to try a field goal. On came the punt team. Jason jogged out to take his spot seven yards in front of Ray Solo, who was standing on the 5-yard line.

A return wasn't likely from here. Powhite would try to punt the ball short of the goal line and down it. Solo's job was to act as if he was going to catch it to slow the defenders a little bit in the hope that the ball would get to the end zone for a touchback.

Jason stood at the 12 and watched as the ball spiraled into the air. Suddenly, a wave of panic hit him. The ball was dropping straight toward him. The punter had kicked it short. Jason had a split second to make a decision. If he let it bounce, it would almost surely be downed inside the 10. A fair catch made the most sense. The 12 wasn't great field position, but it wasn't completely awful.

For some reason, though, he couldn't get his arm into the air to signal the fair catch fast enough. Fully aware that the Powhite punt team was bearing down on him, he caught the ball and—mostly out of panic—began sprinting to his right.

Apparently the defenders were surprised he'd caught the ball without a fair catch. In an instant, he was past the first wall and had gotten to the edge. Remarkably, because most of the punt team had been in full sprint to try to down the ball if it bounced, he had only two Powhite players between him and the goal line.

The first one raced up to meet him at about the 30. Jason made an instinct move, planting his foot to cut inside. The defender flew past, barely touching him. He ran in the direction of the middle of the field, hearing screaming behind him as the Powhite defenders he'd run past tried to recover.

Only the punter was left to beat. Jason simply outran him, flying diagonally across the field, picking up so much speed that the kid couldn't catch him. Once he was in full sprint, he knew he wasn't going to get caught. Still, he didn't look back until he was across the goal line.

Jason turned and saw his teammates bearing down on him. He didn't even know what to do with the football. He fumbled it as he was tackled by what felt like the entire TGP team.

It didn't matter. Jason was a hero—again.

When he came to the sideline, Coach Gutekunst was waiting for him.

"You know you should have fair-caught that ball, don't you?" the coach said.

"Coach, I couldn't get my arm up—"

"Well, thank God for that!" the coach said, giving him a bear hug.

"White Lightning lives!" Tom said, joining the hug-fest.

He was aware of the fact that he had tears in his eyes as he hugged his pal. He hoped they were tears of joy.

· · · · ·

The final was 31–21.

Once again, Billy Bob didn't get a game ball. Tom figured if Billy Bob threw for five hundred yards, he wouldn't get a game ball. Instead, the entire offensive line—including the O-line coach, Marco Thurman—got one for "making the offense go."

Well, Tom thought, *at least Anthony got a game ball.*

The change in quarterbacks wasn't brought up in Coach Johnson's postgame remarks.

Jason also got a game ball.

"Two game balls and you've been in for, what, four snaps on offense all season?" Billy Bob said. "That's impressive."

Even without a game ball, Billy Bob was receiving plenty of congratulations from teammates when Coach Ingelsby walked up. Anthony had already gone off to shower. Jason was standing next to Billy Bob, and Tom was trying to decide whether he needed to shower since he was now zero-for-eight in getting on the field in a game.

"Anderson," Coach Ingelsby said.

Tom wondered if he was actually going to offer congratulations for Billy Bob's performance or Jason's return. He wasn't.

"Jefferson, Roddin, you, too," he continued. "Where's Ames?"

"In the shower," Billy Bob said.

"Well, you can let him know, then. Monday, six a.m., you

report to Coach Winston for your punishment runs." Coach Ingelsby smiled wickedly. "You didn't think you were getting away with your little excursion, did you? We just held off a week because we didn't want to single anyone out after that awful team effort last week. Now we can single you out." He turned and walked away.

"And the hits just keep on coming," Jason said, using a favorite saying of his dad's.

Tom started to take a step in Coach Ingelsby's direction.

"Whoa," Billy Bob said. "What are you doing?"

"I'm gonna tell him he should single *you* out for saving the game tonight."

"No you're not," Billy Bob said. "Just leave him alone. You want to get thrown out of school before you get the chance to dance with Toni?"

"Billy Bob's right," Jason said. "Which reminds me—do we have to go shopping for you in the morning?"

"Shopping?" Tom said. "What for?"

"A ladder," Jason said.

For once, they all laughed out loud in the TGP locker room.

26

THE DANCE WAS SCHEDULED TO START AT SEVEN.

The four boys and four girls decided to walk over together—a good idea, Tom decided, because given the way the four girls looked, and the fact that the four boys were just freshmen, there were bound to be plenty of older guys wanting to ask them to dance as soon as they walked inside.

They strolled up to the front door of the Alumni House at a few minutes after seven and were surprised to find Mr. Gatch standing there, greeting the students as they walked in.

"I forgot," Zoey told the group as they waited in line. "This is one of his traditions. Apparently he tries to remember everyone's name."

Tom, standing next to Toni, felt himself sweating.

"Miss Desheen!" Gatch practically screamed as Zoey walked up to shake hands with him. "What a wonderful win you girls had this afternoon!"

"Thank you, Mr. Gatch," Zoey said. "I think you know Billy Bob . . ."

"Mr. Anderson, of course," Gatch said. "Well done last night, young man. You've earned the right to walk in with Miss Desheen!"

He was practically gushing. It was no different with any of the rest of them. He remembered all their names—even Tom's. He complimented Jason on his punt return and told Toni he was counting on her to lead the girls' basketball team to a great season, no doubt getting his sports confused because of her height.

In the foyer were signs warning students that smoking and drinking were grounds for instant expulsion from the school and that no unruly behavior would be tolerated. Students were also reminded that, "as a courtesy to the dancers and musicians," cell phone use was prohibited inside the building, which was used for alumni events and, Tom knew, had offices for the "development department"—the people who solicited the school's potential donors.

Once everyone was inside, Mr. Gatch formally welcomed them all, talking about what a great start they'd had to the school year and mentioning that the next schoolwide event would be the pre-Thanksgiving 5K turkey trot.

"Start thinking about some original Pilgrim costumes for that one," he said. "Remember, first prize in the costume contest is free food and drink at the coffee shop for the rest of the semester."

"Maybe I'll go as Martin Luther King Jr.," Tom whispered.

"I don't think he was a Pilgrim," Jason whispered back. "I think you should go as Thomas Jefferson."

"I don't think *either* of them was at the first Thanksgiving," Billy Bob chimed in.

The music started; a live band had been imported for the evening. Tom noticed that it looked as if a large number of staff members and almost all of the nonseniors in the school were in attendance. He saw several of the assistant football coaches. Always stiff, Coach Ingelsby had his hands to his ears almost as soon as the music started. There was no sign of Coach Johnson.

Even though the girls had already said they'd dance with them, Tom still felt some butterflies. Apparently, he wasn't alone. All four boys stood with their hands in their pockets, and Tom noticed Zoey dancing with Mitch Knox, the cornerback who had been subjected to the haranguing from Coach Johnson the night before.

"Looks like your girl found someone else to dance with," Tom said to Billy Bob, unable to resist a gibe.

"She probably just feels sorry for him," Billy Bob said. "But you know me—I always come off the bench to save the day."

Three songs in, Tom decided it was time. He took a deep breath and walked over to where Toni was sitting, alone. Much to his surprise, her call that she wouldn't be swarmed by suitors had been accurate.

"May I have this dance?" he asked formally.

"I thought you'd changed your mind," she said, standing, still considerably taller than he was, even in low heels.

He didn't care.

Billy Bob had managed to wrest Zoey away from Mitch, and Anthony was in the middle of the dance floor with Hope.

He hadn't been kidding; he really could dance. Sadly, Jason, for all his grace on the field, clearly could not. When Tom and Toni swiveled over to where Jason and Heather were dancing, he could see that Toni was almost averting her eyes.

"Hey, White Lightning," Tom said over the din of the music, "I'm sure Heather thought you had better moves than this."

"He's terrible," Heather shouted over the music, "but still pretty cute."

Jason shot a wide grin at his friend. Clearly, he was having fun.

Tom was having fun, too, until Aaron Simpkins, who was a starter on the basketball team, tapped him on the shoulder.

"Time's up, frosh," he said, hooking a thumb to indicate it was time for Tom to leave.

Simpkins was at least six foot eight—maybe more. But Tom wasn't going to be intimidated.

"She's dancing with me," he said, looking over his shoulder and continuing to dance. "Because she wants to dance with me."

"Don't think she wants to dance with someone a foot shorter than her," Simpkins said.

"But I do," Toni said, grabbing Tom's hand as he breathed a sigh of relief. Dancing with someone several inches taller than he was? That he could handle. *Fighting* with someone who actually might be a foot taller? That he didn't crave.

Simpkins glared for a second, shook his head in disgust, and walked away.

There were bright strobe lights on the area where people were dancing, and it was now quite crowded. Tom was wondering what he was going to do when the band played a slow song. He figured he'd climb that ladder when the time came. All he knew at that moment was that he and his three friends were dancing with four of the best-looking girls in the school.

One song came and went. Then two. As the band began to play one of his father's favorite songs, an old Commodores hit, Toni leaned in close to Tom for a moment and said, "Anyone ever tell you that you're a really good dancer?"

Tom had never danced much before, except occasionally alone in his room—and that certainly hadn't been to the Commodores.

He smiled and said, "Better than Jason at least."

Toni laughed, and just as she did, Tom felt a second tap on his shoulder. Another basketball player. In fact, it was Trey Broussard, who Tom knew was one of the team captains. Broussard didn't say anything, merely jerked his head as if to say, *Get lost.*

What was up with these basketball players?

Hoping that Toni would interject again, Tom looked to his right and noticed that someone was trying to cut in on Billy Bob: yet another basketball player. The only difference was that it was an African American, Tago Reed. Simpkins and Broussard were both white.

This was no coincidence, Tom *knew.*

"Hey, boy, you deaf?" Broussard was shouting over the music. "I said outta here, pal. You're done."

"Don't think so," Tom answered, not having to look nearly

as far up at Broussard, who was about six-four, as he had at Simpkins. "Ask her."

He pointed at Toni, who shook her head at Broussard. "Like I told your buddy," she shouted, "I'm happy, thanks."

"No you're not," Broussard said. "I got orders."

Orders?

Before he could ask exactly what Broussard was talking about, Tom felt himself being lifted off the ground and tossed aside. He landed, thankfully, on his butt. Sitting there, he saw Toni coming to help him up. He also noticed that Jason, with Heather standing behind him, was squared off nose-to-nose with Paul Franchot, one of the handful of black guys on the soccer team.

Toni offered Tom a hand to help him up. "Stay close to me," she said.

He did as he was told.

Now standing, he looked around the dance floor and saw that Anthony was being held back by several kids while a member of the golf team who was in one of Tom's classes cowered a few feet away as if terrified—justifiably—that Anthony was about to deck him. Zoey had an arm around Billy Bob and was pointing her finger angrily at a handful of kids—all white.

An idea edged itself into Tom's mind: someone—or perhaps several someones—had ordered that the four interracial couples on the dance floor be broken up. But was he just being paranoid? Had all that had happened the last two-plus months completely clouded his judgment?

The music had stopped. Several of the football coaches came onto the floor to prevent complete mayhem from breaking out.

"What the hell is your problem, Jefferson?" Coach Reilly said, ignoring Toni and grabbing Tom roughly by the collar.

"Coach, Trey Broussard wanted to cut in on us and I didn't want him to," Toni said. "Then Trey tried to start a fight with Tom."

"Why shouldn't he cut in?" Coach Reilly said. "What's wrong with cutting in?"

"Nothing, unless the cuttee doesn't want to dance with the cutter," Toni said.

"Well," Coach Reilly said, turning his attention to Tom, "she shouldn't be dancing with you in the first place."

Whoa! Maybe I'm not even a little bit paranoid, Tom thought. *There really is something going on here.*

He then asked aloud, "Why not, Coach?"

For once, Reilly didn't have an answer. Then he found one. "She's too tall for you, Jefferson," he said. "You blind?"

"That's my call, Coach," Toni said. "Not yours."

All over the dance floor, similar arguments seemed to be taking place—coaches and a couple of teachers speaking heatedly to Jason, Billy Bob, Anthony, and their partners about allowing cut-ins.

"When the music starts, you let Broussard dance with her," Coach Reilly said.

Before Tom could answer, Toni did. "Coach, I decide who to dance with," she said. "Not you."

Toni was as gutsy as she was tall.

Tom was hoping and praying the other girls were giving similar responses to being ordered to change partners. He was kicking himself for not thinking something like this could happen.

Coach Reilly glared at Toni. The room had gotten almost quiet.

Suddenly—or perhaps not so suddenly—Mr. Gatch appeared in the middle of the dance floor. The phony smile he seemed to wear at all times was missing.

"Everyone, listen up," the head-of-school said in a voice that was firm but not quite angry. "I'm not certain what's going on here, but let's remember one of our school traditions: when someone in authority tells you to do something, you do it. There's always a good reason why the adults make the decisions they make. We all understand that, don't we?"

He got some nods and a few *Yes, sirs*, but not many. He smiled in the direction of Toni and Tom and then Zoey and Billy Bob.

"Apparently, some of our girls are attracting attention from more than one boy—understandable." The phony smile was back. "So, in order to make sure we don't have any misunderstandings among the boys, we'll let the adults sort this out. Everyone understand?"

By now, Tom was pretty certain he understood. "Mr. Gatch, shouldn't everybody have the right to dance with whoever they want to dance with?" he heard himself say.

Mr. Gatch turned to find out where the voice had come from. His phony smile landed on Tom. "As I said, Mr. Jefferson, sometimes the adults have to resolve disputes. You are dancing with a very popular young lady right now. Perhaps you shouldn't monopolize her."

"I'm not a piece of property!" Toni said, clearly angry.

That seemed to get to Mr. Gatch. He took a couple of steps in Toni's direction, the smile gone. "But you *are* a student here at *my* school," he said, his voice low but his tone menacing. "And when I give an order, you'll follow it."

He was close to cracking.

Tom sensed it, which only made him want to press harder. "So you want people to change partners, is that it, Mr. Gatch?"

The smile came back. "Correct, Mr. Jefferson. It's very simple and very easy."

"No problem, then," Tom said.

He hoped the others would pick up on his cue. He walked over to where Hope and Anthony were standing and took Hope's hand.

"May I have this dance?" Tom asked her.

Anthony didn't miss a beat, moving quickly (for a big guy) to Toni and posing the same question to her.

Jason and Billy Bob were right behind: Jason walked Heather over to Billy Bob and took Zoey by the hand. If this bothered the girls, they didn't show it. They had seen what was going on just as clearly as the boys had, and they were just as upset, if not more so.

Tom turned to Mr. Gatch. "Okay, we've all changed partners, sir," he said. "Can we start the music again now?"

Tom thought he could see steam coming from Mr. Gatch's ears.

The head-of-school spoke slowly, his voice rising in anger quickly. "At *my* school, when I give an order, it is meant to be followed," he said. "It is not meant to be circumvented or ridiculed or . . . trivialized!" His face was turning red.

"Mr. Gatch, with all due respect, you said everyone needed to change partners," Billy Bob said. "That's exactly what we're doin' right now."

"No it's not!" Gatch said. He was yelling now, and Tom could see baffled looks on the faces of a lot of the other dancers.

"What exactly did you mean, Mr. Gatch?" Tom said, trying to sound casual. "How exactly did we misunderstand you?"

"You didn't misunderstand, Jefferson," Gatch said, advancing on Tom, pointing a finger. "I . . . I will tolerate your presence in this school but I will *not* stand here and watch you blatantly break the rules."

"What rules are we breaking by dancing, Mr. Gatch?" Tom said, standing his ground even though he could feel his legs quaking a little bit underneath him. He sensed that Mr. Gatch was close to telling him he couldn't handle the truth. This certainly wasn't the time to back down.

"The rules of common decency!" Gatch roared. "Good God, do you expect me to just *stand* here and watch while you paw this beautiful young girl? And you, Ms. Andrews, and you, Ms. Kaufman, have you no shame at all?"

The looks on most of the students' faces were now almost identical: jaws were dropping. Even Trey Broussard looked confused.

It was Zoey who spoke next. Clearly, she had figured out what was going on. "What about us, Mr. Gatch?" she said. "Should Heather and I be ashamed for getting 'pawed'?"

Mr. Gatch looked at her, then at Jason. "From you, I'm not surprised," he said, pointing to Jason. Then, whirling on Billy Bob, he said: "But *you*, Anderson? A good Southern, churchgoing young man? What is *wrong* with you?"

"Nothing is wrong with me, Mr. Gatch," Billy Bob said. "But clearly, something's wrong with you."

And that was when Zoey surprised them all. She walked a few steps over to Billy Bob, leaned down, and gave him a long kiss on the lips. "Thank you," she mouthed as she pulled her head back and the room erupted in a mix of cheers and jeers.

Too late, coaches and teachers were now moving in, trying to steer Mr. Gatch off the dance floor. Coach Ingelsby and Coach Reilly each had him by an arm and were trying, as gently as possible, to get him away before he could say anything more.

"Let's get some air, Mr. Gatch," Coach Ingelsby said.

Gatch was taking *really* deep breaths now, looking around as if uncertain what to do next. He glared one last time at Tom and Anthony, who were now standing next to each other.

"We let you people into this school because you can perform on the field," Gatch said, now being half dragged by the two coaches but still shouting to be heard. "That does *not* give you the right to interfere with the white girls from decent homes who come to this school. I have to answer to their parents!"

Tom knew there was no need to say anything else. So did Anthony. Everyone was staring at Mr. Gatch, clearly in shock.

The head-of-school opened his mouth one more time to speak. This time, Coach Ingelsby clapped his hand over it, muffling him. Then, he and Coach Reilly lifted Mr. Gatch off his feet and, between them, carried him from the room.

Yes, it turned out, Mr. Gatch *had* ordered the Code Red. Without intending to get him to admit to it, Tom, Jason, and their friends had gotten him to do so. All they'd had to do was dance. Everyone stared after the two coaches and the still-struggling head-of-school in silence.

Thomas Alan Gatch had left the building.

27

FOR SEVERAL LONG SECONDS, EVERYONE IN THE ROOM STARED AT THE
door that Mr. Gatch had exited from or, more accurately, been
carried through.

"What now?" Jason asked, still in a little bit of shock.

Tom, though, felt completely calm. Gatch hadn't said, *I will
never allow my head football coach to play an African American at
quarterback,* but he'd said more than enough. They had him.
Now they had to figure out how to finish him.

"We gotta get in touch with Teel and Robinson right away,"
Tom said. "We have to make sure they're on this before Mr.
Gatch and his people begin to try to spin it."

"Spin it?" Billy Bob said. "How can they possibly spin what
just happened—in front of a hundred-plus witnesses?"

"Half these people will insist it didn't happen," Tom said.
"And the other half may be afraid to go on the record."

"Impossible," Jason said. "I mean—"

He was interrupted by several of their teammates walking into their little circle, clearly angry.

"What the hell was that all about?" Ronnie Thompson said. "What were you guys trying to pull?"

The quarterback had plenty of backup (Tom couldn't help but think that Thompson always seemed to need backup, on or off the field): other football players and guys from other teams nodding in agreement. Almost all of them, Tom noticed, were guys—there were only a couple of girls in the group. All were white.

"What do you mean what are we trying to pull?" Billy Bob answered. "We were all just trying to dance. Is there something wrong with that?"

"You know exactly what was wrong, frosh," Chuck VanDorn, one of the starting linebackers, said.

"What's your point, VanDorn?" Anthony said.

"Where we come from, there are lines you don't cross," VanDorn said. "You ought to know that, Anderson."

"You may be an Alabama boy just like me," Billy Bob said, "but I got no idea where you come from."

VanDorn apparently didn't like that answer, because he took a step in Billy Bob's direction, a fist cocked. He never got there, because Anthony stepped in his path.

"You don't want to do this, VanDorn," he said. "None of you want to do this. What's the deal—you guys behind Mr. Gatch? Seriously?"

VanDorn was a big guy, probably about six foot three and 220 rock-hard pounds. But he wanted no part of Anthony. Once he backed down, things began to calm. There were a couple more shouted insults, but the crowd began to disperse.

Someone apparently told the band to start playing again, and they chose something slow. A few kids started dancing, but almost everyone else either stood around whispering about what had happened or headed for the door.

Zoey, Heather, Hope, and Toni were all still standing there, quizzical looks on their faces.

"Okay," Zoey said. "What just happened here?"

"Come on," Tom said. "Let's all go for a walk."

· · · · ·

They heard a few more barbs on the way to the door but kept moving, except a couple of times when Anthony slowed as if he was going to respond. That shut the talkers up quickly.

Once they were outside, they walked for a while to find a quiet spot to sit down. They ended up back on the same benches where Zoey had told them about the dance a week earlier. Tom recounted the entire story, starting with the first practice. The other three filled in details at different times as the four girls sat and listened, their mouths dropping a little more with each damning detail.

"So Mr. Gatch just walked into a trap you hadn't even set yet," Zoey said.

Tom shrugged. "Pretty much," he said.

"What happens next?" Toni said.

Jason held up his phone. "I just texted Teel and Robinson

while we were talking. They're both in Blacksburg tonight covering Virginia Tech's game against North Carolina. They're gonna drive up here in the morning so we can walk them through what just happened in person."

"How are they going to do that?" Zoey asked. "You know they'll shut the campus down to the media and you guys won't be allowed to leave."

"Already thought of that," Tom said. "All four of us will be going to church tomorrow—even Jason, the godless Jew. Billy Bob and Anthony say that no one ever bothers to check who gets on the bus for which church. Why would they? Teel and Robinson will meet us at Saint Michael's. Then they'll drive us back afterward. The guard on the gate won't know we left without permission; they'll wave 'em through."

"Didn't I hear that you guys are already on some kind of double-secret probation?" Heather asked. "Aren't you risking getting expelled if you get caught?"

Billy Bob laughed out loud. "You don't think we're *not* going to get expelled after tonight?"

"Actually, our only chance to stay—if we want to—is probably to get the story out in public," Anthony said. "Once the media gets involved, it will be hard for the administration to kick us out."

Tom nodded. "Agreed. Like I said inside, they're going to try to claim it was all a misunderstanding. I'm not sure *how* they're going to do that, but that's what they'll do. It's the only way Mr. Gatch can survive."

"What do you mean *survive*?" Hope said. "He *owns* the school."

"Yeah, but if this story gets out and the school can't recruit a single African American athlete going forward, what are the chances it's worth anything in a couple of years?" Tom answered. "What are the chances, if the story's true, that he's able to sell it and get a job fund-raising at Alabama?"

Jason's cell phone pinged. He looked at it, then held it up.

"The reporters will be at the church at nine-thirty," he said. "They'll park on the side."

"That's perfect," Billy Bob said. "There's a side door not that far from the bathroom. We hit the head while everyone's walking inside and duck out after the service starts."

"I'll be in church," Zoey said. "I'll text you if I see anybody looking interested when you disappear."

"You'll let us know what happens as soon as you get back?" Toni asked.

"Absolutely," Tom said.

"For sure," Anthony added, smiling. "*If* we get back."

．．．．．

There were no issues getting on the bus in the morning. There were three buses that went to St. Michael's, the Catholic church, and the boys and Zoey boarded the last one.

Once the bus was moving, though, the trouble began.

Seeing Jason sitting next to Billy Bob, Ronnie Thompson turned in his seat and said, "Hey, Roddin, what's a Hebrew doing going to church?"

They'd been prepared for someone asking the question.

"I'm thinking about converting," Jason said. He had sat next to Billy Bob, away from Zoey, specifically to make it look like they were on a buddy-outing together.

Thompson's eyes narrowed for a moment. Then he looked at Tom, sitting with Anthony. "And you, Jefferson?"

"Same here," Tom said cheerily.

"This doesn't have anything to do with what you guys tried to pull last night, does it?" asked Trey Broussard, the basketball player whose attempted cut-in on Tom and Toni had started everything the night before.

"What'd we try to pull, Broussard?" Anthony said.

"You know," Broussard said.

"It's the Lord's day, Trey," Billy Bob said. "How about giving it a rest?"

Invoking the Almighty seemed to do the trick. They rode in silence for the rest of the trip.

Once they arrived, they joined the people trickling into the church. The boys followed Billy Bob into a pew at the very back corner.

After sitting in silence for a while, Jason said in a stage whisper loud enough to be heard eight rows ahead, "Hey, where's the bathroom?"

"Come on," Billy Bob said. "I'll show you."

They walked down the side aisle together, disappearing through a door beneath a statue of Mary holding the baby Jesus in her lap.

Ten minutes later, with the pews now crammed with congregants, Tom and Anthony pulled the same routine.

"Come on," Anthony said, hauling himself up. "Don't want you climbing over people once we start."

They walked out, Anthony nodding hello to various members of the congregation as they went, and Tom caught Zoey's eye across the center aisle.

After Anthony led them through a maze of back hallways, they walked out the side door, where they saw Robinson waiting a few yards away. Teel had already left with Jason and Billy Bob.

So much, Tom thought, for Jason's Catholic education.

· · · · ·

It was early enough when they got to the Biltmore that the place was half-empty.

Tom had mustered all his self-control to keep from telling Robinson during the car ride what had happened at the dance. He had settled for "You're gonna be amazed."

As they sat down, Robinson told the boys that brunch was his treat.

They all ordered—Tom asking for steak and eggs because he had skipped breakfast and was starving—and then Teel said, "So I understand you guys have got news."

They took turns, occasionally talking over one another. But as the story came out, Teel's and Robinson's eyes grew wider and wider. When the boys finally finished describing Mr. Gatch literally being carried out of the gym by the two football coaches, Teel leaned back in his seat and said softly, "Oh my God."

Robinson looked at the four of them and said, "Are you sure you're all only fourteen?"

"Actually I'll be fifteen next week," Billy Bob said.

Everyone laughed.

"The question is, what do we do next?" Robinson said.

Tom was baffled. "You write the story, right?" he said.

"It's not quite that simple," Teel said. "Before we write, we have to at least attempt to get Mr. Gatch to tell his side of it. We also have to talk to the four girls, and we have to try to get some of the other witnesses at the dance to go on the record."

"The girls will talk to you, I'm sure of that," Jason said. "Not so sure about anyone else."

"There must have been some kids recording the whole thing on their cell phones," Teel said.

Tom shook his head. "We weren't allowed to use cell phones at the dance, remember? I think they wanted to be sure everyone 'socialized.' Teachers and coaches had cell phones, and there were a couple of photographers and a videographer there to record all the merriment."

"We should find out who the videographer was and see what he might have," Teel said.

Tom shook his head again. "*She*, not *he*. It was Mrs. Gatch."

"Ouch," Robinson said. "Plus, chances are good Mr. Gatch will duck us when we try to get a comment from him. He may hide behind the 'It's a private school, and what happens on our campus stays private' excuse."

Tom was a little exasperated. "We *got* him," he said. "He did everything but call Anthony and me the *n*-word."

Teel made a palms-down sign.

"Easy, Tom," he said. "We've got him. He's going down. But we have to do it *right*. When we publish, the story has to be thorough, complete, and—above all—fair. That might take a little while, but we'll get it done."

"How long do you think it'll take?" Billy Bob asked.

"Hard to say," Teel said. "We're both going to have to get our editors to free us up for the next few days. That shouldn't be a problem. It could take a day; it could take a week."

"A week!" Tom said. "Do you know what the next week might be like for us? We're already supposed to be running in the mornings starting tomorrow. Now we're going to be outcasts with a lot of people at the school."

"Like we aren't already?" Jason asked.

"You'll also be a hero with some people," Robinson said.

"Not with any of our coaches," Anthony said.

"Look, if it gets really bad, you let us know," Teel said. "We can rattle their cages in some way if we have to."

"How?" they all asked.

Teel smiled. "I'm not sure, but we'll figure something out."

"That's encouraging," Billy Bob said.

Tom's stomach felt a little queasy. And it wasn't because he'd wolfed down his food. "This is going to be a long week," he said.

"You can bail if you want to," Robinson said. "We can probably take the story from here. You can call your parents and go home right now. No one would blame you."

Tom and Jason exchanged glances, and then all four boys looked at one another.

"Anyone want out?" Tom said.

There was silence.

Finally, Anthony spoke up. "Well, let's eat, drink, and be merry . . ."

"For tomorrow we die," Billy Bob said.

"The Bible quote again?" Jason asked.

"It's actually a combination of several different Bible quotes, and may not mean what you think it does," Billy Bob said.

"Perfect," Jason said. "My religious education continues."

28

THE FOUR BOYS HAD NO PROBLEMS GETTING BACK ON CAMPUS. WHEN the two cars pulled up to the guard gate, they got out and walked through without so much as a question being asked.

"Maybe they've closed down the school," Tom joked.

It certainly felt that way when they got back to the dorm. There was almost no one around—or so it seemed. Tom sent a text to Zoey, Hope, Heather, and Toni, asking if there was a good time when they could all meet.

It was Zoey who responded.

Bad idea. Being watched. Rumor: all of us prob expelled tmrw.

Tom couldn't just let that go. He dialed Zoey's number. She answered on the first ring.

"Expelled?" he said. "What are you talking about?"

"Let me call you right back," she said.

A moment later she rang him. "I didn't want to talk in front of my roommate," she said when Tom answered. "I'm in the common room now. No one around."

"Okay," Tom said. "Expelled?"

"Yes," she said firmly. "Ashley Chase says there's going to be some kind of conference call with the board of trustees tomorrow and they're going to talk about expelling the eight of us."

Thinking about the scheduled six o'clock run in the morning, Tom was tempted to joke, *If they're going to throw us out, why can't they do it before we run?*

Instead, he said, "Who is Ashley Chase and how does she know this?"

"She's a basketball player, and she's the student rep on the board."

Whoo boy, Tom thought, that was probably a reliable source.

"Well, she'll vote on our side anyway, won't she?" Tom said.

"The student rep doesn't have voting rights," Zoey said. "She's just there to give the students a voice."

"Sounds more like a token to me," Tom said.

"Hey, a white kid as a token," Zoey said, her voice lightening. "At least that's a little different." Then she grew serious again: "Tom, if I get thrown out of here, my parents will kill me."

It hadn't occurred to Tom that expulsion might *really* be on the table. Nor had he thought about the fact that some of the others might not be as cavalier about it as he and Jason were.

He felt a wave of guilt.

"Look," he said, "they can't throw us out without some kind

of appeal. Once the story is in the papers, it will be impossible for them to just toss us."

"Tom, it's a *private* school," she said. "They can pretty much do anything they want."

Then she asked about the meeting with Teel and Robinson. He started to fill her in, but she cut him off.

"Someone's walking in, I gotta go," she said. "We'll talk later."

Tom and Anthony went down to Jason and Billy Bob's room. Both were studying.

"You can concentrate?" Tom asked.

"Not really," Jason said. "But the week's going to be tough enough without falling behind in our schoolwork."

"Well," Tom said. "That might not be an issue."

He sat down and relayed what Zoey had told him.

. . . . .

On Monday morning, all four boys reported to the locker room at five minutes before six. Being late, they knew, would only give Coach Winston an excuse to make them even more miserable.

Coach Winston pretty much defined the phrase *strong, silent type*. Tom wasn't sure he'd ever heard his voice other than when he was giving players instructions during their pre-practice stretching drills.

He walked in the locker room door on the stroke of six. "All on time," he said. "Good. Let's get going."

If Coach Winston knew anything about what had happened at the dance on Saturday, he didn't show it. He simply told them to do five laps up and down the stadium steps, take a five-minute break for water, then do five more. When they began to tire and slowed down, he didn't yell, push, or cajole. It occurred to Tom that he wasn't any happier to be here than they were.

"Same time tomorrow," Coach Winston said when they finished.

With that, he turned and walked away, while they all stood, bent over, hands on knees, gasping for breath.

"Maybe," Billy Bob said, "getting expelled today wouldn't be such a bad thing."

They showered, dressed, and headed to breakfast. When they walked into the dining hall, they could hear a murmur. Juan del Potro and company had found a table for the new week in the far right-hand corner of the room.

"We figured the farther from the front you guys are, the better," Juan said when they all sat down.

"We heard the board's conference call is at eight," Jimmy Gomez added.

Apparently the word about the call had spread all over campus. A group of basketball players—all white—walked up to the table.

"Too bad this isn't dinner—you could call it the Last Supper," said Andy Staples, who Tom knew was a senior and the starting point guard.

"Staples, seriously, go climb back under your rock," Juan said.

"We just wanted to say bon voyage," John O'Shea said.

The basketball players all laughed at the hilarity of the comment and moved on.

"Don't worry about them," Jimmy said. "At least half the school is on your side. Maybe more."

The morning passed with no news—not even any whispers. Tom wondered if the information about a conference call had even been correct. During lunch, he sent Teel and Robinson texts updating them—even though there wasn't much to update.

Teel texted back a few minutes later:

Conference call done. Official statement coming this p.m. Board mtg next Sat a.m.

Tom showed the text to the others at the table.

"Sounds like they're really scared," Juan said.

"I think I know why," a voice said behind Tom.

He turned and saw Zoey standing behind him. She was apparently on her way out but had stopped at their table.

"Hiya," Billy Bob said. "What have you heard?"

"According to Ashley, the student rep, several board members were contacted by parents whose kids had called them after the dance to tell them what happened. They're upset—with Mr. Gatch, I mean, not with us—upset enough to go public, pull their kids from school, or both." Zoey smiled. "Apparently expulsion is off the table, at least for now."

"Guess that means we have to run again in the morning," Jason said.

"They've also decided that Mr. Gatch is going to be 'on vacation' this week. That's going to be the reason why he isn't available to talk to the media."

"We could have a media circus at the Fairfax game on Friday if Teel and Robinson get this written by then," Jason said.

"If TGP is putting out a statement, they'll have to write sooner rather than later," Billy Bob said.

Tom knew Billy Bob was right. That, he thought, was very good news.

· · · · ·

The statement came out at three o'clock, just as classes were ending. It seemed to spread instantly around the school because phones began buzzing as soon as people turned them on walking out of classrooms. Tom and Jason had been in their last period history class. Billy Bob had texted them the link.

"Here it is," Jason said. Even though his friend was already looking at it on his phone, Jason stopped in the crowded hallway and read it aloud.

" 'The board of trustees of the Thomas A. Gatch Prep School has been made aware of an incident that allegedly took place at the school dance on Saturday night. There have been varying reports on what occurred and whether there is a need for the small group of students involved in the incident to be disciplined for their actions. We consider this a private matter and will not be commenting further at this time.' "

Jason sighed.

Tom shook his head. "Total stonewall," he said. "They're actually trying to imply that the only ones who might have been out of line were students. No mention of Gatch at all."

Billy Bob, who had been in a math class, and Anthony, coming out of English, walked up.

"What do you think?" Tom asked.

"I think we better not be late for practice," Billy Bob said. "Last thing we want to do is give Bobo any excuse to nail us."

The four boys walked quickly across the campus to the locker room, where everyone was talking at once—or so it seemed. A number of guys greeted them as if nothing had happened; others clapped them on the back to indicate approval. Several glared but went no further since Anthony was more than willing to glare right back.

Coach Ingelsby walked in, which was unusual pre-practice. "Everyone in the meeting room in five minutes," he said.

"Can't be good," Anthony said.

"Maybe Bobo wants to present the game ball to Billy Bob that he forgot to give him Friday," Jason said.

"Certainly possible," Billy Bob said. "Slightly less possible than him naming Tom as the starting quarterback Friday, but still possible."

They all laughed. Gallows humor, Tom figured.

·　·　·　·　·

The entire coaching staff was at the front of the room when they all walked in. Coach Johnson stood at the lectern he used for postgame press conferences. When everyone was seated, Coach Johnson moved away from the lectern and stood in front of the room, silently looking at his players for a moment.

Something in Tom's gut told him this wasn't going to go well.

"Roddin, Anderson, Jefferson, and Ames, would you please come to the front of the room?" Coach Johnson said.

The four of them had been sitting near the back with the other freshmen. They looked at one another briefly, then walked to the front. Initially, they stood off to the side, not sure where their coach wanted them.

"Come on over here," Coach Johnson said. "Front and center."

They did as instructed. The other coaches moved off to the side.

"Now, since the four of you always seem to have all the answers to everything, whether it be what position you should be playing, where and when you should be talking to reporters, or the ins and outs of social behavior, please explain to me, to your coaches, and to your teammates—since clearly none of us is as smart as you are—exactly what you were trying to accomplish at the dance on Saturday night?"

Tom started to answer, but Billy Bob gave him a quick look that clearly meant, *Let me take this.*

Tom realized he was right. There was likely to be less hostility if the response came from one of the white players.

"Coach, I don't understand the question," Billy Bob said.

Coach Johnson smiled his most smarmy smile. "Of course you do, Anderson," he said. "You understand that the four of you decided to directly challenge the authorities of this school on Saturday, and you clearly did it to make some kind of clumsy point. So explain to us what the point was."

Billy Bob looked at his three friends. Tom could tell he was deciding whether to abandon the I-know-nothing approach and tell the truth. He hoped he would just go with the truth, because clearly they weren't going to escape from this room until the truth came out.

Billy Bob apparently agreed. "Actually, Coach, we were just trying to enjoy ourselves with our dates. Mr. Gatch seemed to object that there were four interracial couples on the dance floor."

"The founder of this school is a man who believes that TGP should be a place that honors tradition," Coach Johnson answered. "It's that simple. Do you have a problem with that?"

"Slavery was a tradition, too," Jason said, surprising Tom. "Discrimination and segregation, lynchings and cross burnings—those were traditions. Are you saying he wishes to honor those traditions?"

That seemed to rock Coach Johnson a little bit. He recovered quickly. "Roddin, you're missing the point—"

"No, sir," Billy Bob broke in. "*You're* missing the point. Or you missed the last century. I'm not sure which."

The silence in the room was deafening.

Coach Johnson stared at Billy Bob for a moment. "Among the four of you, you're the one I would have expected this from least, Anderson," he said.

"We all know why that is," Billy Bob said. "Everyone in this room knows it. But maybe you can just say it out loud, for the record?"

Coach Johnson ignored the comment and plowed on, apparently having decided that to continue the dialogue wasn't a good idea. "I'm not going to throw any of you off the team because, frankly, it's not fair to make your teammates suffer for your mistakes, and three of you four are potentially important to our future success on the field." He paused to let that sink in. "The four of you will continue to run on Monday, Tuesday, and Wednesday mornings until further notice. For now, I'd like you to apologize to your teammates, and then we'll put this behind us. We have an important and difficult game on Friday."

"Apologize for what?" Billy Bob said, an instant before Tom did.

"You know for what," Coach Johnson said.

Billy Bob looked at Tom, Jason, and Anthony. "Anyone feel the need to apologize?" he said.

Their response was silence. Billy Bob led the four of them back to their seats.

Coach Johnson wasn't quite finished.

"There will be consequences for this down the road," he said. "For *all* of it."

Tom had the final word. "I certainly hope so," he said.

The four of them sat down. Coach Johnson began talking about Friday's game against Fairfax Prep.

29

THE FIRST STORIES BROKE EARLY TUESDAY MORNING—ON THE
Virginian-Pilot and *Newport News Daily Press* websites and in
the print editions of the two newspapers. Both Tom Robinson
and David Teel had stepped out of their roles as columnists to
each write a story that appeared on the front page.

The two reporters had spent most of the late afternoon and
evening on Monday talking on the phone to the eight principal
students involved. Teel told Tom that they had been able to get
cell phone numbers for the assistant coaches. The only two who
had answered their phones were Mark Cruikshank and John
Gutekunst. Both said the same thing: We'd like to talk to you,
but if we talked for the record, we'd surely be fired. Maybe at a
later time.

The two stories, not surprisingly, were similar and even referred to "a joint investigation conducted by the *Press* and the
Pilot."

The basics of the stories were the same: Thomas A. Gatch, the founder of Thomas Gatch Prep, had apparently had a meltdown at the school's fall dance because there had been four interracial couples on the dance floor—the four boys being freshman football players. The stories included the school's statement and a quote from school spokesman Ed Seaman: "Mr. Gatch was upset with the behavior of a number of football players, who were not, he believed, treating female students with the proper respect." Mr. Seaman went on to say that Mr. Gatch was unavailable for comment because he had left on Sunday for a "previously scheduled" vacation.

All eight students involved in the incident were named and quoted as saying they had been "baffled" by Mr. Gatch's reaction to the fact that they were dancing with another.

Tom, with his steel-trap memory, provided a word-for-word quote: "Mr. Gatch told me and Anthony, 'We let you people into this school because you can perform on the field. That does *not* give you the right to interfere with the white girls from decent homes who come to this school.'"

Both writers used the quote as a jumping-off point to bring up Mr. Gatch's ties to David Duke and to the KKK in Louisiana. Both had tried to coax a response from Ed Seaman. "I think Mr. Gatch's record as an educator speaks for itself," was all the communications director had said.

Reading that line, Jason remembered the famous phrase he had heard repeatedly in *All the President's Men*: "It's a nondenial denial."

The quote from Gatch about "you people" staying away from

"white girls from decent homes" and the Duke/KKK references were what caused the uproar. The national media began storming Scottsville, only to be turned away at the school's entrance by a suddenly increased security force. In response, the cable and broadcast TV networks set up headquarters in an empty field a few yards from the gate and began doing standups with the gate—including shots of guards turning away news trucks—and the school in the background.

Since no one at the school was commenting—or being allowed to comment—Teel and Robinson became TV stars, telling how their suspicions had been aroused when they were told that a very talented freshman quarterback named Tom Jefferson, who happened to be African American, had been converted to wide receiver upon arriving at the school. They never said on-camera that it had been Tom, Jason, Billy Bob, and Anthony who had turned them on to the story, but it didn't take much reading between the lines to know.

The school and its leadership were under siege.

"Something's going to break sooner or later," Juan del Potro said at dinner Wednesday night. "They can't all hide in here or claim to be on vacation forever."

· · · · ·

Unfortunately for TGP—and fortunately for the media—the game on Friday was at Fairfax. There was no reason for the Lions to turn the national media away from their school, especially since they weren't involved in the story, except as the team that had the opportunity to end any postseason dreams the Patriots still had.

Down the road, Middleburg and Roanoke Christian were meeting. Both were 6–0 in conference play. TGP and Fairfax were both 5–1. The winner of their game would have a chance to tie for the conference title the final week of the season, when Middleburg would go to Fairfax and Roanoke Christian would play at TGP.

Someone could win the conference title outright, there could be a two-way tie, or there could be a three-way tie. In the event of a two-way tie, the winner of the head-to-head game would win the conference and advance to postseason. That was why the Patriots were ardently pulling for Roanoke to beat Middleburg. A three-way tie would be decided—oddly enough—by the drawing of lots. The three coaches involved would drive to Richmond, three slips of paper would be put in a hat, and whoever drew the number 1 would be the conference champion.

"Stupid way to decide who gets to play, isn't it?" Jason asked at breakfast on Thursday. "I mean, how do they decide who draws first?"

"Alphabetical," Tom said. "You're right, it's stupid, but how else can they do it? Every other tiebreaker will come up a tie— except maybe point-differential, and that's just about as dumb."

"We're a long way from worrying about any of that," Billy Bob put in.

That was certainly true. Remarkably, there had been very little backlash against the four of them—or against the four girls—since Monday's team meeting or since the story had first broken on Tuesday.

There had been follow-up stories with anonymous quotes from other football players, some backing them up, others saying that all four—particularly the two New Yorkers—had been headaches since day one.

Practice had proceeded the way it normally did: the coaches were no more snarky or nasty than in the past. No less, either.

There had been no discussion about how to deal with the media on Friday. The four boys were assuming they'd be told at some point that they were not to speak to any reporters after the game. Rumor had it that the school was going to pay a bevy of off-duty state troopers to provide security—security from the media—at the game.

"We'll deal with it when it happens, if it happens," Billy Bob said. "If we lose, this might be our last game anyway. There's no reason for them to keep us around if they haven't got a chance to win the conference title next week."

That much was true. All four sets of parents had volunteered to come to Fairfax, and all four boys had asked their parents not to come. Tom and Jason's parents—horrified—asked if the boys wanted to come home.

"Not *yet*," they had both said.

"The temptation to just get in the car and go home with them might be overwhelming," Tom said. "I want to ride this out to the end, one way or the other."

They all agreed.

They left for Fairfax early in the afternoon—the traffic, they knew, would be even worse there than around Middleburg— although there were no plans to go to a hotel this time around.

There was a place called P. J. Skiddoo's in Fairfax where they would stop to eat at around three o'clock. From there, they'd go to the stadium.

The rumors had been true about the extra police presence. In the restaurant, as they were finishing their meal, Coach Johnson stood up and explained it to the team.

"You all know that there's been a media frenzy around our school this week," he said. "Unfortunately, the Fairfax people turned down our request not to grant credentials to those organizations that have no interest in covering a football game. So we've brought some extra officers with us to protect you guys, and there will also be Fairfax County police—in uniform—to keep the buzzards away from you before and, more important, after the game. We will decide exactly who will and who won't talk to the media and under what circumstances after the game. Now let's flush all that and get ready to play."

The game was not much different from the games they had played against good teams all season. Fairfax took a quick 7–0 lead as the TGP offense continued to flounder. Then, early in the second quarter, a poorly thrown Ronnie Thompson pass led to a field goal for the Lions and a 10–0 lead.

Coach Cruikshank walked over to where Billy Bob, Jason, and Tom were standing.

"Warm up, Anderson," he said. "If we don't move the ball on this series and he won't make a change, I'll quit on the spot. I'm tired of these silly games."

It was, without question, the most fire or anger the mild-mannered quarterbacks coach had shown all season. Sure enough, the Patriots went three-and-out. As the punt team took the field, Tom saw Coach Cruikshank talking to Coach Johnson. It was clear the exchange was getting heated. Coach Ingelsby and Coach Gutekunst both joined the conversation. Finally, Coach Johnson threw his arms into the air and walked away.

Coach Cruikshank and Coach Gutekunst walked over to where Billy Bob was tossing a ball to Tom. Jason was watching.

"Next series, you're in," Coach Cruikshank said to Billy Bob.

Coach Gutekunst turned to Jason. "If they punt, you're the deep guy," he said. "We need a boost."

Billy Bob took the news with his usual humor. "Did you threaten to quit?" he asked.

"Almost," Coach Cruikshank said. He turned and walked away.

Jason wasn't nearly as calm. He had practiced as the deep returner a little but had never done it in a game.

"You okay?" Tom asked.

"Absolutely not," Jason answered. His heart was pounding.

The defense held, and Jason heard the dreaded words: "Punt return team, let's go."

The ball was on the 42-yard line. Based on their scouting report, the deep man was supposed to be forty yards from the line of scrimmage. That meant the 18. His mind going in a hundred different directions, Jason lined up at the 13.

Ray Solo, standing on the 25, turned and saw him. "Roddin," he said. "Move up five yards!"

Jason looked down, realized where he was, and moved up.

Thank goodness Solo was a good guy and wasn't sulking about suddenly becoming the short man.

The punt spiraled down, and Jason had to move up a couple of yards to field it. One defender—the gunner, who was always the first man downfield—was coming straight at him. He dodged him and started left. Solo got a crunching block on another man coming to meet him, and Jason was able to get to the outside. They pinned him to the sideline and pushed him out of bounds, but he had crossed midfield to the Fairfax 48.

"That's the way!" Coach Gutekunst said as they came to the sidelines. "Great block, Solo."

"Yeah," Jason said. "Great block."

"All for the cause," Solo said, smiling.

Whether it was Jason's return or Billy Bob's presence at quarterback—or both—the Patriots were a new team. The offensive line began blowing Fairfax off the line of scrimmage and, with Billy Bob carrying the ball himself several times, they quickly moved down the field, until Billy Bob scored from the 1—running into the left tackle hole directly behind Anthony—to make it 10–7.

A couple of minutes later, the defensive line broke through en masse and sacked Fairfax's quarterback Ben Fay. He fumbled at the 14-yard line, and that set up a touchdown in the final minute that gave TGP a 14–10 halftime lead.

Coach Johnson was clinical during the break, almost subdued. His message was pretty simple: Keep doing what you're doing. There was no talk about who would start the second half at quarterback. There was no need. If anyone but Billy Bob had been the starter, Coach Cruikshank might have led a full-scale revolution.

Billy Bob at quarterback made the Patriots a much better team, but Fairfax wasn't going to just fade away. The Lions returned the second-half kickoff to midfield and moved steadily down the field to score and take a 17–14 lead.

At that point, both offenses stalled. Fairfax was keying on Billy Bob's runs and had enough speed to keep the slotbacks from getting to the outside easily. They also put consistent pressure on him when he tried to pass.

One drive stalled when fullback Danny Nobis was stuffed on fourth-and-one at the Fairfax 41. Another was stopped when a rushed Billy Bob overthrew Wally Joyner and was intercepted. Each time the TGP defense dug in and kept the deficit at three.

Then, midway through the quarter, Fay, the Fairfax quarterback, faked to his fullback, rolled right, and threw a perfect, deep strike to his best wide receiver—Andrew Cantelupe, who had already caught at least half a dozen balls on the night. Cantelupe was well covered, but Fay laid the ball in to him perfectly and he pulled it in at the 12-yard line, rolling to the 9 as he fell.

The defense dug in again and kept Fairfax out of the end zone. The field goal kicker came in and drilled a twenty-four-yarder with 2:12 to go, making the lead 20–14.

"Well, old buddy, this is do-or-die," Tom said to Billy Bob. "No pressure, though, none at all."

"We'd probably be better off with you in there at this point," Billy Bob said. His confidence had been shaken a bit by the poor throw that had caused the interception.

Before Tom could think of an answer to that one, Coach Gutekunst raced up to Jason. "Hey, Roddin, ever return a kick-off?" he asked.

"No, sir," Jason said.

"Well, it's time. We need some field position. We need your speed."

"But, Coach, I don't know—"

"Nothing to it," Coach Gutekunst said. "See the ball into your arms like on a punt. It's easier, no one right on top of you. Just be aware the ball will be traveling end-over-end, not spiraling." He paused for a moment as if trying to be sure he wasn't forgetting anything. "The return's left," he said finally. "Catch the ball and start running left as fast as you can."

Jason stood rooted to the spot.

"Go!" Coach Gutekunst ordered.

Jason went.

Coach Gutekunst looked at Billy Bob and Tom. "What'd I hear you say, Jefferson? Do-or-die? Might as well go down swinging."

30

JASON JOGGED OUT TO JOIN THE KICKOFF RETURN TEAM. IF ANYONE WAS surprised to see him, they didn't show it. Again, Ray Solo was there to help him out.

"Stand on about the five," he said. "That's where he's been kicking it."

He went to take the up-position.

Jason stood on the 5-yard line taking deep breaths. He heard the referee's whistle behind him, signaling the kicker to put the ball into play.

A moment later, the ball was coming down to him, end-over-end, just as Coach Gutekunst had explained. He moved back a yard and slightly to his right. The ball fell into his arms—and he dropped it.

"Oh my God!" he heard himself say aloud. Desperately, he reached down for the ball and just managed to scoop it up before a tackler took off airborne, clearly going for the ball. That gave Jason a split second to gather his wits.

Run left, he told himself.

The blocking wall had formed in spite of his drop and he managed to get to the 20 untouched. Someone dove at his feet. He dodged him, swerved farther left and made it to the outside. A couple more blocks and he was at the 35. He tried to cut back inside, and someone plowed him down from behind. Still, he had gotten the ball to the 39.

"Scared the living daylight out of me when you dropped the ball," Coach Gutekunst said as he came to the sideline, batting him on the head.

"How do you think I felt?" Jason said. He was smiling, as much because he'd survived as because he'd had a decent run-back.

"Well," Tom said, coming up to stand next to him as Jason pulled his helmet off, "now it's up to your roomie."

The clock was under two minutes and TGP had two time-outs left. Billy Bob twice threw quick out passes to Terrell Davidson, the fastest man on the field for TGP. Respecting his speed, the defenders were playing back on him. Davidson picked up eight yards on the first pass, eleven on the second. But he couldn't get out-of-bounds the second time, and TGP had to spend a time-out with the ball on the Fairfax 42. There was 1:27 left.

Billy Bob came to the sideline. He was met there by Coaches Ingelsby and Cruikshank. Coach Johnson stood to the side, listening. Tom inched up so he could hear the conversation. Jason followed.

"Remember, you've only got the one time-out left," Coach Ingelsby said. "If you have to, spike the ball rather than call time."

Billy Bob nodded. This was obvious stuff.

"What do you think, Mark?" Ingelsby said, surprising Tom because he'd never heard him defer to the quarterbacks coach that way.

"We gotta go over the middle," Cruikshank said. "There's time. Send Davidson deep as a decoy, and circle one of the slots into the seam."

Ingelsby nodded, put his arm on Billy Bob's shoulder, and called two plays.

Billy Bob trotted back. He called the play, brought the team to the line, took the snap, and dropped quickly, only three steps because Fairfax's three-man rush was giving TGP trouble on the right side. Anthony was a rock on the left, but right tackle Bart Blessing was struggling.

Billy Bob stepped away from the rush and found Emmet Foley—younger brother of center Conor Foley—over the middle. He led him just a bit too much, but Foley, wide open, dove and caught the ball, rolling to the 26.

The clock was running. The coaches were all screaming at Billy Bob to spike the ball. It took several seconds to get everyone lined up; by the time Billy Bob took the snap and spiked the ball, the clock was down to thirty-one seconds.

Billy Bob looked to the sideline. Coach Ingelsby simply

screamed "White!" which meant to run the second play they'd decided on during the time-out. This time, Foley was also a decoy, running the same pattern down the seam. Danny Nobis, the fullback, delayed a moment, then circled out of the backfield and caught a pass underneath from Billy Bob. He began sprinting on an angle—in the direction of the goal line and the sideline.

He didn't make either, pulled down at the 9, a few yards from the sideline. Tom glanced at the clock. The coaches were hysterically screaming at Billy Bob to spike the ball again.

"There isn't time!" Tom said. "He's got to use the time-out."

The Fairfax players were taking their time to get back across the line of scrimmage, which was the right thing to do. The clock rolled under ten seconds, and they still weren't lined up.

"Time!" Billy Bob screamed with six ticks left.

He walked to the sideline.

"Why didn't you spike it?" Coach Johnson demanded.

"Coach, the clock was going to run out—"

"Forget that," Coach Cruikshank said. "We've got one play left."

The three coaches began debating what play to call. Finally, Tom heard Billy Bob interject.

"Fullback draw," was all he said.

All three coaches looked at him as if he had said, *ET phone home.*

"It's wide open," Billy Bob continued. "We split everybody wide as if we're going for an end-zone lob. I start back, Nobis acts like he's blocking, and I slip him the ball."

"If he doesn't score, the clock's going to run out," Ingelsby said.

"It's going to run out regardless of what we call, Coach," Billy Bob said.

Coach Cruikshank jumped in. "I like it," he said. "I think it's our best chance."

There was no time left to debate further. The officials had started the play clock, which was under twenty seconds. Billy Bob sprinted back to the huddle and made the call, and they came to the line. The play clock was at five.

Conor Foley snapped the ball with one second on the play clock. Billy Bob started to drop, then slipped the ball to Nobis. He'd been right. There was *no one* in the middle of the field. Nobis was untouched until he got to the 2, when defenders frantically coming from the outside closed on him. He put his head down and used his 230 pounds to bull the final six feet. He cleared the goal line with a foot to spare.

The officials raced in, looked at one another for a moment, then threw their arms into the air, signaling touchdown. The clock was at 0:00. Nick Stover came in for the extra point—the most nerve-racking extra point Tom had ever witnessed—and calmly kicked the ball through the uprights. The game was over. TGP had won, 21–20.

Tom wasn't exactly sure why he felt so happy, after all he'd—again—contributed nothing. Maybe he was just happy for his pals: Jason, Billy Bob, and Anthony had all played key roles in the stunning win.

Danny Nobis was being mobbed, but Tom and Jason headed straight for Billy Bob.

"What a genius call," Tom said.

"*You* should coach this team," Jason said.

Billy Bob smiled wearily. "If I did," he said, putting an arm around Tom, "you'd be the quarterback."

They all laughed, went to shake hands with the crushed Fairfax players, and wondered what would happen next.

. . . . .

They found out quickly. Coach Johnson had little to say in the locker room. He talked about the great comeback and the poise "shown by everyone" during the last drive. He gave game balls to all three linebackers and to Danny Nobis. Hardly a surprise at this point. *That* was it on the game.

Then he gave the players their postgame instructions: Only he and Nobis would speak to the media. Everyone else was to shower and be on the bus in thirty minutes. Then he added, "Anderson, I'd like to see you and your three buddies in the coach's office right now."

No one had to ask which three buddies he was referring to.

"Think he's going to apologize?" Billy Bob said, grinning, as they headed to the front of the room, where they knew there was a single office for the visiting coach.

Coach Johnson was sitting in a chair behind the desk in the small office when they walked in. It was barely big enough for all of them to squeeze through the door. There were two chairs on the other side of the desk, but Coach Johnson didn't offer anyone the chance to sit down.

"I just want to make it clear to all four of you what's going to happen tonight and going forward," he said, barely looking up at them. "First, you're going to be escorted, one by one, to the bus by the Fairfax County officers—who are in uniform, so no one will get confused and think they're *not* cops.

"Anyone from the media tries to get close to you or ask you a question, you just say, 'No comment,' and keep moving. That doesn't mean you say, 'I can't talk' or 'Coach says I can't talk.' You say, 'No comment.' You say anything other than that, the cops will report back to me and you'll run at five tomorrow and on Sunday—at least the two of you who don't go to church anyway. We'll be home after midnight, so that'll leave you maybe four hours to sleep before you run.

"*If* any of this leaks to your two newspaper buddies, you'll be running in the mornings and be doing up-downs in the afternoon until you puke.

"Roanoke Christian just beat Middleburg, thirty-eight to thirty-one, so we can win or at least tie for the championship next week. If I didn't need three of you to win that game, you'd be long gone. Jefferson, you're completely worthless, but I know if I throw you off the team you'll start screaming racism, so you'll be kept around until season's end, too."

"And then what happens?" Tom said.

"Honestly, I don't know and I don't care," Coach Johnson answered. "The stories you've heard are true. I'm going to Alabama.

Everything is done except actually signing the contract, which can't happen until Coach Daboll signs his new contract."

"Where's he going?" Billy Bob asked, even though it really didn't matter to any of them.

"None of your business, Anderson," Coach Johnson said. "I made a terrible mistake when I recruited you two." He pointed at Tom and Jason. "I should have known New York kids would be a couple of know-it-alls. But your dad's a cop, Roddin; I thought you'd have some respect for authority.

"So I got that wrong, and poor Tom Gatch is paying the price. He can't sell the school now or go to Alabama with me because of all this Klan stuff you've managed to sell people. I have no idea what will happen to the school down the road or to the football team." He smiled and leaned forward. "Fortunately, it's not my problem. It probably won't even be your problem. I'm guessing that, one way or the other, you won't be back next semester." He looked down at his phone as if something very important had just popped up. "Have to go meet with the media," he said. "That's all."

The boys turned to leave, only Billy Bob lingering. "By the way, you're welcome," he said.

"For what?" Coach Johnson asked.

"For saving your butt—again—tonight."

They all walked out—smiling in spite of themselves.

. . . . .

The decision not to defy Coach Johnson on the way to the bus was a fairly easy one.

"We'd accomplish nothing," Tom said. "The cops won't let us talk anyway, and we'd just be hurting ourselves. Let's hold our fire for now."

After getting out of the shower, Tom had gotten a text from Teel saying that Coach Johnson was being peppered with questions about the dance but was using the "I wasn't there" and "I have complete faith in Tom Gatch" dodges to every question.

A swarm of media was waiting as they exited. Tom was the lucky one—almost no one wanted to talk to him. It took four cops—two Fairfax officers and two state troopers—to get Billy Bob to the bus.

Once aboard, they headed to the back rows only to find Coach Ingelsby sitting there.

"You boys don't mind some company, do you?" he said with his ever-present sneer.

So much for discussing what to do next on the trip home.

Since there was no point in talking or texting, Tom tried to sleep. It didn't work. His mind was churning. He was happy for his three friends because they'd all played a key role in winning the game, but part of him wished they had lost, if only to get the whole mess over with one way or the other. Now they had at least one more important game to play, so they'd have to put up with Coach Johnson and drones like Coach Ingelsby for another week.

"What now?" Anthony asked as they all walked wearily from the bus back to the dorm. It was almost one o'clock in the morning.

"I honestly don't know," Tom said. "Gatch can't stay on vacation forever, can he?"

"At least it looks like we screwed up his sale of the school," Jason said.

"Temporarily probably," Billy Bob said. "Bad guys always figure a way out of trouble."

"Good point," Tom said. "Alex Rodriguez got a standing ovation in his last at-bat at Yankee Stadium."

"Different kind of bad guy," Jason said.

"True," Tom said. "But Donald Trump got elected president."

There was no real answer for that, so they walked silently to their rooms and fell into bed. Tom's last thought before he fell asleep was the same one he'd had for more than two months in response to so many of the things that had happened at TGP: *How in the world did we get ourselves into this?* At least, as Coach Johnson had pointed out, it was almost over.

31

TOM AND ANTHONY BOTH SLEPT IN THE NEXT MORNING, CHOOSING shut-eye over breakfast. Shortly after ten o'clock, they were awakened by someone banging on their door.

"Did you lock it?" Tom said, looking wearily at Anthony.

"Yeah," Anthony said. "Friday night, after a game, all that's been going on, I thought some of the guys might try to mess with us."

Tom nodded. "Then you open it," he said.

"Hey," a voice came from the other side of the door. "Wake up in there!"

It was Jason.

Anthony pulled himself up and opened the door. Jason and Billy Bob, both in sweats, were standing there. Tom guessed they hadn't been up for long either.

"What in the world is so important?" Anthony said as Jason and Billy Bob pushed past him into the room.

"This," Billy Bob said, holding up his phone. "It's a text from Coach Cruikshank. He says he's on his way over here to see us and it's important. I told him to come here because I figured you guys would still be sleeping."

"What could possibly be so important?" Tom asked.

"Maybe Bobo's finally given in and is going to start you"—Anthony pointed at Billy Bob—"on Friday."

Billy Bob shook his head. "No. He wouldn't come racing over here for that. It has to be something bigger than that."

"Maybe Bobo's not even sticking around for the last game," Jason said.

"Nah, he wants the shot at the title," Tom said. "You heard him last night."

"Even if he did leave, we'd just get Ingelsby," Anthony pointed out.

Fortunately, they didn't have to guess for long at what the news might be. Coach Cruikshank knocked on the door less than five minutes later.

"It's open," Tom said.

Coach Cruikshank pushed the door open and walked in. His face was flushed and he appeared to be out of breath. He was carrying a travel cup of coffee.

"Shouldn't be drinking this," he said. "Fourth cup. But I needed it to get going this morning."

"You okay, Coach?" Billy Bob asked. He got up to offer him his chair, but Coach Cruikshank waved him off and sat on the edge of Tom's bed.

"I'm fine," he said, taking a sip of the coffee. "But I thought you guys needed to know right away what's going on. I know you and those two reporters have been going after Mr. Gatch, and I know what you believe about Coach Johnson."

"You mean, what we believe isn't true?" Billy Bob asked.

Coach Cruikshank held up a hand. "Of course it's true. It's all true. But I need you to listen to something and then we can talk."

He pulled his cell phone from his pocket, pressed several buttons, and then put the phone on Tom's desk.

"We had a coaches' meeting this morning," he said. "We never meet on Saturday, but Coach Johnson told us to all be in his office at eight-thirty. Except it wasn't *all* of us. It was just the white coaches. Once I saw that, I thought it might be a good idea to tape the meeting. Something was clearly up. So I excused myself for a second to get more coffee, turned on the recorder on my phone, then just put it on top of my notepad like I normally do during meetings."

The boys were rapt now.

"I think it's pretty self-explanatory."

He pressed the Play button and sat back on the bed. Loud and clear, Coach Johnson's voice boomed through the room.

"I'm pretty sure y'all know why we're here this morning. Sorry to wake you, but this has to be dealt with right away and without our darker-skinned colleagues."

There was a pause, and for a panicked second Tom wondered if the recording had somehow cut off at that moment. It hadn't.

"I talked to Gatch a little while ago. The board's meeting at

two o'clock this afternoon. He'll be back for the meeting. It's already been decided what we're gonna do."

Another pause, this one a little bit longer.

"I'm gonna hold a press conference on Monday afternoon before practice to announce I'm goin' to leave at the end of the season. I can't actually say I'm takin' the Alabama coordinator's job because Daboll hasn't announced where he's gonna be goin' yet. But I'll say that there have been stories written about my future and I'm not prepared to deny any of them, and that I'm very excited about what the future holds."

Another pause. This one the longest of all.

"And then . . . Gatch is gonna introduce my successor. He's gonna say he's consulted with me, with all the coaches, and with the board of trustees and that there's no doubt the right man for the job is . . . Marco Thurman."

The four boys all looked at one another in shock. Marco Thurman, the offensive line coach? The *black* offensive line coach?

They heard a cacophony of raised voices on the recording, and then Coach Ingelsby's voice rose above the others.

"Hang on, Bobo! You said the job was mine."

"It was, Don, you know that," Bobo's voice answered. *"But things have changed. Tom Gatch is fighting for his life right now, and this is probably the only way to save the school and the football program."*

Ingelsby responded, *"Well, I sure as hell am not working for a goddamn . . ."*

And then he said it, the *n*-word. It hit like an electric shock.

"Me neither," another voice said.

"That's Coach Reilly," Coach Cruikshank said, in case they were wondering.

No surprise there.

Coach Johnson began speaking again. *"Look, fellas, I don't blame you one bit. But we all have to make sacrifices in today's world. Bad enough we had to put up with a black president in this country. Hell, bad enough I'll have to work with black quarterbacks at Alabama. Every man has his price, and Coach Saban is going to meet mine . . . Don, Terry, I will help you find jobs. Anyone else who feels the same, let me know and I'll try to help."*

"I'm fine with it," a voice Tom recognized as Coach Gutekunst's said. *"I think Marco's a fine coach and a better man. I'd be proud to work for him."*

"Not surprised to hear you say that, Rich," Coach Johnson said. *"You and Mark have always had your notions. I assume you're fine with it, too, right, Mark?"*

"Absolutely, Coach."

"Well, then, there's one more thing you'll like. We're also moving the Jefferson kid to quarterback this week. He'll back Anderson and Thompson up on Friday. That way it'll be tough for anyone to say I won't play a black quarterback."

"I don't think making a black kid your third-string quarterback is going to fool people," they all heard Coach Cruikshank say on the tape.

"Mark, did I ask you what you thought?" Bobo said. *"You coach him up in case—God forbid—we need him."*

"Why would we need him?" Coach Ingelsby said.

"Because something could happen to Anderson and, honestly, I

don't know how long we could afford to leave Thompson in the game if it came to that. I've pushed that envelope as far as I can. Jefferson does have some talent—long as we call plays that don't require any deep thinking."

"He's a straight-A student, Coach," Cruikshank said.

"I couldn't care less," Coach Johnson said. "They can study and get by. It's thinking they have trouble with."

"What do we say if someone asks why he was moved to quarter-back?" Coach Gutekunst asked.

"Or why he wasn't there in the first place?" Coach Cruikshank added.

"Under normal circumstances, Gatch wouldn't let me play a black boy at quarterback, even if I wanted to. Which I don't. But these are not normal circumstances. We'll say he'd shown some talent in seven-on-seven there and we needed some depth at the position this week because Thompson got banged up at Fairfax and we already lost Dixon in preseason. We thought he'd have a better chance to contribute as a receiver because of his speed."

"He's got no speed, Coach," Cruikshank said.

"Okay then, because Bobo Johnson is color-blind when it comes to football."

There was some laughter in response to that line. Coach Cruikshank turned the recording off.

There was silence in the room for a moment. It was the coach who spoke first. "You guys got your smoking gun on Mr. Gatch last week. This is your smoking gun on Coach Johnson."

Tom stood and began to pace, which he did when he was nervous and wound up. "Question is, what do we do with it?"

he said. "Do we nail him with it now, or do we wait until after the game on Friday?"

"Personally, I'd like to play the game on Friday," Billy Bob said, and then turned to Tom. "Especially with you as my backup."

"I'm not your backup, I'm third string."

They thought about it some more.

It was Jason who spoke next. "Here's what we do," he said. "Let Coach Johnson have his press conference on Monday. They'll obviously let all the media onto campus for that. We e-mail this file to Teel and Robinson and tell them *not* to use it before Monday. As soon as the press conference is over and Coach Thurman's been named coach, they play it for everybody there. Hold their own impromptu press conference." He paused, then added, "That will blow them all up at once."

"Only problem is, Coach Johnson will know that I was the one who recorded him," Cruikshank said. "He'll fire me on the spot."

"No he won't," Billy Bob said.

"Why not?" Coach Cruikshank said.

"Because he won't have a job. They'll *have* to fire him immediately. There's no way to spin this. This gun's not smoking; it's still firing."

Once Billy Bob's words sank in, the boys and Coach Cruikshank decided not to take any chances. The coach e-mailed the voice recording to all four of them, and the boys decided to leave the dorm before taking any further action. The coach left first, and a few minutes later the boys followed. Once they'd crossed the campus, Jason and Tom called Teel and Robinson and told them the latest. Then they e-mailed *them* the recording.

· · · · ·

After that, it became a waiting game. Over the weekend and in classes on Monday morning, there were congratulations from some students and the ongoing glares from others. At lunchtime on Monday, everyone on the football team received a text:

Mandatory: At end of classes today, come to team meeting room; press conference to begin at 3:10. Please stand in back; media will take up seats. Start of practice delayed until 4:00. BIG NEWS!

The dining hall was immediately filled with speculation about what the big announcement could be. Most of the football players seemed to be in agreement: Coach Johnson was going to take the job at Alabama at season's end and Coach Ingelsby would be his replacement.

Tom, Jason, Billy Bob, and Anthony listened in silence as people ran various theories by them. They played dumb. Their afternoon classes seemed to last forever.

Finally, they followed the crowd of players down the hall from the locker room to the meeting room, everyone buzzing in anticipation.

Only one person, Ronnie Thompson, made any sort of

derogatory comment. "If whatever this is happened because of you four, you better be ready to run," he said.

Anthony looked like he was about to say something, but Tom grabbed his shoulder. No sense starting anything right now.

The room was absolutely packed. A line of TV cameras perched on a platform at the back of the room. Every seat, as predicted, was taken. Tom spotted Teel and Robinson sitting near the front, a row apart, both on the aisle.

At the front of the room, on either side of the riser, several campus security guards stood, apparently there to ensure that no one tried to approach the participants once the press conference was over.

The players spread out, finding places in the back or along the walls on either side of the room.

"I hope nobody calls the fire marshal," Jason whispered to Tom.

At 3:15, five minutes late, a side door at the front of the room opened and five men walked through it: Tom Gatch, Coaches Johnson and Thurman, Ed Seaman, and someone Tom didn't recognize. Seaman walked to the podium; the others took seats alongside.

Seaman introduced himself, thanked everyone for coming, and then introduced the panel, as he called it. The fifth man, it turned out, was Harrison Ballard III, chairman of the board of trustees.

Seaman then turned the podium over to Coach James "Bobo" Johnson.

Tom heard a smattering of applause from some of the players

as Coach Johnson approached the podium and, from the front row, some more applause. He noticed that none of the people in the very front row were holding digital recorders or notebook computers.

"Rest of the board down there," Billy Bob said softly, apparently reading Tom's mind.

Coach Johnson launched into a lengthy speech about how much TGP meant to him, about how proud he had been to be its head football coach, and about how much his friendship with Tom Gatch also meant to him. Finally, after a couple more minutes of filibustering, he came to the point: "At season's end, I'll be leaving this great school. I've been offered another opportunity, one I can't talk about today, but one that is simply too challenging to turn my back on. I can assure you that, even though I won't be physically present at TGP anymore, my heart will always beat within these walls."

Cameras flashed, reporters pecked at their notebooks, and pockets of applause sounded in the room.

"I'm going to be sick," Billy Bob said.

The head coach went on about his great staff and then said, finally, "There's not a man coaching here right now who isn't capable of carrying on the Gatch football tradition. But when Mr. Gatch and I sat down and talked, there was one man we kept coming back to as our choice to succeed me. I will now turn it over to Mr. Gatch to introduce that man."

More applause came from players and board members as Gatch walked up and hugged his soon-to-be-former coach.

"Thank you, Coach Johnson, from the bottom of my heart

for everything you've meant to this school. You do, however, have one last job to complete, and that's leading us to a win on Friday so that we can go on to take the state championship!"

Now there was *lots* of applause from around the room.

"Bet the media didn't know they'd been invited to a pep rally," Jason said.

Mr. Gatch waited for the applause to die before plowing on. "It's been a long week," he said, smiling. "A lot of rumors, virtually all of them completely false. A lot of strife and heartache. But that's not what today is about. Today, it is my honor to tell you that our new football coach, effective as soon as we win the state championship will be"—he paused for effect—"a remarkable man whom I consider a good friend"—another pause—"Marco Thurman!"

There was something of a gasp around the room. Then some claps, then some more claps. The offensive linemen were whooping happily. Tom looked around and noticed that neither Coach Ingelsby nor Coach Reilly was in the room. They had slipped out, apparently, as soon as Coach Johnson had finished talking.

Coach Thurman stood up and shook hands with the others on the platform. He approached Mr. Gatch, who hugged him awkwardly—at least in part because Coach Thurman, at six foot six, towered over him. The circumstances certainly played a role in the awkwardness, too.

"You surprised he took it?" Tom whispered to Anthony. "He's gotta know what this is about, right?"

Anthony shrugged. "Not sure, to be honest."

Coach Thurman nodded at the applause, then smiled. "I'm

not much of a talker," he said. "And this should be Coach Johnson's day. So let me just say that I look forward to having the chance to lead the young men in this room and, once the season's over, I'll have a lot more to say to all of you. For now, we've got to get to practice today. We have a big game to get ready for on Friday." He then stepped aside.

Mr. Seaman came back to the podium. "As Coach Thurman mentioned, the players and coaches have practice, so they'll be leaving right away. Mr. Gatch has asked that any questions specific to the school be directed to me."

Players and coaches stood to leave, the security people making their presence between the media and those who had spoken very evident. Tom saw David Teel jump to his feet and say something he couldn't hear that got Coach Johnson's attention. Quickly, Tom walked down the side of the room, against the flow of the crowd, to get within earshot of the two men. His three friends followed.

"You can stay and listen to this or not," Tom heard Teel say. "But you might want to get your side on the record."

"I've got practice right now," Coach Johnson said.

"The recording is eight minutes long," Teel said. "I'm playing it starting in five, one way or the other."

Tom saw a look of panic cross Coach Johnson's face.

Game on, Tom thought. *Game on.*

32

TEEL WAITED UNTIL MOST OF THE PLAYERS HAD EXITED. HE INVITED THE board members to stay. Several stalked out; a couple of others kept their seats. Tom Robinson had been moving through the media crowd, telling them they might want to wait a minute before packing up their gear.

Tom noticed that Coach Thurman had walked off the podium and then had gone to the side of the room instead of out the door with Mr. Gatch and the security retinue. Coach Cruikshank and Coach Gutekunst had also stayed.

Coach Johnson stalked out, but returned a minute later—one security officer by his side. He sat down in one of the chairs on the podium.

Coach Thurman walked up to where Tom, Anthony, Jason, and Billy Bob were standing. No one had said anything to the four of them to indicate that they couldn't stay. Several other players also lingered, sensing something was up.

"I know you've heard the recording, too," Coach Thurman said quietly. "This should be interesting."

Teel was now standing in front of the platform, addressing the room. He was holding a digital recorder in his hand.

"This is a recording that was made two days ago during a meeting in Coach Johnson's office that was received via e-mail by myself and by Tom Robinson of the *Virginian-Pilot*. The stories we've written will go up on our papers' websites at four o'clock—that's fifteen minutes from now. We think the words on this recording are self-explanatory."

Tom looked at Coach Johnson. He was—appropriately enough, Tom thought—as white as a ghost.

Teel walked to the podium, unimpeded by security, and put the recorder on top of it next to the microphone, asked for complete quiet, and turned on the machine.

For the next eight minutes it felt to Tom as if no one in the room was breathing. A couple of times he thought Coach Johnson was going to bolt for the door. His body went almost rigid as his own words were played back to him.

When it was over, nobody moved. Or so it seemed.

Finally, Teel shut off the recorder, turned to Coach Johnson and said, "Any comment?"

Coach Johnson stared straight ahead for a moment. "That tape is out of context," he said, grasping at the most familiar straw available.

"How so?" Teel asked. "What is missing that will make the facts any different?"

Coach Johnson stood, pointing a finger at Tom, Anthony, Jason, and Billy Bob.

"The four of you did this!" he roared. Then he seemed to remember where he was. "I have to go get ready for practice," he said, stalking from the room through the side door with the security officer trailing in his wake.

"Come on, let's go," Coach Thurman said. "We'll never get to practice if the media stops us right now. We can talk to them afterward."

They sprinted to the back of the room and out the door, a few people shouting questions in their direction.

"Now what?" Tom asked once they were out of the room and into the locker room, which was off-limits to the media.

"Now you boys go get dressed for practice," Coach Thurman said. "We have a game to get ready for, and I suspect we're going to be doing it without several members of the coaching staff."

. . . . .

Coach Thurman was right.

Coach Winston and the two captains already had the team stretching when the four freshmen—and the others who had hung around to hear the tape—arrived. No one said anything.

There was no sign of either Bobo Johnson, Don Ingelsby, or Terry Reilly. Coach Thurman wasn't there either. Finally, just as they were wrapping up their stretching and Tom was beginning to wonder who was going to run practice, Coach Thurman and Bill Stiller, the athletic director, came walking onto the field. Harrison Ballard III, the board chairman, who had never opened his mouth during the press conference, was with them, too.

As soon as they got to the TGP logo at midfield, Coach Thurman blew his whistle. Confusion followed. Some players reacted the same way to Coach Thurman's whistle as to Coach Johnson's whistle, moving right away to stand in a circle around him. Others traded glances as if unsure what to do next. Some moved slowly to the circle; others stood talking quietly among themselves as if deciding what to do.

"If you want to know what's going on, I'd suggest you all get over here," Coach Thurman called, his voice booming around the empty stadium.

The stragglers walked over and joined their teammates.

"I know you're all confused and probably a little upset," Coach Thurman said once he was surrounded by the entire team and the remaining coaches. "I don't blame you. This has all happened very fast.

"Let me turn this over to Mr. Ballard and Mr. Stiller, who will update you."

Stiller nodded at Thurman and, in a shaky voice, said, "Thank you, Coach." He paused and took a deep breath. He was struggling to keep his composure.

"As of ten minutes ago," he finally said, "Coach James Johnson is no longer TGP's head football coach."

A number of players gasped and a couple cried out, "No, that's not true!"

Stiller plowed on. "At the request of the board of trustees, he is submitting his letter of resignation, effective immediately. Coach Ingelsby and Coach Reilly are also resigning, effective immediately."

Now everyone was silent.

"I know a handful of you were in the room after the press conference, so you know what took place. Those of you who don't know will find out soon—it will be all over the Internet and social media when practice is over. Suffice it to say, Coach Johnson has made some comments that make it impossible for him to continue as coach." He paused again. "This is a tragic turn of events for all of us."

Tom almost laughed out loud at that one. *Tragic?* he thought. *A racist football coach being forced to resign is a tragedy?* He started to whisper something to Jason but resisted.

"I have asked Coach Thurman to take over as your head coach for the rest of the season. Coach Cruikshank will double as offensive coordinator and quarterbacks coach, and Coach Williams"—he looked at slotbacks coach Mo Williams—"will double with the slots and the wide receivers. I have complete faith in them and in you."

Mr. Stiller was near tears. He turned to walk away. Mr. Ballard had never said a word.

"Does he talk," Jason asked, "or just walk around in an expensive suit?"

In a barely audible voice, Coach Thurman thanked the two men as they exited. Then he returned to normal.

"I know this is traumatizing for some of you and it's

shocking for all of us," he said. "But we have the biggest game of the season to play Friday. We're off to a late start today, but this time of year, length of practice isn't as important as quality of practice. So let's get started. Report to your coaches."

Tom wasn't sure where he was supposed to go.

Coach Cruikshank solved that quickly. "Jefferson!" he shouted. "Over here with the other quarterbacks."

Ronnie Thompson was glaring daggers at him as he jogged over to join the quarterback group. Jason was a step behind him until they heard Coach Williams's voice.

"Roddin!" he said. "Over here, with the other receivers."

Tom saw Jason's face break into a wide grin.

He looked at Tom. "Well," he said, "better very late than very never."

Looking as if he'd just won the lottery twice, he went to join the receivers. Tom felt the happiest he'd been since he'd stopped for dinner with his dad and his best friend at the Aberdeen Barn on the way down from New York.

· · · · ·

Seven players quit the team that night. Led by Ronnie Thompson, they put out a statement via social media:

We came to TGP to play for Coach Johnson, not for someone who, with all due respect, has never been a head coach. We understand mistakes were made, but we

believe Coach Johnson's forced resignation was an over-reaction to media pressure by the TGP board of trustees.

They went on to say that they intended to finish the semester academically but—none of them being seniors—they would transfer to play football someplace else the following fall.

Six seniors also put out a statement saying they, too, were unhappy with the change in team leadership but because they were so close to the end of their high school football careers and to graduation, they would remain in school and on the team—and would dedicate Friday's game to Coach Johnson.

Tom was looking over Jason's shoulder at the computer that night, reading the seniors' statement.

"Did Coach Johnson die?" he asked, reading the final line.

"Sort of," Jason said.

Tom and Anthony had come downstairs to Jason and Billy Bob's room to follow all the various reactions. Different kids were in and out, many to offer congratulations, others just checking to make sure they were all okay after the events of the afternoon.

The Internet had gone completely wild with the story, as had national TV. ESPN had devoted an *Outside the Lines* show to the question "Can it be possible that race is still such a huge issue in athletics today?"

The answer, of course, was yes. On MSNBC, Rachel Maddow—whom Tom's and Jason's parents both watched every night—devoted her whole show to the same question. John Thompson Jr., the former Georgetown basketball coach, who had been the first African American to coach a team to the NCAA championship, was asked: "Thirty-three years after you won your title, how can this still be going on?"

Thompson smiled and said, "Because racism didn't die when we won the championship, just as it didn't die when Barack Obama was elected president. Sometimes it goes into hiding in today's world, but it is very much alive."

. . . . .

"Do we have any chance to win on Friday?" Anthony asked at one point. "Four of the guys who quit were starters. And who knows how those six seniors will play."

"They're dedicating the game to Coach Johnson," Billy Bob said. "They'll play."

The one question unanswered anywhere was what had become of Mr. Gatch. He had apparently disappeared after the press conference, and no one had seen or heard a word from him since. All the official statements from the board of trustees were coming from Harrison Ballard—who could apparently release statements as long as they didn't involve actually speaking, or answering questions.

"I'm gonna make a prediction," Billy Bob said. "Mr. Gatch has run for the hills. We won't see him again."

"He's probably pulling his old Klan outfit out of mothballs as we speak," Tom said.

"What makes you think it's been in mothballs?" Jason asked. "He probably sleeps in the thing."

They all laughed. Tom had no idea what the future held, but he suspected his and his friends' days at Thomas Gatch Prep were numbered. It was also possible that the days of Thomas Gatch Prep were numbered. That was fine with him.

· · · · ·

There was still a game to play, and though the team was divided over the issue of Coach Johnson's departure, it was bonded by one thing: wanting to beat Roanoke Christian.

The two captains addressed the issue after practice on Thursday. Daylight saving time had ended the previous Sunday, so the sun was down by the time practice finished and it was cold on the field, with a few snow flurries in the air. Still, when Conor Foley and Ford Bennett asked Coach Thurman if they could speak to their teammates, he readily agreed.

It had already been a difficult week. The seven players who had quit the team had willingly spoken to the media about how unfair it all was that Coach Johnson had been "run off," and many of their parents had been making the rounds on the national news shows. Fox News was having what felt like a field day with the story, the issue to them being that the United States was being destroyed by "chronic political correctness."

President Trump had even weighed in, saying, "If I ever own an NFL team, which I will one day, Jim Johnson will be my coach!"

"Jim?" Jason said as they watched Trump blather.

"I'm sure they're *very* close," Tom said.

Coach Johnson had been everywhere, saying that, yes, maybe he was a little slow to the table dealing with "change," but that his record on racial equality was clear: almost half his team was African American, and four of his assistants were African American. Yes, he could probably use some counseling on the issue and he planned to get it, but, as he declared over and over, referring to himself in the third person, "Bobo Johnson isn't perfect, but he is *not* a racist."

Coach Thurman had told the players they could talk to anyone in the media they wanted to talk to and say anything they wanted to say *after* the game. "I'm not stonewalling," he'd said. "I just want you to focus as much as possible on the game. Once it's over, we can all speak our piece."

Foley and Bennett, the two captains, spoke theirs to their teammates. They talked about how none of what had gone on mattered between now and the last whistle the next night.

"We're going to remember this week and this game the rest of our lives," Bennett said. "We owe it to ourselves to make this last memory a good one." He paused. "And I'm not just talking about the seniors, I'm talking about all of us. If there is a football team here next season, if there's a *school*, things will be entirely different. We all know that."

Neither Bennett nor Foley had signed the statement put out by the six seniors. In fact, Foley's parents—who had two sons on the team—had appeared on several shows to say that their sons had wondered why, on a team that was half African American, every team captain the last four years had been white.

Foley wrapped up his talk emotionally. Looking in the direction of the six seniors who had written that they were dedicating the game to Coach Johnson, he said: "*I'd* like to dedicate this game to *us*—all seventy-four of us who are left—and to the coaches who have stuck with us. *We* deserve this. So let's go out and win it."

33

THE STADIUM WAS PACKED ON FRIDAY NIGHT. THERE APPEARED TO TOM and Jason to be three constituencies: the TGP fans, the Roanoke Christian fans, and the media—many of whom were forced to sit in the stands because the press box couldn't possibly accommodate all of them.

Ed Seaman, who had stayed on as the school's communications director at least for the moment, had been quoted as saying he had more than three hundred requests for credentials. Apparently he'd been told to honor them all.

For the first time all season, Tom was tingling with anticipation as the players assembled outside the locker room to take the field. He had started the week sharing second-team snaps with Frank Kessler and had ended it actually taking some first-team snaps when Billy Bob was rested.

Jason was equally fired up. He was listed as the number two receiver at the Z spot, but it was apparent he was going to play a lot. He had caught a number of deep balls in practice from both Billy Bob and Tom.

Roanoke Christian was undefeated, 9–0. A win, and the Bengals would be the outright conference champion. A loss and—depending on the outcome of the Middleburg-Fairfax game—it would tie for the title with one or two other teams.

The first half was an offensive show on both sides. Roanoke's quarterback, Billy Doughty, had already committed to Virginia. He was six foot four, left-handed, and had a cannon arm. TGP, with Billy Bob starting at quarterback, didn't go through any of its normal Ronnie Thompson early sputters. It was 17–17 at the half, one of the Patriots touchdowns coming on a forty-four-yard strike from Billy Bob to Jason.

At halftime, Coach Cruikshank pulled Tom aside. "You have to stay ready," he said. "We bog down at all, you're going to be in there."

"I hope we don't bog down," Tom said, meaning it—not because he was nervous about playing, but because he didn't want Billy Bob to fail.

They traded touchdowns in the third quarter, and then the Patriots drove to the Roanoke 19 late in the quarter before stalling. On came Nick Stover to nail a thirty-six-yard field goal for a 27–24 lead.

The defense promptly held as the fourth quarter began and Jason, fielding a punt on the 22, returned it to the 43 to set the offense up in prime field position.

As Jason came to the sideline, Coach Gutekunst met him.

"Catch your breath for two plays, then get back in there," the coach said. "We have a chance to drive a stake through their heart on this drive."

Sure enough, Billy Bob began moving his team again. Jason came back on a third-and-two from the Roanoke 49 and made a catch down the seam for seventeen yards. The Roanoke defensive backs were playing way off him because, by now, they had figured out he was the fastest player on the field.

The game clock was ticking toward ten minutes. A two-score lead might be enough.

But then, just when another score seemed inevitable, Billy Bob made a mistake. On second-and-three, with the ball on the 14-yard line, he spotted Jason open over the middle in the end zone. Only he wasn't really open. He had the cornerback beaten, but one of the Bengals linebackers had dropped deep in coverage and he stepped in front of Jason just as the ball was about to reach him and made a diving interception.

It was the first turnover of the game. Roanoke took over with 8:43 left and began marching methodically down the field—mixing runs with short passes. Billy Bob was berating himself on the sideline for the mistake, but there was nothing to be done at that moment except watch and hope.

"The way this is going, they're going to run the clock to almost nothing," Jason said.

"We might have to start using time-outs *now*," Tom said.

"We gotta save one or two for when we get the ball back," Billy Bob said.

It seemed as if Roanoke was picking up four yards on every play. The Bengals converted four straight third downs as the clock kept ticking.

"If we can hold them to a field goal, we're fine," Tom said. "Even if we don't score, we can win in overtime."

On a third-and-eight from the 14, Doughty dropped and then ran straight up the middle on a quarterback draw, picking up nine—for a first down at the 5. The clock was now under three minutes. Coach Thurman used a time-out as much to rest the defense as stop the clock.

It didn't help. Two plays later, Doughty faked to his fullback, then ran a bootleg to the right and scored with nobody from TGP in the same county. The extra point was perfect and, with 2:09 to play, Roanoke led 31–27. It would take a TGP touchdown to win the game. A field goal would be worthless.

"Just like in the Fairfax game," Tom said.

"Exactly," Billy Bob said. "Which means, roomie, we need a good return."

Jason understood. Only Roanoke wasn't going to give him the chance to give his team some momentum with a return—it had seen enough of him. The Bengals kicker sailed the kickoff well out-of-bounds, meaning TGP would start from the 35-yard line. Not bad field position, but time was short.

"One more time, Billy Bob!" Tom yelled as the offense took the field. "You can do this."

Billy Bob nodded, checked with Coach Cruikshank, and jogged to the huddle. Just as in the Fairfax game, the first two plays were quick outs to speedy receivers: one to Jason, who picked up seven yards before stepping out-of-bounds; one to Terrell Davidson. He picked up seven more and got out-of-bounds at the TGP 49. The two plays had only used up nineteen seconds, but the clock was now at 1:48.

Coach Cruikshank signaled in two more plays: the first one a little risky, Tom thought—a draw to Danny Nobis—because it would definitely use some clock. The second was a fake spike play they'd worked on all season. Billy Bob would race to the line signaling "spike" to his teammates; then he would fake spiking the ball and throw a quick turn-in pass to either Terrell Davidson or Jason. Depending on how fooled the defense was, the play could pick up ten yards or it could go all the way. Tom liked the strategy but understood the risks.

Billy Bob handed to Nobis, who burst through a big hole for nine yards. The clock ticked down while Billy Bob frantically made the spike signal to his teammates as they rushed to the line. Tom could see that many of the Roanoke players weren't even in stances as Billy Bob moved under center. They were expecting the spike. The clock rolled under 1:20.

Billy Bob took a step back and made a motion with his arm to spike the ball. Tom could see that both Jason and Davidson were virtually uncovered. Roanoke had bought the fake entirely.

And then disaster struck.

Somehow, as he made the motion to spike, Billy Bob lost control of the football. It slipped from his hand and began bouncing wildly on the ground. He spotted it right away and dove for it, but so did a couple of Roanoke defenders, who had seen the ball come loose.

Billy Bob got there first and landed on it as about a half dozen white jerseys followed. A huge pileup ensued. The officials signaled for time—the clock stopped on a fumble—with fifty-nine seconds left. Then they dug into the pile to see who had the ball.

Apparently Billy Bob did, because the officials came up signaling that it was still TGP's ball. Tom breathed a sigh of relief. A lot of time had been lost, along with about three yards, but they were still alive.

Everyone untangled and got up from the pile.

Except Billy Bob. He was lying on his back, holding on to his right leg, writhing in apparent agony.

"Oh, no," Tom breathed. "Oh, no."

The officials were waving at the TGP sideline for the trainers to look at Billy Bob. As they raced to help, followed by Coach Thurman, Tom had a realization: By rule, once the medical staff goes on the field, the player has to come out.

You're going in, he thought, *for at least one play.*

Tom turned and saw Danny Nobis, who had come out to catch his breath, standing there, staring, like everyone, at Billy Bob.

"Nobis, quick," Tom said. "You gotta warm me up!"

Nobis froze for a second, then understood. They walked to the bench area and grabbed a ball. Tom stood fifteen yards from Nobis and began lobbing passes to him. He wasn't even looking at the field. He put more zip on the ball after about five throws, then moved back five yards. As he did, he heard a cheer rising from the stands.

He looked at the field and saw that Billy Bob was on his feet or, actually, on one foot. His right foot was off the ground and he was leaning heavily on two of the backup linemen, who had come out to help him off.

"Jefferson!" he heard Coach Cruikshank shout. "Where the hell is Jefferson?"

"Here, Coach," Tom said.

Coach Cruikshank saw him and waved him over. "It's up to you, Tom," he said.

"How bad—"

"Bad. Ankle is either broken or badly sprained. Someone fell on it. He's absolutely done for tonight. You ready?"

Tom had no idea if he was ready, but that wasn't the right answer. "Hundred percent," he said instead.

As he spoke, Billy Bob reached the sideline, his face a mask of pain. Coach Thurman was behind him, the referee behind Coach Thurman.

"Hang on a second," Billy Bob said. He put one hand on Tom's shoulder. "I can't believe I put you in this position," he said, his voice filled with pain. "But you can do this. You *know* you can do this."

Tom nodded, unable to think of a response. The referee was explaining to Coach Thurman that because the injury had occurred in the last two minutes, TGP had to lose either a time-out or ten seconds off the game clock.

"Take the ten seconds off," Coach Thurman said.

"Coach, I don't think—" Coach Cruikshank said.

Coach Thurman waved him off. "You gotta trust me, Mark," he said.

He turned to Tom. "You get warmed up at all?" he asked.

"Enough, Coach," Tom said. "I'm okay."

"Good," Coach Thurman said. "Run Z-curl. They still gotta respect Jason's speed. Send X on a fly. If it works, spike the ball and look at Coach Cruikshank for your next play."

The X-receiver was Terrell Davidson. He would go deep to create some space for Jason in the middle of the field.

Tom ran to the huddle. The referee started the play clock. The game clock was at forty-nine seconds after the runoff.

"You've got this, Jefferson," Conor Foley said as Tom stepped into the circle of players. "We believe in you."

That made Tom feel good. He called the play. As soon as he took the snap, he felt as if he'd been playing quarterback all fall. He dropped three steps and snapped the pass to Jason, who caught it in stride coming across the middle. Jason raced to the 24 before he was brought down.

"Spike!" everyone was screaming.

Tom got them lined up and spiked the ball with twenty-two seconds left.

He looked to Coach Cruikshank. He was signaling for a draw play and for Tom to call time as soon as the play was dead. Tom wasn't crazy about the call, but there was no time to argue.

He handed the ball to Nobis, who picked up five yards to the 19. The clock was at thirteen seconds when Tom got the officials to stop the clock.

He came to the sideline. "Two pass plays," Coach Cruikshank said. "You don't have to throw in the end zone because we have the time-out left."

Five receivers were now in the game. The backfield was empty. Tom dropped and saw no one open. He couldn't scramble because, if he did, the clock might run out. Finally, he saw Emmet Foley come back to him and he found him at the eight.

Foley caught the ball and Tom screamed for time. He got it—with two seconds left.

"They're going to put their entire defense on the goal line or in the end zone," Coach Cruikshank said when Tom ran over one last time. "Terrell's our best leaper. Send him to the corner and throw the lob. It's our only chance."

Coach Thurman nodded. Tom went back to the huddle. Davidson was their strongest leaper, but he wasn't all that tall. The chances of completing the pass were slim—at best. All eyes were on him as he reached the huddle.

He looked at Jason, then made a decision.

"Listen to me, we're going to try something crazy."

No one said a word.

"Everyone run Flood Fly"—that meant flooding the end zone with receivers—"except you, Jason. You fake like you're running Flood Fly, then come behind me. The rest of you *block* your men like your lives depend on it. Because they do."

It was a play Tom and Jason had run in Riverside Park all the time, setting up the other receivers as blockers downfield and then letting Jason outrun everyone else. It was insane to call it at this moment. Which was why, Tom thought, it could work.

"On the first sound," Tom finally said, and they came to the line with the entire stadium on its feet. Tom knew it was loud, but he heard nothing.

He screamed "Omaha!" in honor of Peyton Manning, and took the snap.

Roanoke was only rushing two men. Everyone else was in the end zone. Tom watched his receivers sprint to the end zone and cocked his arm as if to throw the ball up for grabs. Out of the corner of his eye he saw Jason flying past him. He pulled the ball down and pitched it to him.

Jason had a full head of speed. It took a split second for the Roanoke defenders to figure out what had happened. Jason was around the corner and at the 5 before anyone started in his direction. It looked as if someone had a shot at him at the 3, but Davidson dove in front of him and knocked him aside. Jason planted a foot and cut to the outside. Three defenders closed on him. It was a race to the corner.

At the 1-yard line, Jason left his feet and dove. A blur of white uniforms collided with him in midair. Jason was knocked sideways but kept lunging. Tom saw him reach with the ball at the goal line and then go down in a huge pile.

Everyone raced in the direction of the pile. Two officials got there first. They looked at each other for a moment, and then their arms went into the air.

Touchdown!

Tom fought through everyone and reached Jason just as he was climbing to his feet.

"I get there?" he asked, uncertain for a moment.

Tom pointed to the kids in the white uniforms, all of them on a knee or lying flat on the ground.

"What do you think?" he asked.

A few seconds later, they were both on the shoulders of their teammates, being given a crazy ride around the field. When they were finally put down, Coach Thurman and Coach Cruikshank were both standing there, hands on hips. Billy Bob, on crutches, was a half step behind them.

"What the *hell* kind of crazy call was that?" Coach Thurman asked.

For a split second Tom thought the new head coach was angry, but he could see both coaches were fighting grins.

"New York City schoolyard," Tom said. "Works all the time."

"I *love* New York!" Billy Bob said.

He dropped his crutches and reached for Tom and for Jason, and they group-hugged, someone grabbing them from behind to join in. It was Anthony.

"I told you," Billy Bob said, tears rolling down his face. "I told you that you could do it. Even if it took the stupidest, craziest call I've ever seen in my life."

Coach Thurman was laughing. "Actually, it was an amazingly smart call," he said. "Caught them totally by surprise."

"Yeah, I guess that was some pretty deep thinking," Billy Bob said.

With that, they all burst out laughing, and the hugging and the celebrating began all over again. The two black kids and the two white kids. The two Southerners and the two New Yorkers. All celebrating, as one.